Jeff clutched the railing, squeezing until his fingers ached.

How could he have kissed her?

"Jeff, what's wrong?" Andie asked, placing a hand on his arm.

He jerked away. "Go inside. We'll be leaving soon. In the meantime, just stay out of my way."

"Stay out of *your* way? You're the one who—"

"Don't say it," he growled, glaring at her. "Damn you, don't you say it."

She stared at him as if he'd gone crazy. Perhaps he had. He'd also hurt her. He read that in the slight slump of her shoulders as she turned and walked into the house.

He closed his eyes against the memories, but that didn't help. He could still see her, still taste her.

This was his punishment. Once again, his sworn enemy had won—because he was lusting after his enemy's woman....

Dear Reader,

Welcome to another month of fabulous reading here at Silhouette Intimate Moments. As always, we've put together six terrific books for your reading pleasure, starting with *Another Man's Wife* by Dallas Schulze. This is another of our Heartbreakers titles, as well as the latest in her miniseries entitled A Family Circle. As usual with one of this author's titles, you won't want to miss it.

Next up is *Iain Ross's Woman* by Emilie Richards. This, too, is part of a miniseries, The Men of Midnight. This is a suspenseful and deeply emotional book that I predict will end up on your "keeper" shelf.

The rest of the month is filled out with new titles by Nikki Benjamin, *The Wedding Venture;* Susan Mallery, *The Only Way Out;* Suzanne Brockmann, *Not Without Risk;* and Nancy Gideon, *For Mercy's Sake.* Every one of them provides exactly the sort of romantic excitement you've come to expect from Intimate Moments.

In months to come, look for more reading from some of the best authors in the business. We've got books coming up from Linda Turner, Judith Duncan, Naomi Horton and Paula Detmer Riggs, to name only a few. So come back next month—and every month—to Silhouette Intimate Moments, where romance is the name of the game.

Yours,
Leslie Wainger
Senior Editor and Editorial Coordinator

Please address questions and book requests to:
Silhouette Reader Service
U.S.: 3010 Walden Ave., P.O. Box 1325, Buffalo, NY 14269
Canadian: P.O. Box 609, Fort Erie, Ont. L2A 5X3

THE ONLY WAY OUT

SUSAN MALLERY

Published by Silhouette Books

America's Publisher of Contemporary Romance

SILHOUETTE BOOKS

ISBN 0-373-07646-0

THE ONLY WAY OUT

Copyright © 1995 by Susan W. Macias

This edition published by arrangement with Harlequin Enterprises B.V.

Printed in U.S.A.

SUSAN MALLERY

makes her home in the Lone Star state, where the people are charming and the weather is always interesting. She lives with her hero-material husband and her two attractive but not very bright cats. When she's not hard at work writing romances, she can be found exploring the wilds of Texas and shopping for the perfect pair of cowboy boots. Susan loves to hear from her readers. You may write her directly at P.O. Box 1828, Sugar Land, TX 77487.

To Jan. Okay, so it was tough at first. It's turned out to be more than worth the trouble. I wish I could find the words to say how much your support and friendship have meant to me. You're terrific. (I know it's supposed to be a secret, but hey!) Here's to being R&F, to maids, summer homes and bright futures.

Prologue

He was less than twenty feet from the car when it exploded. The deafening blast threw Jeff Markum up against the side of a clothing shop. Glass, chunks of wood from a corner fruit stand and pieces of twisted metal from the car itself peppered his body like buckshot. He couldn't breathe, couldn't see, couldn't hear anything except the powerful echo of the explosion. The blackness around him grew, humming louder and louder until he felt himself losing this world. Not yet, he thought desperately.

He forced himself back to consciousness, driven by the need to rescue the two people inside what had once been a small red Ford. As he tried to push himself to his feet, pain ripped through his left leg. A quick glance confirmed the injury. Blood seeped from a tear in his trousers, and his knee bent at an awkward angle. Broken.

Around him, people stirred to life. He heard faint cries and louder screams. The uninjured scurried for cover in case the blast came again. Jeff knew they hid in vain. There was no need for another blast.

He gathered the little strength he had left and crawled along the littered sidewalk. Glass cut his hands. His broken leg dragged behind him. His shoulder was dislocated, but he couldn't worry about any of that now. He had to get to the flaming, twisted heap that had once been his car.

Toward the inferno that housed his wife and child.

Fury drove him. Sorrow and guilt fueled his need. He was less than five feet from the car when he heard the sounds of the sirens.

They were too damn late, he thought looking at the flames licking skyward as if they could consume the heavens. No one inside could have survived. Even as he tried to comfort himself with the thought that they would have died instantly, he imagined he heard their screams.

Each high-pitched shriek of terror pierced him deeper and deeper until his soul started to bleed. He stared at the wreckage as black smoke began to obscure it from sight.

Then the siren stopped next to him and the medical team jumped out. Strong hands pulled him away from the fire, away from his wife and son. He fought the medics, but he had no strength. All too soon he was in the medical van and on his way to the hospital.

Jeff closed his ears against the clanging of the siren, and closed his eyes against the medic's penlight. He would get the report tonight, but he already knew what they would find.

A car bomb. Nothing odd about that in a city that claimed hundreds of lives each year. Yet he'd been arrogant enough to assume that the statistics would never touch him. That he could pursue his enemy with all the fervor of a saint chasing the devil and that it would never get personal. Jeff had known Kray had marked him for death, but he hadn't thought his family would have to pay because he loved his job.

"J.J. needs to be near his father," Jeanne had insisted when her plane had landed in Lebanon. "And I need to be near my husband."

Jeff had tried explaining the situation to her, and when that hadn't worked, he'd resorted to anger. Jeanne had listened quietly, then continued unpacking. As far as she was concerned, it didn't matter to her that she was in the middle of something ugly, something she would never understand. The rules in her life were simple. A wife's place was at her husband's side.

So he'd let her stay. Because a part of him had enjoyed the moments of normalcy in an otherwise chaotic life. Because he loved his wife and son almost as much as he loved his job, and because he believed he could keep them safe. Kray had warned Jeff he would pay. Until this moment he hadn't known how much.

Jeff let go of his thoughts and concentrated on the pain because the alternative was too horrible. Kray had ordered one of his men to place the bomb in Jeff's car. The car Jeanne had borrowed that morning so she and J.J. could run errands. Jeff had grown complacent and overly confident. He'd killed his wife and child as surely as if he had set the bomb himself.

Then the buzzing in his ears grew louder and his thoughts more erratic. He couldn't focus on Jeanne's face or the sound of J.J.'s laughter. They were getting lost in the pain. Suddenly not finding his way back didn't sound so bad.

"We're losing him," a disembodied voice called. "Pressure's dropping. He's lost too much blood."

Jeff let himself sink further into the blackness. He didn't care if he died. Jeanne was gone already, and with her, Jeff Jr. Dying might solve his problem. He would simply wait for Kray to join him in hell.

Chapter 1

Five years later

Jeff Markum lay on his belly in the sand. Waving sea grass, bougainvillea and wild fig trees hid him from view. His powerful binoculars allowed him to see into the open windows of the exclusive villa situated at the far end of the hotel grounds.

Three men gathered around a table, as was their morning custom. They'd finished breakfast and were talking. A soft, tropical breeze carried with it the faint sound of laughter. Jeff couldn't hear what they were saying, but he watched their lips moving and deciphered most of the words.

They were going fishing.

Jeff turned his head slightly to the right and saw the dock jutting out into the deep blue of the Caribbean sea. A well-equipped powerboat sat bobbing in the water. The crew was preparing for their day of fishing. Jeff looked back at the villa. The path from the front door to the boat was about fifty feet long. Nothing obstructed Jeff's view of the area, so nothing would get in the way of his shot.

Kray would walk those fifty feet. He was a head taller than both his bodyguards. It would be easy to take him out.

Jeff lowered the binoculars and rolled onto his back. His hip bumped the gleaming rifle he'd laid out in preparation of what had to be done. Timing. This whole damn thing was about timing. Today it would happen. He could feel it in his bones, especially in his knee, which often ached if the weather was right.

It was early enough that the temperature was still pleasant. A rainstorm had passed through during the night, washing everything clean. He inhaled the thick air of the island, smelling the tropical flowers, the sea and his own sweat. He'd thought he might hesitate or be weighed down by indecision, but he wasn't. Today. Now. Kray would die.

Jeff brushed his arm across his forehead and tried to relax. He'd killed men before. He wasn't afraid to watch someone die. He wasn't even afraid of dying himself. The plan was flawless. He was the ultimate weapon—an assassin willing to sacrifice himself for the target. Kray didn't have a chance.

Jeff knew what would happen afterward. He hadn't spent much time planning his escape, mostly because he didn't expect to get away. Kray practically owned the island. He came here often enough to make the locals pliable to his wishes. While he was on St. Lucas, Kray liked to pretend he wasn't a dangerous criminal, but instead, a wealthy businessman on holiday. So the villa had no alarm system, no heat sensors, no obvious security. It was perfect for Jeff's plan. The three bodyguards who went everywhere with Kray wouldn't even notice the single bullet that flew past them to find its victim. No doubt Jeff would be caught. So be it. He wanted Kray dead—nothing else mattered.

Jeff rolled onto his stomach again. Instead of the villa, he saw the small red car exploding into unrecognizable pieces. He felt the heat and smelled the burning wreckage.

He held himself very still and waited until the vision passed; then he picked up the rifle and stared through the scope. It had been five long years. In all that time Kray had never crossed the line. He'd never tried to kill Jeff again, and he'd never been caught. One of the most powerful crime lords in the world walked free because he was too smart and too lucky. Jeff smiled slowly. Kray's luck was about to change for the worse. A single bullet to the head. That's all it would take.

He was cynical enough to know Kray's death wouldn't change the world. Someone else would step in his shoes. But Jeff didn't care about that. Part of the reason he was here— hell, *all* of the reason he was here was personal. Maybe when Kray was dead, his dreams about Jeanne and J.J. would haunt him less. Maybe then he could finally forget.

The sound of the boat engines cranking over caught his attention. He adjusted the rifle, shifting his arm on the sand, then stared through the scope. He closed his left eye. He could see the crew preparing to cast off.

Slowly he turned the rifle toward the villa's front door. Within a few seconds, the first of the bodyguards appeared, carrying a canvas bag. The man was talking. Jeff couldn't decipher his words. A second man stepped out onto the path. Kray's assistant. Jeff waited.

A third man moved onto the path. Jeff stiffened. Kray. He stared intently through the rifle's scope. The crime lord looked like what he pretended to be: a successful businessman on holiday. His brown hair was short and brushed straight back. Thick eyebrows arched over light brown eyes. A full mouth curved into a smile at something one of the bodyguards said.

Jeff adjusted the scope until the cross hairs centered on Kray's head. He touched the trigger. He'd been practicing with this rifle for over a year. He knew exactly how much pressure to apply, knew how heavy the loads were in the bullets and knew precisely what would happen to Kray at the moment of impact. He'd always been a good field agent, even if he'd spent the past five years behind a desk.

He thought about Jeanne and J.J. one last time, then cleared his mind. Nothing existed except the target. Nothing mattered. His breathing slowed, as did his heartbeat. His body stayed perfectly still in anticipation.

The fourth man stepped through the door and onto the path. He, too, carried a canvas bag. The group started moving toward the boat. Now, Jeff told himself. He drew in a breath, held it and started to squeeze.

"Monsieur Kray!" a female voice called.

Jeff froze, then forced himself to relax. There was still time.

Kray and his men turned toward the house. A dark-haired woman in a gray-and-white uniform ran down to the dock. She was holding a piece of paper. Kray waited impatiently as the woman approached him.

They spoke briefly.

The woman, her dark hair pulled away from her face, stepped between Jeff and his target. Jeff waited. Kray read the paper, then handed it back to her and nodded. The woman started toward the villa.

Before he could adjust his sights on Kray again, a flicker of movement from behind the villa caught his attention. He tried to ignore it, but years of training kicked in. Cursing silently, he swung the gun back toward the villa, using the scope as a magnifying lens.

A woman crept up to the rear of the villa, toward the French doors by the breakfast room. She wore jeans, a white T-shirt and running shoes. Despite her casual attire, she was as out of place as a mouse in a cage full of cats. Tourists didn't go creeping around behind the crime lord's villa, and operatives didn't sneak around in the middle of the day. Who the hell was she? Her long blond hair and pale skin told of her Anglo heritage; she wasn't a native. But she *was* trying to get in to Kray's villa. Jeff knew enough about his enemy to know she wasn't part of his entourage.

Jeff glanced at the maid. The dark-haired woman had paused at the front of the building to light a cigarette. He looked at the blonde and saw she was fitting a key into the

French doors and cautiously pushing them open. If the maid smoked one cigarette, that gave the blonde less than two minutes before the maid interrupted her. Damn it all to hell.

He turned his attention back to the men at the end of the dock. In about ten seconds, when the bodyguard climbed into the bobbing boat, he would have a clear shot at Kray. If he killed his old enemy now, the woman would be trapped inside the villa and caught at whatever she was trying to do. He told himself she wasn't his responsibility. He was here to take out Kray, civilians be damned.

Except that wasn't his policy. He trained his men to protect civilians. He couldn't expect any less from himself.

Jeff closed his left eye and gently moved the rifle until the cross hairs centered on Kray's ear. He touched the trigger.

"Bang, you're dead," he said softly, then lowered the rifle to the ground.

Kray spent at least six weeks every spring on the island. He met with his managers, talked money with the various banks that laundered his funds, gave expensive parties. Jeff was also going to be here for six weeks. This was only day five. He had plenty of time to deal with Kray.

He glanced at the maid. She'd finished about half of her cigarette and was watching the men on the boat cast off. One of the bodyguards called out to her. She smiled and waved.

Jeff quickly broke down the rifle and slipped the weapon into his backpack. As he put on his cap and picked up the binoculars, he heard the boat engines roar as they powered the vehicle out toward the open ocean. Blue skies and bluer water beckoned. They wouldn't be back until late afternoon. He thought about the bags the bodyguards had carried. They might even stay away overnight.

He turned his attention back to the villa. The woman hadn't reappeared. The maid was down to the last third of her cigarette.

"Come on," Jeff said quietly. "You've got less than thirty seconds until she goes back inside."

He didn't know why he was rooting for the mysterious woman, except if she was Kray's enemy, then she was *his* ally. He waited, counting out the seconds. The maid finished her cigarette and stubbed out the butt in the decorative sand-filled jar beside the door. She opened the front door and stepped inside.

Damn. Jeff picked up his backpack and rose to his knees. With a last glance at the departing boat, he crawled through the low-lying bushes around the beach and toward the back of the villa. The blonde hadn't come back out yet. If the maid caught her, she would have a lot of explaining to do. If she did manage to escape, he would follow her and try to find out what she was doing here. Ally or not, he wasn't going to let anyone get in the way of what had to be done.

Andie Cochran promised herself that when she was safely out of danger, she was going to find a quiet place out in the bushes somewhere and throw up. She hadn't known it was possible to be this scared and still function.

Her muscles quivered and twitched. Her hands shook, her knees trembled. Even her breathing was ragged. Her stomach lurched threateningly and her heart raced. Nerves had kept her going for the past three weeks and she was hanging on by sheer force of will.

She glanced at her watch. She had no time left. She'd seen the nanny run down the dock toward Kray and his men. It had given her only a moment to act, but she'd taken it. There might not be another chance. Kray and his goons were gone on an overnight fishing trip. The villa was at the far end of the resort and the hotel housekeeping staff wasn't due for a half hour. No one else was around. The building was empty except for the nanny and Bobby. She had the perfect opportunity to rescue her son.

Andie moved quickly through the silent house. It had changed some since she'd been here last. Of course, that had been over six years ago. She'd been young and innocent. A fool. As she passed by the elegantly appointed living room, she noticed that the cushions and draperies had been replaced, but the heavy carved mahogany furniture was the same. She and Bobby could live for three years on what

Kray had paid for the sofa and love seat alone. But then he'd always wanted the best, the most beautiful, the rare. She must have been such a disappointment to him.

It didn't matter, she reminded herself. None of it mattered. She turned toward the long hallway and ran quietly toward the back bedrooms. Kray would take the master suite for himself, with his bodyguards on either side and across the hall. That left only the last three bedrooms empty for her son.

Most of the doors stood open and she glanced in them as she moved past. Unmade beds, piles of luggage, luxurious furnishings, but no people. When she approached the end of the hallway and the last three rooms, she heard a voice.

"I'm not afraid, I won't be afraid."

The soft singsong crooning stopped her in her tracks. Instinctively Andie clutched her hands to her midsection as if she could hold in the pain. Oh, God, what had Kray done to her child?

She flew down the last few feet of corridor toward the sound. When he was frightened, Bobby would huddle in the middle of his bed and rock back and forth, singing the refrain over and over again. It happened during rare Los Angeles thunderstorms, or when he'd snuck downstairs while she was studying and watched a scary movie. She would hear the soft singing, then curl up next to him on the bed, holding him close until he forgot to be afraid.

No one knew that, she thought, fighting the tears. No one knew anything about him. He'd spent the past three weeks alone in a terrifying world. Living with strangers, missing her, not knowing how desperate she'd been to be with him.

She opened the last door on the right and stepped into the darkened room. Drapes had been pulled closed over the wide window. There was a bed in the center of the room, along with stacks of toys, many of them still in their boxes. An untouched breakfast tray sat on a low table.

Her son lay huddled in the center of the bedspread, his back to her.

"Bobby," she said softly.

The boy turned toward her. His hazel eyes widened; then he sat up slowly as if not able to believe what he was seeing. "Mommy?"

She moved toward him, holding out her arms. He stood up and launched himself at her. She caught him in midair. He wrapped his sturdy legs around her waist and his arms around her neck. Familiar little-boy smells assaulted her, as his warm, small body pressed against her.

"Bobby," she murmured, clutching him closer. His hair was longer, but still felt the same. Her palm moved up and down against his bony spine, feeling the ridges and thin muscles that would one day make him as big and broad as his father.

He cried, clinging to her as if he would never let go. His relief was as tangible as his thin arms, as real as his words.

"I missed you," he said between sobs that nearly ripped her in two. "I called for you, but you didn't come. Didn't you hear me?"

"No," she said, pressing her cheek against his. She felt the moisture there, then realized their tears mingled. "I wanted to be here, sweetie, but I couldn't find you right away. I'm here now."

Bobby leaned back and stared at her. He sniffed. "I don't wanna stay, Mommy. I hate Daddy." He said it defiantly, as if expecting her to scold him. At five, life was simple. Bobby loved his mother, his friends and his teacher. He liked school and tolerated bath time. He hadn't yet learned to hate. Until Kray had torn him away from the only world he'd ever known. But his anger and fear obviously troubled him. Boys weren't supposed to hate their fathers.

Most fathers weren't Kray.

"It's okay," she promised, then prayed she wasn't lying. "I'm going to get you—"

The front door slammed closed. Andie's heart thumped loudly against her chest as she realized she'd wasted precious time. The nanny had returned. What now?

She glanced at the open bedroom door. The nanny's footsteps sounded loud on the tiled floor. She and Bobby couldn't go back that way. She'd hoped her luck would hold and they could walk out the way she'd come in. But that wasn't going to happen. Still, she would find another way. She had to; Bobby was depending on her.

She set him down. He started to protest, but she touched her fingers to his mouth. "Hush," she whispered. "We have to escape. You must be very quiet. Do you understand? Not a word."

He nodded, wide-eyed.

She moved silently to the door and peered out. The nanny was in the great room by the front door. Andie could see the hem of her dress as she bent over a sofa. They still had a few seconds.

Andie closed the door quietly and turned the lock in the knob. Then she glanced around to find another way to escape. There were two doors. She tried them both. One led to a closet, the other to a bathroom. That meant they were trapped. Her gaze lingered on the pulled drapes. Unless they went out the window.

She looked down at her son. He was dressed in shorts and a T-shirt, both new. Kray had taken nothing when he'd stolen her child from her. His athletic shoes were sturdy. He would be fine.

She took his hand tightly in hers, and led the way to the window. "Come on, Bobby. We've got to go right now."

He stared at her while she opened the drapes, then fumbled with the catch. The glass slid open. She pushed out the screen.

"Are we 'scaping?"

"Yes, we're escaping." She released his hand so she could lower the screen to the ground. A blooming azalea bush provided a small amount of cover. From the front of the villa she could hear the tap-tap of the nanny's heels. The sound kept advancing. Andie didn't know how much time they had left. They just needed a few seconds. Please, God, grant them that.

The window was about chest height on her, which meant she needed a step up. She glanced around the room, then saw the child-size chair by the low table. She grabbed it, along with the roll from the untouched breakfast tray. She stuffed the bread in her jeans pocket and placed the chair below the window.

Andie looked outside. When she didn't see anyone, she reached for Bobby, picking him up under his arms. He was heavier than he looked, but she was used to his growing weight. She heaved him onto the windowsill, then stepped onto the chair. The plastic seat sagged under her, but didn't give way. She had him scoot around so his legs were hanging outside the window, then stretched as far as she could, lowering him to about ten inches from the ground.

"Jump for the last bit," she said.

"Okay." He hunched up for the drop. She released him and he hit the ground in an exaggerated crouch. "Made it, Mom," he said, grinning up at her.

His familiar smile made her weak with relief. Whatever Kray had done to him in the past three weeks, it hadn't destroyed his spirit. Now they just had to get away and off this damned island.

Using her arms as leverage, she pushed hard off the plastic chair and turned as she moved through the air so that she landed on the windowsill on her hip. She pulled one leg up and through the window, then the other. Motioning Bobby to step back, she dropped to the ground, then picked up the screen.

The footsteps were definitely louder now.

"Bobby?" a female voice called. "You can't stay in your room all morning. It's a beautiful day. Would you like to play in the water?"

The footsteps got closer. Andie ducked down behind the building, knowing at any second the nanny was going to try the door and find it locked. She glanced around frantically, wondering which path would be the safest. Fear gripped her, but she had to stay calm. She couldn't let Bobby know the danger they were in. He'd been through enough.

A sharp ringing cut through the silence. At first she thought she'd imagined the sound. Then she leaned against the villa and exhaled her relief. The footsteps moved away from Bobby's room as the nanny went to answer the phone.

After closing the window, Andie leaned the screen against the glass, hoping it would take the nanny some time to figure out how Bobby had escaped. With any luck the other woman would search through the house before realizing her charge was gone.

They had a few more seconds reprieve. It would be enough. She took Bobby's hand and led him around the villa, back toward the way she'd come. She'd left her rented Jeep about a half mile away. It was parked on the side of the highway. All they had to do was get away from the villa and into the low bushes and trees. The undergrowth would protect them. She should know. She'd spent most of yesterday and the four hours since dawn hidden by a small bush, praying no one would discover her. Just thinking about it made her feel itchy all over. For all she knew the plant had been poisonous, but it hadn't mattered. Getting Bobby out alive was her only priority.

She kept moving and kept low, hugging the building, making sure they couldn't be seen from the windows. Bobby trailed behind her. She reached back and pulled him close to her body. He looked worried. Why wouldn't he be? They were escaping from the man who had casually walked into their town house and kidnapped him on the day of his fifth birthday.

Big hazel eyes stared up at her. She took the time to brush the hair from his flushed face and smile.

She picked him up. They would move faster with her carrying him. Besides, they were about to cross open ground. If someone did shoot at them, her body would protect Bobby. She shuddered, not able to believe what she was thinking. This was so far from her regular, boring life. Yet it was painfully real. Kray had threatened to kill her if she came after her son. She believed him.

"I love you, pumpkin," she said.

"I'm not a pumpkin," he answered, slipping into the familiar game. "I'm a boy."

"Really?" She pretended to be surprised. After dropping a quick kiss on his forehead, she took one last look around. "We're going to run to those trees there," she said, pointing.

Bobby looked over his shoulder. "Are you going to go fast?"

"Yup."

"So Daddy can't find us?"

He was so young to have had to deal with everything that had happened. Her heart ached for him. But there was no time to discuss it. That would come later. When they got away. If they got away.

"Yes, Bobby. So Daddy can't find us."

He gripped her arms and buried his head in her shoulder. "I'm ready. Let's go."

Let's go, she echoed silently. She moved between two large windows and stood up. The stucco building felt warm. She could feel the sweat on her back. Shorts would have been cooler, but she'd been afraid of getting scratched as she crawled through the brush on her way to the villa.

"Here we go," she said softly, and took off across the manicured lawn.

She moved as quickly as she could, keeping low. Bobby clung to her like a burr, but his weight pulled at her and she could feel the strain on her back and shoulders. Her breath came in rapid pants. At any second she expected to hear the nanny yelling at her to stop. Her muscles tensed in anticipation of the gunshot that would follow, because she sure as hell wasn't going to stop for anyone.

She ran hard and fast into the low brush and trees, slowing only to avoid a fall. Just a few more feet, she told herself. Then they would be out of view of the villa.

She circled around a tall mahogany tree and ducked behind it. Coming to a stop, she leaned against the massive trunk to catch her breath.

In between her rapid panting, she listened for the sound of someone following. Nothing. Just the call of the gulls and the crash of the waves on the shore. They'd made it.

Andie clutched Bobby closer and nuzzled his neck, making him giggle. She chuckled with him, then raised her head and took off to her right. After going about ten feet, she turned and doubled back.

Something moved. She spun around.

Her scream never got further than her throat. The man had appeared from nowhere. She'd never seen him in all the time she'd been waiting by the villa or heard him moving through the trees. Now he stood in front of her, dressed in military camouflage with a pistol pointing directly at her head.

Chapter 2

"Who the hell are you?" Jeff asked, staring at the woman clutching the child to her chest.

She blinked at him but didn't answer. The boy in her arms twisted until he could see Jeff; then his mouth dropped open and fear filled his big hazel eyes.

"Mommy, that man has a gun."

"Hush, Bobby, I know."

The child looked to be about five or six. Not much older than J.J. had been when he'd been killed in the car explosion. Jeff didn't want to think about that now. He glared at the woman in front of him. What was going on here? Who was the woman and what was she doing with that kid?

"Is he going to hurt us?" Bobby asked.

"I don't know." She adjusted her hold on the boy, pulling him more securely against her. Long blond hair had been pulled back into a braid. Her face paled under her slight tan, her eyes were wide, her mouth trembling.

"Who are you?" she asked with an obvious effort to keep the fear from her voice. "What do you want?"

"That's what I'd like to know about you. I saw you climb out of the villa with that kid."

His gaze drifted over her cotton T-shirt and jeans. She wasn't concealing a weapon. He flicked on the Beretta's safety, then shoved the pistol into the holster attached to his waist.

Her breathing increased and he could smell her fear. The boy was confused, but not frightened. His mother looked as if she expected to have her throat slit.

"It has nothing to do with you," she said, desperation adding an edge to her voice. She sidestepped him and continued moving away from the villa. "Please just let us go."

"I can't do that," he said. Not after she'd seen him. Whatever kind of game she was playing with Kray, he didn't want any part of it. Once his old enemy knew he was on the island, Jeff would be marked and hunted until they found him. Some woman with a grudge against her old lover wasn't about to interfere with what he had to do.

She spun toward him. Blue eyes met his. He saw her panic. "Oh, God, you work for him."

He didn't answer.

"You're going to kill me. No, you can't. I won't let you. He can't have Bobby back. He can't."

She took off running. At first, Jeff was too startled to do more than stare after her. What the hell was she going on about? He didn't look like one of Kray's men. They dressed like businessmen and tourists. He glanced down at his camouflage fatigues. He looked as if he were going to lead jungle warfare exercises. But if she was with Kray, she should know all that. And if she wasn't—

He loped after her, moving quietly through the dense brush. As he got closer, he heard the sound of her breathing. Bobby clung to her shoulder and stared behind them.

"I don't see him, Mommy," he said quietly.

"Good."

"Was he going to hurt us?"

Jeff didn't bother listening to her response. He circled around them and stepped into her path, two feet in front of her. She saw him and stopped instantly.

Perspiration had collected on her forehead and upper lip. A single drop rolled down to her damp T-shirt. It was barely after ten in the morning, but the temperature was already in the mid-eighties. Warm for late April in the Caribbean.

Her lips moved, but there was no sound. He realized she was praying. She started backing away from him.

"No," she whispered. "No. No. No." Her breathing came in rapid pants. The child clung to her.

"Mommy, I'm scared."

This was more than a lover's spat, he realized. She was genuinely terrified. "Who *are* you?" he asked, frustrated and confused. "What are you doing on Kray's island and who is that kid?"

The woman stared at him, then bent over and let the boy slip to the ground. "Run," she ordered him.

The child hesitated, hovering near her.

"Run!" she screamed.

Bobby took two steps away. Jeff moved toward him. The kid could get lost in the tropical jungle and not be found for weeks, if ever.

The woman sprang between him and her child. She raised her fists in front of her and balanced on the balls of her feet as if she expected him to physically fight her.

"Listen, lady, let's just calm down." He didn't need a hysterical woman on his hands.

"Run, Bobby," she called and lunged forward.

Jeff sidestepped neatly, letting her run harmlessly past him. The boy hovered by a large mahogany tree and clasped his arms tightly in front of him. He began to rock back and forth.

Jeff started toward him when he saw a movement out of the corner of his eye. He turned to the right as the woman barreled into his left side. Before he could reach out and steady her, she'd curled her fingers into claws and started going for his eyes.

"Damn it, woman, be careful," he muttered, grabbing her upper arms to hold her off.

She wrenched free of him and kicked at his knees. Great. She's had just enough self-defense training to hurt herself, he thought grimly as he jumped out of the way and caught her neatly around her midsection. She screamed and fought him, her hands pulling at his hold. He hauled her hard against him. Her heel came down on his foot. He barely felt the impact through his heavy boots. Her elbow connected with his belly. He exhaled audibly.

Then something or someone rushed him. Small hands grabbed his shirt.

"You let go of my mommy. Let go!"

Jeff turned toward the boy. The woman took advantage of his distraction and went for his gun. He read her intentions before she even got close to the pistol, but it was enough. His brain shut down and he reacted instinctively.

His left hand clamped down hard on her right wrist. With one quick, fluid movement he jerked her arm around behind her, pinning her hand to her back. She winced in pain. He spun them both, putting the woman between him and the boy, then wrapped his right arm around her neck, cutting off her supply of air. He applied enough pressure to frighten her, but not enough to kill.

"Now that I have your attention," he said softly, "you're going to answer a few questions."

He could feel the heat of her body and the curve of her breast where it brushed against his elbow. She trembled against him.

"I'm going to let you breathe enough to talk, but I'm not going to let you go. If you give me any more trouble, I'll make you very uncomfortable. Do you understand?"

She nodded.

He loosened his hold on her throat. She gasped in a breath of air, then coughed. Bobby rushed at her. "Let her go! You let go of my mommy. My daddy will come back on his big boat and he'll hurt you."

Sunlight filtered through the trees and brush around them. The scent of the saltwater and the faint crash of the surf drifted toward them. Jeff stared at the boy, hearing his words, but not wanting to believe them.

The child moved closer and angrily swiped at the tears on his face. Sunlight caught the brown of his hair, then highlighted the shape of his nose and chin. Raw anger radiated from the child's eyes. Anger so like another man's rage.

"Let her go," Bobby demanded again.

Jeff released the woman and stepped back. He bumped into a tree and grasped its smooth trunk for support. Bobby continued to glare at him. Those eyes, so large and expressive. So like his father's.

Jeff swallowed hard, remembering another child with big eyes, a boy about four years old, laughing as he climbed down the plane's steps and flew into his father's arms.

"I crossed an ocean," J.J. had said proudly as Jeff had swooped him up.

"Did you?"

"I wasn't afraid."

Jeanne had followed her son down the steps, moving a little slower, the long flight and time changes making her weary. "He's not afraid of anything."

Fierce pride had burned through Jeff, as though he had something to do with his child's bravery. Perhaps he had taught him something about courage, but more likely, J.J. hadn't encountered anything to be frightened of. He'd been surrounded by loving parents and family from the moment he'd been born.

So much life snuffed out by a single explosion. An explosion meant for his father.

Jeff stared at the boy in front of him, and at the woman crouched down beside him. She held the child to her and watched him fearfully, as if he'd gone mad. He *had* gone mad.

Loathing rose up inside of him until he could taste the bitterness. Hatred, anger, rage. Revenge.

He advanced slowly. "What's your last name, Bobby?"

"C-Cochran," the child answered.

There had been rumors, of course. Whispers of a brief marriage, hints of a child. But few had seen the mysterious woman or her son. Word on the street was that she'd left Kray after six months of wedded bliss. Kray had kept his secrets. And the woman had kept hers.

Jeff continued to approach. The woman stood up and moved the boy behind her.

"You can't hurt him," she said. "He's just a boy."

"He's Kray's son."

"No. He's mine. Until three weeks ago, he'd never even seen his father. He thought he was dead. Bobby is nothing like Kray. Nothing." Her voice grew louder with each word.

"Mommy?" Bobby clung to her leg and whimpered.

Jeff reached for the custom grip of his pistol. His hand brushed against the cool steel. He froze. What the hell was he doing?

He shook his head to clear away the anger, then tamped down the remaining emotions. He couldn't let his personal feelings get in the way of his job.

He gave the boy a half smile. "Don't be scared, son. I won't hurt you."

Bobby sniffed, but didn't release his death grip on his mother's jeans.

Jeff returned his attention to the woman. She, too, had large eyes. High cheekbones sculpted her face. For the first time he realized she was beautiful enough to stop a man in his tracks and make him think about the forbidden. Or beautiful enough to tempt a man to try to own her, much as Kray owned objects from all over the world.

"How old are you?" he asked Bobby.

"F-five."

His gaze narrowed as he studied the woman. That meant she'd married Kray about six years ago. Six years ago, when J.J. had been three and growing faster than he'd believed possible. Six years ago, when Jeff's marriage with Jeanne was crumbling around them and it didn't seem to matter how much they'd been in love. Six years ago when his wife had accused him of loving his job more than he'd loved her and he'd known in his heart she was right.

Jeff moved closer. The woman froze in place. Fear flickered across her features, tightening her jaw and making her body tremble. But she didn't back away. She kept herself between him and the boy.

Her run through the jungle and wrestling with him had loosened her braid. Strands of hair drifted across her shoulders. He reached forward. She flinched. Slowly he grabbed the loose hair and pulled it away from her face. His gaze narrowed as he studied her features. Six years ago she hadn't been blond. He pictured her eyes green instead of blue, her hair cropped above the ears and bright red. His gaze flickered over her T-shirt and jeans. She hadn't been as curvy then, or dressed so casually. He searched his memory recalling all the pictures of Kray he'd pored over, memorizing everything he could about the man.

One photograph clicked into place. He stared at the blonde, seeing instead a tall, painfully thin party girl in a designer gown. She'd been clinging to Kray's arm, gazing up at him adoringly. The powerful telescopic lens had caught her perfect features, her wide eyes and mouth. He remembered everything and knew exactly who she was.

Jeff stepped back from her. "You're the bimbo model."

"And you're some macho jerk who gets a kick out of frightening little boys."

He raised his eyebrows. "I'd always assumed Kray liked his women submissive and decorative. Guess I was wrong."

"I was a great disappointment to him."

He glanced at Bobby. "Obviously not. You're the wife," he said, wondering how any woman could become involved with low-life scum like Kray. Was it the money? The power? He shook his head. It didn't matter. He didn't have time for this.

"Ex-wife," she said.

He ignored her, then glanced back the way they'd come and wondered how long it would be before someone noticed the kid was missing. Kidnapping Kray's only son wasn't going to make the crime lord happy. The woman was in a lot of trouble. No doubt she already knew that.

Damn. If only she hadn't picked today to try her heroics. Kray would be dead by now and all their problems would be solved.

"Are you going to turn us over to him?" she asked.

He returned his attention to her. She'd squared her shoulders and folded her arms over her chest. Bobby still stood behind her, watching him warily. The kid had spunk, he thought, then frowned. It wasn't right. Kray's child lived and breathed while J.J. was long since dead and buried.

The familiar sense of loss swept over him, making him wonder if he would ever be able to look at a young boy and not think of his son.

"I won't turn you in," he said shortly and shifted his backpack. He wasn't going to turn them in, but if he let her go, and she was captured by Kray's men, she would tell them about him. Once they knew he was on the island, he would be dead before he got another shot at Kray.

He glanced up at the sun in the clear blue sky, then back at her. "You've got the boy. How did you plan to get away?"

She clamped her lips shut.

Great. "Listen, lady, I just saw you kidnap Kray's son. If I was one of the bad guys, don't you think I'd turn you in and get some kind of reward for my trouble? Kray would pay big money to get you and the kid back."

She balled her hands into fists. "He doesn't want me back. I told you, I'm his ex-wife. It's been over five years since we—" She shook her head. "Why am I explaining this to you? I don't even know who or what you are. Look at how you're dressed. My God, you're probably some paramilitary psycho who gets his kicks out of torturing innocent women and children." Her voice trembled on each word, and by the end of her speech he could see she was fighting tears.

"Mommy?" Bobby looked up at her. "Mommy, what's wrong?"

"Nothing." She blinked several times, then smiled down at her son. "I'm fine. We're going to go now." She took Bobby's hand and turned away.

"Not so fast," Jeff said, starting after her. "Not until I know exactly what is going on here."

She looked at him over her shoulder. "It's not your business."

"You made it my business when you crashed my party. I don't trust you. You're not going anywhere without me."

"I don't need your help."

Help? If things hadn't been so twisted, he would have laughed out loud. "Who said anything about help? Lady, I don't care what happens to you. I just want to stay alive on this stinking island. You're in my way. I want you out of my way. End of story."

The woman recoiled visibly. "Don't hurt my son," she pleaded. "I don't matter, but he does. Please, please just get him away from Kray. Bobby's the innocent one in all of this. Surely you can see that. He didn't even know who his father was. Kray had never even seen him until three weeks ago. I'm begging you, help him."

"I won't hurt the kid," Jeff said in disgust. She was Kray's ex-wife. She'd known what the man she'd married was and now she was paying the price. That wasn't his problem. But he understood about the child being a victim. Like J.J. had been a victim. "I can't let you tell Kray I'm here."

She laughed. The sound had a slightly hysterical edge to it. "Mister, if he finds me, he's not going to bother with questions. Trust me."

"It's not that simple."

They stared at each other. The woman blinked first.

"I guess we have a standoff," she said. "What happens now?"

"You tell me your plan and then I decide what to do with you."

She swallowed hard. He could see her weighing her alternatives. Her gaze strayed to the gun at his waist.

"If I wanted you dead, it would have been done by now," he said.

"Thanks. That makes me feel better."

He shrugged. "If you don't want me coming with you, then you're coming with me. Willing or not."

"I don't trust you."

"That's smart. But the way I see it, you don't get a vote. I'm stronger, armed and I know what I'm doing."

He could see her weighing her alternatives, and knew the moment she'd realized she didn't have a choice in the matter. She must have figured out that he'd been telling the truth when he'd said if he'd wanted to kill her, she would be dead by now.

She'd been strong so far, but she was beginning to unravel around the edges. She had a lot of nerve to keep talking back to him. He would guess she was so close to the edge she either had to fight back as best she could, or fall off the other side. He gave her about four more hours on her own before she lost it completely. She didn't know it yet, but he was her best hope for survival. What irony. Here he was, standing in the middle of some goddamn tropical jungle talking to Kray's ex-wife. Somebody somewhere was having a good time at his expense.

"What do you want to know?" she asked quietly.

"A short version of the truth."

She nodded. "I met Kray six and a half years ago while I was in Europe. I was young and stupid and... I suppose that's no excuse, is it?"

Bobby crept out from behind her and stared up at him. Jeff forced himself to smile at the boy. The woman rested her hand on the child's head.

"It was a whirlwind courtship. We were married for a short time. When I realized he wasn't—" She paused, then grimaced. "When I found out what he was, I left."

"I find it hard to believe he let you go."

She shrugged. "I wasn't nearly ornamental enough and was far too outspoken. I came back to the States and— Why are you looking at me like that?"

"Like what?"

"Like I'm not fit to clean your boots. You have a real attitude problem."

Jeff stared at her. She was right. He did. He hated everyone involved with Kray. "An occupational hazard."

"I'll bet."

"Mommy, I'm hungry."

She crouched down next to her son. "I know you are, Bobby. You haven't had any breakfast yet, have you?"

He shook his head.

She placed one knee on the ground and pulled a mangled roll out of her jeans pocket. "Here. Have this. We'll get some more food later."

"Get to the point," Jeff said.

The woman looked up at him. Wide blue eyes, the color of the Caribbean sky, held his gaze. Fear flickered there. Concern, anger, but no subterfuge. His gut told him she wasn't lying. At least not yet.

"I came home, then my doctor confirmed my pregnancy. Kray divorced me. He never said anything about the baby. I wasn't even sure he knew. I got on with my life. Three weeks ago, he showed up." She turned away, but not before he saw the tears. "It was Bobby's fifth birthday. Kray said he was old enough to learn about the business and took him."

"Just like that?"

She nodded. "He said if I tried to get him back..." She glanced at Bobby. "I got the message."

So did Jeff. Kray threatened to kill her if she tried to get her son back. "Apparently you don't know how to listen."

She rose to her feet. "What was I supposed to do? Just let him keep my son?"

"You could have done a hell of a lot better than sneaking in to save him yourself."

She stiffened and cleared her throat. "Do you think I'm crazy? I didn't come out here alone."

Her first lie. "Listen, lady, I don't—"

"My name isn't 'lady.' It's Andrea Cochran. Andie. I'll thank you to call me that."

"Fine, Andie. The way I figure it, the maid back at the villa already knows the kid is not in his room. She's about finished searching the house and grounds, and is going to call Kray on his boat. We can stand here talking about who and what you are, or we can move out of here and stay alive."

She glared at him. "May I remind you, Rambo, you're the one who asked about my past."

"And you told me. Let's go." He bent down and picked up Bobby. "Wanna bet you and me together can go faster than your mom alone?" He ended his sentence with a quick wink, forestalling the child's fear.

Bobby eyed him warily, then nodded slowly. "Mommy can't go real fast."

"I'm not surprised. Let's see if she can keep up."

Andie grabbed his arm. "Give him back to me."

Jeff started walking. "He's too heavy and you're already exhausted. How far is your car?"

"I'm not sure." She fell into step behind him. "I left it off the side of the road."

"Camouflaged?"

"I didn't hack down a tree and bite off the branches with my bare teeth to cover it, if that's what you're asking. I did pull into a turnout and park behind some brush."

"That's something."

"Your faith in my ability is overwhelming."

"How are you planning on getting off the island?"

She didn't answer.

He ducked around hanging vines, then stepped over a log, not letting either slow him down. Andie didn't have the advantage of his training or endurance. He could hear her labored breathing and she struggled to keep up. Bobby held on tightly, his skinny legs wrapped around his waist, one hand holding on to Jeff's backpack. The kid wasn't too heavy, but he was awkward. Jeff shifted so Bobby's weight rested on his hip and kept moving.

After a few minutes, he eyed the sun overhead, then turned slightly east. They would come out on the road about a half mile from the villa. It was unlikely she would have been willing to hike much farther on her own. He hoped she remembered where she'd parked her Jeep.

The temperature rose steadily, and with it the humidity. The call of birds and the drone of insects provided background noise for his tangled thoughts. None of this felt real. Not the boy, or the woman. Not the circumstances in which he found himself. Somewhere in the past few minutes he'd made the decision to get her off the island, mostly because the alternative was being identified before he'd finished what he'd come for. But he sure as hell didn't want to be saddled with an inexperienced, volatile party girl and her bratty kid.

He glanced down at Bobby and smiled. Okay, so the kid wasn't so bad. Bobby smiled back shyly and offered the last bit of his roll. "Want some?"

"No, thanks."

When they neared the road, he paused, waiting for her to catch up. Perspiration coated her face and her cheeks were flushed bright red. More strands of hair had escaped from her braid.

He reached behind him and ripped open the Velcro strap that held his canteen in place. He opened the top and handed it to her.

"Thanks," she said, between pants. She took a small mouthful of water and swished it around in her mouth before swallowing. "If you were trying to prove a point, you did. Aerobics doesn't equip you for jungle combat. I see that now. I'll be sure to have a word with my instructor when I get back."

In spite of himself, he admired her spunk. "You're some mouthy woman, you know that?"

"Yeah." She took another drink, then handed him the canteen. "I know."

After Bobby had drunk his fill, Jeff took a couple of sips, then slipped the canteen back in place. He shifted the boy to his other side. "The road is about ten feet that way," he said, pointing. "Which way is your Jeep?"

She walked through the brush to the edge of the road. Once there, she looked to the left, then to the right. He rolled his eyes. "Let me guess. You can't remember."

She turned around and glared at him. "Listen, Rambo, I'm not having a good day here. You didn't kill me, so I assume you're either toying with me, waiting to turn me back over to Kray or you're genuinely trying to help. As you pointed out, you're stronger than me, you're armed and right now you're holding my son. I think you've got enough of an advantage without resorting to giving me a hard time, as well."

"The name's Jeff," he said.

Her gaze narrowed. "Is there a last name, or don't I need to know?"

He didn't answer.

"Figures." She returned her attention to the empty road. "That way," she said, pointing.

He followed her out of the brush. A hundred feet or so up the road there was a turnout. As she'd mentioned, the Jeep was parked behind a tree, partially concealed by brush. Someone driving by quickly wouldn't spot it. Someone looking for it would see it in a minute.

He moved closer, then stopped dead. "That's your car?"

She nodded cautiously. "What's wrong with it?"

He looked from the vehicle to her. "It's a rental."

"I know. I wasn't able to bring my own car across the Gulf of Mexico. The water was a little too deep for my convertible."

"Let me guess. You flew in on a commercial flight, flashing your passport and credit cards at will." He swore under his breath. "Stupid woman."

"Don't call me stupid."

"Don't yell at my mommy."

Kray's ex-wife and child both glared at him. He bent over and lowered Bobby to the ground. The boy scampered over to stand next to his mother.

"He's mean," Bobby announced.

The childish pronouncement shouldn't have mattered, but Jeff felt a slight sting. Andie laid a protective hand on the kid's shoulder.

"I may be inexperienced, but I'm not stupid," she said. "I flew into San Juan, then took a series of tourist boats from one island to the other. I haven't had to use my passport and I've paid for everything in cash."

"Except for the rental," he said.

"They wouldn't let me pay cash. Besides there's a hundred just like it on the island. The rental company only has Jeeps."

"Did you pay cash at the hotel in town?"

"I haven't been to a hotel."

He raised his eyebrows. "When did you arrive?"

She brushed her hair out of her face. "Two days ago."

"Where have you been staying?"

"In the Jeep." She gestured wearily to the jungle around them. "I've been sleeping out, when I could sleep. Are there snakes on St. Lucas?"

"Some." He looked her over, more thoroughly this time. Weariness lined her face. There were shadows under her eyes, and her jeans weren't as clean as they could have been. Camping out in the jungle for two nights. Not bad.

He walked over and popped the trunk. She'd brought a small bag of clothing. He unzipped it. A pair of jeans, shorts for Bobby, T-shirts and underwear for herself and the boy. No makeup, no impractical shoes or fancy dresses. Next to the satchel was a cardboard box filled with bottled water, fresh fruit and a half-eaten loaf of bread.

"You buy this in a local store?" he asked.

She shook her head. "I went to the port when the cruise ship came in and shopped with the tourists. I'm obviously not a native. I figured it was the only way I would be able to blend in."

"I'm impressed."

He'd thought she might say something smart, but instead she smiled. A warm genuine smile that exposed perfect white teeth and made his gut clench. She'd been a model in Europe, earning a living on runways and in print ads. She'd never made it big, and after her marriage to Kray, she'd disappeared. God help the advertising world if they'd ever seen her smile. She could have made millions.

He ignored his typically male reaction to a pretty face, reminding himself it didn't mean a thing. It sure as hell wasn't about her specifically. She'd once belonged to Kray. He would rather be roasted over open coals than be attracted to a woman Kray had been with.

He walked around the vehicle. The glove box was locked. He held out his hand for the key. She reached into her jeans pocket and pulled it out. He opened the vehicle's door, sat on the passenger seat and unlocked the glove box. Her purse spilled out. He dug around in it until he found her wallet. She murmured a protest, but didn't try to stop him. He looked at her California driver's license.

"Not a great picture," he said.

"I was having a bad hair day."

He flipped through the credit cards. There was enough plastic here to buy a car. She had a couple thousand in cash, and no traveler's checks. He put the wallet back and searched until he found her passport. It was in her name. Bobby was listed on the document. That was something at least.

"What do you do in your real life, Andie?" he asked, stuffing the purse and its contents back in glove box and finally looking at her.

She stood by the edge of the Jeep. Her spine was straight, defying her weariness. "I go to law school."

He laughed out loud.

Andie glared at him. "Why are you so surprised? Even bimbos have brains."

He cleared his throat. "Look, I'm sorry I called you a bimbo. I'm sure you're a great person, even if you have lousy taste in men. Does Kray know you're studying law?"

"I don't care if he does. Despite what you might or might not think of me, until three weeks ago I hadn't seen or spoken to my ex-husband in over five years."

Jeff stepped out of the car. "Kray doesn't let go easily. Especially not a woman like you."

She rubbed at her damp cheek, then stared at the dirt on her fingertips. "I'm a real prize. You can see the men lining up for miles. It made it hard to get away, as you can imagine."

He had a feeling that if she stopped mouthing off, she would start crying. He couldn't deal with her tears. It would make him feel sorry for her, and he didn't want that. He didn't want to think of her as a person. Not now, not after what had happened with Jeanne. He couldn't forget and he wouldn't forgive. It might not have been Andie Cochran's fault, but he still blamed her for being alive when his wife wasn't.

"How are you planning to get away?" he asked. "Back the way you came?"

She stared at him without answering.

He walked over to her, stopping so close that she had to tilt her head back to meet his gaze. Fear battled with exhaustion and determination.

"Kray controls this island," he said quietly. "He comes here several times a year to relax."

"I know that," she said. "That's why I was able to find Bobby."

"You don't get it. He owns the ground we're standing on. He owns or controls all the hotels, half the banks and most of the people. He's everywhere. You've been lucky, but don't expect your luck to hold out. How are you planning on getting off of the island?"

"I won't tell you. How do I know you're going to help me? How do I know you aren't with Kray? Maybe you're keeping me hostage until he gets back and then you'll turn me over to him. I won't tell you anything." She glared at him. "Not a word. I don't care what you do to me."

Before he could decide whether or not to just leave her to her own devices, a sound caught his attention. He cocked his head, trying to identify it.

He swore under his breath.

"Mommy, that man said a really bad word."

"I know, honey."

Jeff ignored them both and slipped off his backpack. He pulled out his powerful binoculars. There was a clearing a few feet to the left. He walked to it, then looked out toward the ocean.

Sunlight sparkled off the clear water. Rocks jutted out to meet the sea, while waves crashed over the uneven formation. He waited patiently. In less than a minute, he saw that he'd guessed correctly.

"You're about to find out if your theory is true," he said, holding the binoculars out to Andie.

"What do you mean?"

"Look."

She took them and stared out at the ocean. "So?"

"See that boat? The one that's followed the coast of the island and is making a wide turn and heading back in the other direction?"

"Yes."

"Does it look familiar to you?"

She adjusted the focus, then gasped. "Oh, God. Kray."

"They're heading back here in a hurry," Jeff said, then glanced over his shoulder at Bobby. "Looks like somebody figured out you took his kid. It'll take them about forty minutes to get back to the house. So if I'm with Kray, this is where I make my move."

Chapter 3

The man leaned casually against the front fender of her rented Jeep, watching her. Waiting for his words to sink in. Waiting for her to crack. Andie swallowed the fear, wondering if she would ever be able to forget the bitter taste of it or let go of the memories.

She'd been nervous before in her life; she'd even been afraid. When she'd been eighteen and had been in the back seat of the car with her parents when an oncoming car had crossed into their lane, she'd been terrified. Not just in those brief seconds before the collision, but in the months afterward. She'd walked away, physically unhurt while her parents had died, leaving her alone in the world. Later, she'd been afraid when she'd married Kray, only to find he wasn't the suave businessman she'd imagined, but was instead a cold-blooded killer.

But none of those experiences, none of those fears, prepared her for the heart-pounding terror that had gripped her ever since her ex-husband had stolen her son. She'd lived with the fear, had even grown used to the sweaty palms and jumpy nerves. Until today. Until she'd come so close to escaping with Bobby, only to be captured by a stranger who looked at her as if he hated her.

So if I'm with Kray, this is where I make my move.

Andie still clutched the binoculars in her hand. She lowered them to her waist, prepared to throw them at him if he made a move. Not that being hit by them would slow him down much. As he'd already pointed out, he was bigger, stronger and armed. He also moved through the jungle with the casual competence of someone who had been through this before.

Was he with Kray, or someone else? She didn't know. He hadn't killed her. Yet. She took a step back toward Bobby. Her son was her only concern. He had to get away from Kray. If he stayed with his father— She shook her head. She couldn't think about that.

Jeff didn't budge from where he leaned against her rental. She moved back again, then held out her hand. Bobby slipped his palm against hers as his fingers closed around hers trustingly. They would run, she decided, trying to pick a direction without actually looking around them. She would have to count on adrenaline to give her speed.

Jeff pushed off the vehicle and placed his hands on his hips. He didn't tower over her, so he couldn't be more than six foot one or two. His hat shaded his face, hiding his eyes and concealing his expression. He wore a camouflage-colored shirt and pants, heavy boots and a holster. There were several compartments attached to his leather belt. She studied them to avoid looking at the pistol.

"Once they dock, it'll take them about two minutes to get mobilized," Jeff said, his low voice calm, as if he were discussing the weather. "He'll call for reinforcements from around the island. They'll be looking for a woman and a child traveling alone. Within the hour he'll know about the rental car charge on your credit card, and by nightfall he'll figure out you flew from the States into San Juan."

"Who are you?" she asked.

"Someone who's willing to help."

Andie wanted to believe him. She'd spent the past six years looking over her shoulder, always afraid that Kray would show up to take her child away from her, or maybe even drag her back. She hadn't dared get close to anyone because she couldn't explain about her past. One mistake, she thought for the thousandth time. How long was she going to have to pay for one mistake?

"Are you with the U.S. military?" she asked, hoping he would say yes.

He shook his head.

"Let me guess. You're some sort of spy."

His posture didn't change, nor did the straight line of his mouth. *I can't do this anymore,* she thought, clinging desperately to her fragile grip on reality. It was too much. She was so far out of her element; she didn't know the rules anymore.

"How were you planning to get off the island?" he asked again.

If he was with Kray, he would already be taking her back to the house, she told herself. If he was with Kray, she wasn't getting off the island anyway, so what did it matter if he knew her plan? And if he wasn't, well, she could use a little expert assistance.

"I still don't trust you," she said.

"Good. You don't have to trust me. Just pay attention to my instructions and we'll all get out of this alive."

That's all she wanted. To get Bobby and herself out of here alive. Once they were back on American soil, she could disappear.

"I've hired a private plane to fly us to San Juan. There are several flights from there to Florida tonight."

"How do you know you can trust this guy?"

"I don't trust him, but I'm paying enough."

"What if Kray pays more?"

She didn't have an answer for that. She couldn't bear to think about it.

"What time are you supposed to meet the pilot?" he asked.

"One o'clock."

He glanced up at the sky as if he could use the sun to tell time. "Then we'd better get going." He bent down, picked up his backpack and flung it into the back seat. When she didn't move, he glanced at her. "You driving or do you want me to?"

"Where are we going?" Now that she'd thrown in with him, she was nervous about getting into the Jeep. What if he had been toying with her?

"We need to get out of here. My Jeep is about two miles down the road. It isn't a rental, so it can't be traced. We'll leave yours there and then—"

"I can't just leave this at the side of the road."

"Why not?" he asked as he sat in the passenger seat.

"The rental company will assume I stole it. I don't need them looking for me as well as Kray."

"If you're worried about that, you can call the car rental company when you get to Florida. Tell them that you've returned home unexpectedly and that they should come and collect the car. We'll leave the key under the seat mat."

She couldn't think of any more excuses, so she led Bobby over to the Jeep and opened the driver's door. The boy scrambled in to the back seat. Andie then slid in and inserted the key into the ignition.

"Drive back the way you came," Jeff said, not bothering to look at her. "In a few minutes you'll see a dirt turnout, like this one, only deeper. My Jeep is concealed behind some trees. We'll leave yours in its place. With any luck, Kray and his men won't find it before you've left the island."

"I think I used up all my luck getting Bobby," she said and backed the vehicle up so that she could turn it around and head toward town.

Jeff didn't answer her. She wasn't surprised. She could feel the disdain radiating from him. He judged her by Kray's standards. She supposed she couldn't blame him. She still judged herself for what had happened six and a half years ago. She should have known. She should have seen the clues.

But she hadn't. She'd been young and stupid, and now she and her child were paying the price.

The steering was stiff on her rental. Andie gripped the plastic wheel tightly and concentrated on the road ahead. There wasn't any traffic this far out on the island. She hadn't seen anyone when she'd driven in, either. That was something. The man beside her sat comfortably in the bucket seat. Almost as if he were relaxed. If she hadn't noticed the watchful pose of his head or the way his right hand was never far from his gun, she would have assumed he wasn't worried about what they were doing.

They rounded a bend in the narrow two-lane road. "Over there," Jeff said, pointing toward a turnoff.

As she turned off the ignition, he opened the passenger door. He bent over and collected her purse from the glove box, then grabbed his backpack from the seat behind him.

"Through here," he said, leading the way without bothering to make sure she followed.

Andie wondered if it was because he assumed she would trail after him, knowing he was her greatest chance at survival or if it was because he didn't care if she came with him or not. Then she frowned. He'd taken her purse, which had all her cash. Subtle but deadly. That's how she would describe Jeff-with-no-last-name.

She opened the trunk and removed the small suitcase she'd brought. Bobby climbed out of the rental and stood next to her.

"I'm hungry," he said.

She opened the bag of bread and pulled out a slice.

He grimaced. "I want a hot dog."

"Later, honey. This is all we have now. When we get to San Juan, I'll buy you a hot dog."

"He needs to get changed," Jeff said.

"Why?"

"Kray has a description of what he's wearing. It won't put them off much, but it may help if he has on different clothes."

"That makes sense." She opened the suitcase and took out the shorts and T-shirt she'd brought with her.

While she helped Bobby change his clothes, Jeff pulled away several large branches, exposing his Jeep. The vehicle was about ten years older than her rental. The tan paint had given way to rust. The tires were muddy, but closer inspection showed them to be new. The seats were torn and damp from the recent rains. There were a hundred vehicles exactly like this one in the capital city of St. Lucas, all of them belonging to poor locals. She saw instantly that between the new paint and rental sticker, her vehicle had stood out on the roads, even though she'd been trying to blend in.

"Did you buy that?" she asked, repacking the suitcase and zipping it closed.

"Yeah. It's more expensive, but easier in the end. Cash can't be traced."

"I should have thought of that."

"Why? You've got no experience at this."

"And you have?"

He didn't answer.

Figures. Rambo types were always monosyllabic. She wondered if they got a pay deduction every time they spoke.

"We've got to get out of here," Jeff said.

"I'm ready. Let me just get the box of food." She set the suitcase down next to his Jeep, then returned to her own vehicle. After slipping the key under the mat, she did a quick check to make sure she wasn't leaving anything behind. The rental agreement was still in the glove box. She pocketed that, then closed the trunk and picked up the cardboard box containing her meager supplies.

"There's plenty of room," Jeff said, jerking his head toward his open trunk.

She glanced inside, half expecting to see some powerful long-range weapon or a secret decoding device. There was nothing but an oily rag, a jack that looked rusty enough to collapse at the first sign of use and a baseball cap advertising a local beer. She set the box down.

Jeff pulled off his hat and ran his hand through his hair. With the brim shading his eyes and covering his short, cropped hair, she hadn't seen his coloring, but she'd expected him to be dark, like Kray. Instead, Jeff was blond with blue eyes and the clean-cut good looks of a California surfer. The image was so contrary to what she'd just experienced that she almost smiled. Almost.

Their gazes locked. She saw a flash of cold determination flicker in his gaze, the confidence and willingness to do anything to get the job done. He wasn't some guy on holiday; he was a professional at this. She didn't know why he was here, and she didn't want to know. Better for both of them if she just got out of his way.

"I'm ready," she said quietly.

He nodded, then dropped his gaze to her legs. "You don't have any shorts, do you?"

"No. Why?"

"We obviously can't pass as natives. The next best thing is to go as tourists."

At that she did smile. "Yeah, right. No one's going to notice your unusual outfit there, are they?"

Bobby, who'd been following their conversation, sidled over to her and peered at Jeff. "Why's your shirt all funny like that?"

Jeff glanced down at the fatigues he was wearing. He winked at the boy. The friendly act, so incongruous when compared with who he was and what he'd done, made Andie feel as if she were trapped in a carnival fun house. Everything was distorted and nothing was as it seemed.

"I was playing hide-and-seek," he said. "With this shirt and these pants, it's harder for people to see me."

"Mommy didn't see you."

"That's right," Andie said. If she'd seen him, she would have taken off in the opposite direction.

"There's a baseball cap in the trunk," Jeff said as he started unbuttoning his shirt. "Bobby can wear it." He nodded his head toward the boy.

When he had unbuttoned the shirt to the waistband of his fatigues, he jerked it free. Andie didn't know if she should turn her back or run like hell.

"What are you doing?" she asked.

"Trying to fit in. As you pointed out, I don't look like a tourist. Yet."

He pulled the shirt off, exposing a red tank top. He sat on the bumper and unlaced his military boots. After taking off the boots and his socks, he unbuckled the thick leather belt at his waist and laid it on the driver's seat. He unzipped his pants and slipped them down. Underneath he wore wrinkled white shorts. He pulled the pistol from its holster. For a split second Andie thought she'd made a life-threatening mistake, but he tucked the weapon in the waistband of his shorts, against the small of his back, and pulled the tank top over the bulge.

From his backpack, he dug out a second baseball cap. This one advertised a local brand of rum. He slipped one on his head, then took the other from her hands and adjusted it to the smallest size, then gave it to Bobby. A pair of worn leather sandals completed his outfit. In less than two minutes he'd gone from trained military expert to beach bum.

He was tanned, with long legs and strong arms. She could see the ripple of muscles as he moved. The shorts fitted over his narrow hips, then hung loosely past his thighs. He was right—he did look like a tourist. She glanced at his face, but the brim of the hat hid it from view. It also covered most of his blond hair. Only a half inch or so stuck out the bottom. Conservative haircut, familiarity with weapons, knowledge of Kray and his line of work. If Jeff wasn't military, he sure was government. She didn't know if that piece of information made her feel better or worse. She shrugged. At this point, she couldn't afford to be picky.

Working quickly, he put his fatigues in his backpack. He transferred money and a mean-looking knife to his shorts pocket, then dropped the backpack into the trunk and closed it.

"Let's go," he said.

Andie nodded and picked up Bobby. Instead of letting him climb into the back seat, she sat down and pulled him onto her lap. Just in case, she thought. She wanted to be able to run with him, if she had to. Despite the fact Jeff hadn't taken her to Kray, she still didn't trust him.

Jeff slipped in beside her and started the engine. He pulled the Jeep in a tight circle, then headed toward the road. As they drove out of the brush, she held her breath, afraid that Kray's men would be waiting. There was no one on the side of the road. Just her rental sitting in the shade.

He stopped long enough for her to drive it back into his vehicle's hiding place; then he glanced both ways and hit the gas. They took off toward town.

Andie fought the urge to glance behind them. With the Jeep's open top and low doors, she felt as if they were completely exposed. That as soon as they were spotted, they would be gunned down.

Violent pictures filled her mind. Not just her wild images about what Kray would do to her if he caught her, but ugly memories from six years ago. From the moment when the pieces had clicked into place and she'd realized her husband wasn't the man she'd thought him to be.

"Just a couple more hours and you'll be safe," Jeff said. "Once you get off the island, you'll be okay. When you get back to the States, you're going to have to lay low."

She nodded. She already knew that much. She had money stashed in a couple of safety deposit boxes in different cities. After Kray had stolen Bobby, it had taken her three weeks to figure out parental kidnapping wasn't high on anyone's list of crimes to be solved. Especially when the father in question had taken his son out of the country. Once she'd realized no one was going to help her, she'd come up with her own plan and had quickly put it into action. Ironically, the generous settlement Kray had given her at the time of the divorce would pay for her escape from him.

Bobby leaned back against her and closed his eyes. "You tired, honey?" she asked.

"Nope."

But his eyelids fluttered shut. She couldn't blame him. After the morning they'd had, she was exhausted, as well. She wished she could trust someone enough to watch Bobby so *she* could curl up and sleep for a week, but she couldn't. She only had herself to depend on.

"There's a private airstrip north of town," Jeff said quietly, a few minutes later. "Is that the one you're going to use?"

Andie glanced at him. He slowed the Jeep and met her gaze. Dark blue eyes, almost the color of her own, stared back at her. His lashes were thick and only a couple of shades darker than his hair, although the tips were lighter, as if they'd been bleached by the sun. He squinted slightly and lines fanned out to his temples.

He was good-looking enough to be the poster boy for the local tourist commission. Come to St. Lucas and find romance. Only, she wasn't looking for romance, and from what she'd seen of Jeff, he wasn't too fond of her. She wondered how much of that was because she was obviously in over her head and how much was because she was Kray's ex-wife. Did it matter? As long as he helped her get away, he could think what he liked.

"Yes," she said, after a moment. "I'm supposed to meet a pilot there named Michael."

"How will you know him?"

She wrinkled her nose. "He has a tattoo of a snake on his left wrist."

"That should inspire confidence."

She smiled. "I'll admit I would feel better if it had been of a flying creature rather than one that slithers. But he didn't ask any questions."

Jeff returned his attention to the narrow dirt road. "That doesn't mean he won't."

"I know."

"Do you have a story prepared?"

"Yes."

"You want to try it out on me?"

"Not really."

He chuckled. "Good."

She stared at him. He was smiling. Honest to God smiling. "What's so funny?" she asked.

"Nothing. It's good that you've already learned not to trust anyone unless you have to. At least you're not as dumb—" His lips straightened.

"As I look," she finished for him. "Thanks for the compliment."

She was twenty-seven years old. She should be used to it by now. The average male assumed pretty equaled stupid. No doubt from Jeff's perspective, her coming to Kray's island and kidnapping Kray's only son by herself did seem pretty stupid. So what? Kray hadn't caught her yet.

Andie stared out the passenger side, watching the tropical trees and vines give way to flatter plowed fields. Her eyes burned. She told herself it was fatigue and the wind, nothing else.

"Look, I'm sorry," Jeff said abruptly.

"Forget it."

"It was just a knee-jerk reaction."

"I'll accept the 'jerk' part of the apology."

"I guess I am, huh?" The Jeep slowed to a stop.

She turned and looked at him. He angled himself toward her, resting his left forearm over the steering wheel. Bobby murmured softly in his sleep. Andie shifted him so her legs wouldn't go numb.

She studied Jeff's short haircut, the lines of weariness around his eyes, the firm set of his jaw. She wanted to look lower, but she was suddenly aware of the fact that his loose tank top and shorts left very little of his lean, tanned body to the imagination.

Something flickered in her belly. Horror filled her as she realized it was attraction. Unnecessary, unwelcome, ill-timed attraction. Oh, God, not now.

"Who are you?" she asked.

"Nobody you want to know."

She was willing to believe that.

"There's a road to the airport that goes around the town. We can avoid most of the city. We'll take that."

"Fine with me."

He reached his right hand toward her face. He was going to touch her. She didn't know whether or not to bolt or lean forward. Bobby prevented her from doing the former and panic from acting on the latter. So she simply stayed still as he touched a loose strand of hair.

"People are going to remember this," he said, then frowned and turned back to the road.

"Am I expected to cut it off?" she asked.

"We don't have to be that extreme. There'll be several carts selling things for the tourists just outside the city. I'll get something there to help disguise you."

"But I'm going to be getting on a plane in a couple of hours. No one's going to see me but you and the pilot."

"Exactly," Jeff said, pausing to read signs at a crossroads, then turning left. "Better for all of us if the pilot can't describe you in detail."

"Oh." She hadn't thought of that.

Jeff drove through the narrow streets, careful to keep within the speed limit. As they neared the city, three- and four-story buildings rose up on either side. Wide wrought-iron balconies jutted out several feet above the ground. The architecture dated back to the first Spanish explorers, but its beauty was lost on Andie. She tried to look straight ahead and not draw attention to herself. At the same time, she wanted to look around and see if anyone had noticed them. It was hard to tell who was watching whom. Shoppers crowded together on the almost nonexistent sidewalks. Drivers blasted horns as they fought for small parking spaces on the busy road.

From open-windowed restaurants and bakeries, Andie could smell food and exotic spices. Her stomach gurgled.

"Sounds like Bobby isn't the only one who's hungry," Jeff said.

"I'm fine."

Being near town made her nervous. She didn't want to stop and eat. They could do that once they got to San Juan. There it would be easy to get lost in the large tourist areas. Several cruise ships docked every day and unloaded thousands of passengers who crawled over the old city. From there, it was only a short hop to Florida and safety.

Jeff took a right turn, leaving the busy street behind them, then turned right again and came out on a paved two-lane road.

"We can circle around the rest of the city from here," he said.

"Great."

Up ahead was a freestanding stall manned by an old woman in native dress. Hats, printed T-shirts and locally made dresses hung from the rickety sides of her place of business. Jeff slowed the Jeep and pulled onto the red clay shoulder. He angled the nose of the vehicle in slightly, so that the passenger side was blocked from the woman's view by a large tree.

"I'll get you a hat," he said, stepping out and moving toward the stall.

Andie stared after him, watching his long, bare legs cover the distance in a matter of seconds. She could see the power in his stride. His blond good looks and clothing tagged him as an American tourist. The old woman could see there were other people in the Jeep with him, but she wouldn't be able to identify the occupants and she hadn't seen a woman and young boy traveling alone together. Jeff had thought of everything.

Andie glanced down at the driver's side and the key dangling from the ignition. Except he'd left her with a means of escape.

She could simply drive off and leave him stranded. By the time he could arrange other transportation, she would be away from St. Lucas.

She shifted slightly, ready to lift Bobby off of her. Her gaze drifted to the stand where Jeff was buying her a hat. He could have left her on her own, or even turned her in to Kray but he hadn't. Obviously he wasn't overwhelmed by her feminine charms. If anything, he seemed to alternate between disgust and ambivalence. She trusted those feelings more than she would have trusted an unreserved effort of assistance. She didn't know why he was on the island and she didn't want to know. Was he part of some agency's plan to capture Kray? She wouldn't want to interfere with that. The sooner Kray was locked up for his crimes, the sooner she and Bobby would be safe from him.

Her indecision cost precious time, and before she could make up her mind, Jeff had paid the old woman and was starting back toward them.

She glanced from the dangling key to him, and saw the exact moment he figured out what she was thinking. His pace didn't increase or his stride lengthen, but his shoulders straightened slightly and his gaze narrowed.

"You made the right decision," he said, tossing her a paper bag and sliding into the driver's seat.

"What would you have done if I'd gone?" she asked, then told herself she was a fool for wanting to know. The way her luck was running, Jeff would tell her the truth.

"Either fired a shot and blown out one of the tires, or told Kray where you were going."

"Whatever happened to chivalry?"

"Put on your hat so we can get out of here." He waited until she'd set the large-brimmed straw hat on her head before starting the engine and pulling out onto the road.

The bag also contained sunglasses and a gauzy cotton shirt in bright blue. "What's this for?" she asked.

"When you get to San Juan, dump the jeans. Buy some shorts. You'll look more like a tourist. The shirt is something for you to wear until you can stock up on supplies. If the pilot describes you to Kray, you don't want to make it easy for his men to find you."

Even as he gave her instructions, his voice was edged with contempt. "Why do you hate me?" she blurted out.

Jeff was silent so long, she decided he wasn't going to answer. Just as well. It didn't matter what he thought of her.

She needed to concentrate on Bobby and how to keep him safe.

The road narrowed and a small plane flew overhead. The thick island air seemed to press down upon her. Six and a half years ago, she'd thought St. Lucas was paradise. Now it was a prison.

They rounded a bend in the road. Up ahead was a collection of wooden buildings, all small and in need of paint. Tin roofs rusted from the elements. An assortment of planes stretched out next to a long single runway. The plane she'd seen in the air came down slowly, drifting like a leaf on a breeze. Its engine got louder as it descended; then the plane touched down and rolled to a stop.

"We made it," she said, shaking Bobby gently. "Come on, honey, wake up."

Bobby stirred on her lap. "I'm hungry."

"I know. There's some bread."

He shook his head. "I wanna hot dog."

"In a couple of hours we'll be in San Juan and I'll buy you three hot dogs."

Hazel eyes stared sleepily up at her. "With 'tato chips?"

"Sure, and a soda, too. But not yet, okay?"

Bobby nodded.

Jeff pulled up in front of the large building and turned off the engine. Andie gave him a tight smile. "Thanks for the lift and the lesson in survival." She touched her wide-brimmed hat. "We'll be fine from here."

He nodded. "I'll stay to see that you get off all right."

"It's not necessary."

"It is to me."

"Yeah, right. That's why you've been so friendly to me."

Blue eyes met and held her own. Something ugly and painful flashed across his expression. Something that made her want to touch him and ease the suffering. Then it was gone and she was looking at the cool expression of a handsome, but deadly stranger.

"It's not you. It's your lousy taste in men."

If he was talking about Kray, she had no rebuttal. She understood why he made his judgment, but she didn't have to like it. "Everybody gets one mistake. He's mine," she said flippantly, so he wouldn't know how his words had stung. "Come on, Bobby. Let's go find our pilot."

She collected her small cloth suitcase and filled it with the remaining water bottles. Bobby refused any bread or fruit, stubbornly insisting he wanted a hot dog. Andie prayed for patience.

When she'd settled her purse strap over her shoulder, she looked at the buildings, then started out toward the largest. It wasn't much bigger than a two-car garage, but she could hear voices from inside. Before she entered the building, Jeff touched her arm.

"Let me keep the boy," he said.

She stared up at him as her heart began to pound against her ribs. Oh, no. Not that. She'd *trusted* him and now he was going to steal her child? It wasn't fair. She glanced around wildly for a weapon or something to hold him off.

He grabbed her arm. "Dammit, that's not what I meant." His fingers bit into her. "Stop it, Andie. I'm not going to hurt you or Bobby."

She swallowed the fear and struggled for control. "Then what are you saying?"

"I don't like this." He jerked his head toward the building. "It's been too easy and I have a bad feeling. What I'm saying is that I'll stay here with Bobby while you go make your deal with the pilot. If something happens—I'm not saying it will—but if something happens, he won't know about Bobby."

"What could happen?"

From Jeff's shuttered expression, he could probably name her a hundred things, but he didn't detail them. Instead, he shrugged as if to say it was up to her.

He made sense. She hated that. He didn't like her because of Kray and he expected her to leave her son with him? She couldn't.

She didn't have another choice.

"Stand just outside the door so I can see you," she said, then looked at Bobby and tried to smile. "Stay here with Jeff. I'll be right back."

"But I'm hungry."

"I know." Andie left her suitcase beside Bobby, then straightened her back and marched into the building. When she crossed the threshold, she looked back to make sure Jeff was right where she'd left him. He was.

Inside the building, several large airplane engines lay in pieces. Four men were bent over different workbenches. The room smelled of sweat, beer and machine oil. Andie walked to a cleared section in the center and waited for someone to notice her. Finally, the dark-haired man closest to her looked up.

"Can I help you, lady?" he asked, getting to his feet and smiling at her.

She smiled tightly back and was grateful Jeff's hat hid her hair color. The way this man's gaze was roving over her body, he would have every detail memorized.

She glanced at his wrist, but didn't see a snake tattoo. "I'm here to meet a pilot. His name is Michael."

The dark-haired man frowned. "Michael no here."

"We were supposed to meet at one."

"Michael no coming in."

She didn't like this one bit. Andie glanced over her shoulder. Jeff and Bobby weren't in the doorway. She was about to panic, when she saw a flash of red from Jeff's tank top. They were just outside the door, keeping out of sight. She hadn't completely agreed with the precaution before, but the bad feeling growing in her stomach told her it was for the best.

"Why won't he be in?"

Dark brown eyes met hers. "None of the pilots are coming in today. All flights out have been canceled."

"Canceled? Why? The weather's perfect."

"Not weather, lady." The man pulled a rag out of his pocket and started cleaning his hands. "Orders. No flights leave today. Maybe not tomorrow, either."

Kray. He'd ordered the airport closed. Damn.

"You tell me what you want," the man said, moving closer. "I can help."

"I don't need anything," she said, backing up slowly. "Really. Michael was just going to...ah, he was going to give me a tour of the island from the air. He was recommended by my boss back in New Jersey."

"Michael no give tours," the man said. "Who are you? What's your name?"

From behind her came a sharp cry. "Let me go! Mommy, make him let me go. I'm hungry. I want a hot dog."

The man whirled toward the sound. "Who's that? Your boy?"

He said something in a language she'd never heard before. The other three men rose from their benches.

"Dammit, run," Jeff called to her.

She turned and ran. The mechanic raced after her.

By the time she reached the open door, Jeff already had the Jeep started and was circling around toward her. She heard the man behind her gaining. She dug deep for her fading last reserves and lunged for the vehicle. Jeff leaned across and opened the passenger's door. Bobby was in the back seat, clinging to the sides, crying.

"Mommy, he's right behind you. Mommy!"

The man reached for her. She felt the brush of his fingers against her back. She shrieked and dove for the seat. The man grabbed again, this time tugging off her wide-brimmed hat.

As the Jeep sped off, she glanced back and saw him staring after them. His expression hardened as he took in her features. A blond woman with a boy. He would be able to identify her to Kray.

She was trapped on Kray's island, trying to kidnap Kray's only son. She was alone with no way to escape. She looked at Jeff. He didn't spare her a glance as he drove expertly over the winding roads, turning again and again, as if he feared they were being followed.

"You all right?" he asked at last.

"Yes," she whispered, knowing she had to lie for Bobby's sake at least.

"You can kiss your plane ride goodbye," he said.

"I figured that."

"Now what?" he asked.

Now what? she echoed silently, then bit down on her lower lip to stifle the sob that threatened. Now she looked until she found another way out.

Chapter 4

Jeff continued driving north, away from the city and away from Kray's villa. He circled around small villages, turned onto one-lane roads, always keeping the ocean in sight and on his left.

The woman trembled. Every few seconds a tremor swept through her. She clasped her hands tightly together, her fingers squeezing so hard, the skin around her knuckles turned white. Even Bobby was quiet, as if he somehow understood the danger.

At the top of a rise, Jeff pulled into a dirt turnout. There weren't any other cars or people around. With a quick jerk of the key, he shut off the engine. Instantly the silence swallowed them.

Straight ahead was the blue Caribbean sea. Below, waves slowly slipped ashore, aimlessly flowing onto the beach before retreating. Lush plants surrounded them. Large palm trees provided shade. After a few moments, the birds and insects scared off by the Jeep's presence returned. The low hum of wings and sharp calls of separated mates filled the air.

He should have been able to smell the flowers, perhaps even the salty sea. Instead, there was only the scent of a woman's fear. Andie Cochran had run out of options.

He glanced over his shoulder. Bobby was lying on the back seat. The boy had found a few leaves on the floor of the open-air vehicle and lined them up like soldiers.

Jeff knew the easiest thing in the world would be to walk away. They weren't his responsibility. Maybe Andie would get lucky and find another way off the island. Maybe he would be able to finish the job he was here to do before she got caught. Or maybe Kray would choose not to be merciful when he found her. Maybe he wouldn't kill her quickly, but instead would punish her for taking his son.

Jeff rubbed the bridge of his nose. "You have another plan?"

"Of course," she said brightly. "Just drop us at the edge of town. We'll be fine."

"And pigs fly."

She turned to look at him. "I'm telling the truth." She made an X over her left breast. "I swear."

"You don't know how much I want to believe that," he mumbled under his breath.

"You can, Rambo. Look, I don't need to be with someone who thinks I'm slightly less worthy of life than the local variety of cockroach. So get us back to town and forget you ever saw us."

He was surprised at her vehemence. He shifted in his seat, wondering how she'd been able to read him so easily. There'd been a time when no one had known what he was thinking. Of course it had been five years since he'd been in the field.

Rusty instincts or not, he was the best Andie and the kid were going to find on this island. Letting her go wasn't an option. Not only because she could identify him, but because she was an American citizen. He didn't have to like her, he only had to get her away from Kray. He started the engine.

"Where are we going?" she asked.

"Back to town."

"You're going to let us go?"

He glanced at her. The sunglasses hid her eyes, but he knew what she was thinking. He was going to take her at her word and dump her. The problem was she couldn't decide if she was relieved or terrified.

"Let's get some food and more supplies. Then we'll discuss your options," he said. "The man at the airport didn't get a good look at me, so that helps. We'll head to the shopping center by the harbor. The cruise ships stay in port until around six so the whole area will be crawling with tourists." He shifted into gear. "Your braid's come loose."

He pressed on the gas, easing the vehicle out into the narrow road. As he headed back toward town, Andie dug through her purse for a brush. He tried not to notice as she drew her blond braid over her shoulder and brushed the strands free. He stared straight ahead as she raised her arms to begin refastening her hair in its neat style. But from the corner of his eye he could see the way her T-shirt tightened over her breasts.

His fingers clenched on the steering wheel as he swore under his breath. He didn't want to notice she was a woman. He sure as hell didn't want to feel his blood flowing hotter and faster through his aroused body. In the five years Jeanne had been gone, he'd avoided women and any connections, even the brief impersonal kind. He hadn't needed anything but his pain and memories. He hated that his body chose this moment to come back to life. So what if she was attractive? She was Kray's wife. She'd chosen to marry a killer. She and her kid were alive while his family was dead.

Refusing to look at her or acknowledge her, he drove down the coast toward town. As they got closer to the port, he began to check his mirrors. Up ahead, a white cruise ship sat in the harbor, an elegant vessel dwarfing not only the other boats, but the harbor itself.

"Do you think Kray already has men in town?" Andie asked.

He was still angry about getting turned on. "Yes," he said, the single word curt.

"If the man at the airport phoned about me, they'll be looking for us in a Jeep."

"I know that."

He continued on the waterfront road until they reached the edge of the shopping district. On the left were ancient stone buildings with low ceilings and small windows. Tourists swarmed along the narrow sidewalks. Laughter and bits of conversation carried to him. Everyone was having a wonderful time. Brightly flowered dresses and shopping bags blended into a kaleidoscope of colors. Tour buses lined up across from the shops, while cruise passengers disembarked.

Jeff scanned the vehicles in front of him, then checked the mirrors again. Kray's men could be anywhere. There was an alley between a linen shop and one of the many jewelry stores. He turned left into the alley and parked next to three other Jeeps. Only then did he look at Andie.

She clutched her purse to her stomach. Her skin was pale under her tan. Her sunglasses hid her eyes, but the fear was still tangible.

"Look like you're having a good time," he said, getting out of the driver's side. Bobby scrambled after him.

"I wanna hot dog!" the boy announced.

"I know you do, sport." Jeff tugged on the brim of the kid's baseball cap. "We'll find one here."

Bobby's smile was brilliant. And exactly like his mother's. Jeff stared at the child, seeing instead another boy. J.J. had had Jeanne's smile. The flash of pain was an explosion in his chest. Jeff swallowed hard and fought to keep his face expressionless. When this was over, when Andie and her kid were gone, he would remember one last time. He would recall the face of his wife and his child, remember their laughter; then he would have his vengeance. Maybe then he could lay his ghosts to rest.

Andie joined them. She settled her purse on her shoulder and took Bobby's hand. "I'm ready," she said.

Jeff pocketed the key, then led the way out of the alley.

Bright sunshine flooded the shopping district of St. Lucas. Cruise passengers jostled for position on the narrow sidewalks. Jeeps and buses filled the streets. The sound of horns, conversations and vendors filled the air. The scent of suntan lotion, expensive perfume and sweat mingled with tempting aromas from tiny restaurants. Jeff ignored it all as he carefully searched the crowd, looking for any of Kray's men. So far, he hadn't seen anyone suspicious. If Kray knew Andie hadn't been able to get a private flight off the island, he knew she would be looking for another way out. How? What would his old enemy think a frightened woman would do?

The cruise ship? She could easily pass for one of the passengers. Perhaps a fishing vessel or a private boat. Maybe a commercial flight. Jeff doubted he would expect her to be in town. That was to their advantage.

Behind him, Bobby chatted with his mother. The boy took an interest in everything he saw, laughing at some of the funny hats people wore, gasping with delight as a native man walked by with a colorful parrot on his shoulder. Andie responded quietly, as if afraid to draw attention to herself. For the hundredth time Jeff wished she'd picked another day to rescue her son, or even another time. He'd only needed two more minutes to finish what he'd come to do.

The narrow street ended abruptly at a large, square, open-air market. The crowds were thicker here, the call of the vendors, louder. Jeff was jostled by a group of tourists, one of whom turned and smiled an apology.

"There's a hot dog stand over here," Jeff said, pointing. "Let's feed Bobby first."

"Good idea."

Within ten minutes they'd bought several hot dogs, potato chips and icy cans of soda. Jeff paid for everything with American dollars, knowing most of the tourists wouldn't bother to get any money exchanged for local currency. There were picnic tables set up under a woven grass awning. He led the way, then paused to pick a seat. A couple of tables were empty, although most were filled with cruise passengers. He spotted an older couple sitting by themselves and headed in their direction.

"Afternoon," he said, as he took a seat on the vacant end of the bench.

"Hello," the man replied and smiled. He was short, with gray hair and a ruddy complexion. His wife, also in her sixties, was dressed in a floral print sleeveless dress that fell loosely over her considerable bulk.

Andie gave Jeff a confused look, then urged Bobby to slide onto the bench. She took the seat next to him, directly across from Jeff.

He introduced them, being careful to avoid last names. The subtle implication was that they, too, were on the cruise ship. The Colemans were from Omaha. After a minute or so, Jeff got them to talk about the small town they lived in and their grandchildren. Conversation flowed around them. Jeff didn't bother to do more than pretend to listen. He concentrated on watching the square. If one of Kray's men came looking for a woman and child alone, or with a single man, he wouldn't find them. Instead, he would see tables of happy cruise passengers all chatting together, including this one. For the moment, they were safe. But he still had to get her and kid off the island.

Mr. Coleman pointed to an ice-cream stand. Bobby shoved the last bite of hot dog in his mouth and nodded vigorously.

"Can I, Mom?" he asked, already scrambling out of his seat.

Mrs. Coleman rose also. "I think I'll have an ice cream, too," she said, leaving her purse on the table and smiling at Bobby. "Chocolate's my favorite flavor. What's yours?"

"Strawberry," the boy said and smiled.

"Here." Jeff dug a bill out of his shorts' pocket.

"Nonsense," Mr. Coleman said, placing a hand on Bobby's shoulder. "We haven't seen our own grandchildren the whole time we've been on the cruise. Let us treat the boy."

"Be sure to say thank-you," Andie called after her son. She'd pushed her sunglasses on to the top of her head. Jeff could see the worry in her eyes.

"He'll be fine," Jeff said. "Mrs. Coleman left her purse with us." He pointed to the large straw bag in the center of the table. "Besides, they aren't going to hurt him."

"How do you know?" she asked, giving him an angry glare before turning her attention back to the older couple.

"I can tell. They've never been out of Nebraska before. Mrs. Coleman's idea of doing something wicked is putting walnuts in her chocolate-chip cookies."

"So she's not a really bad person, then. Nothing like me. That *is* what you're saying, isn't it?"

Once again he was surprised at how well she could read him. "We don't have time for that now. I want to leave you here with the Colemans while I do some shopping. You need some clothes—so does Bobby—and we need supplies."

The older couple and her son were having a discussion with the ice-cream vendor. Apparently the decision about which topping to put on the ice cream was not one to be made lightly. Jeff stared at the trio and felt a twinge of longing. Had he ever taken the time to buy his son ice cream?

There'd been so many months spent away from his family. That was one of the reasons Jeanne had come to Lebanon. She hadn't liked the long separations. Jeff hadn't enjoyed them, but they were a part of his job and he'd accepted them as such. It was only after Jeanne and J.J. were gone that he'd wondered about all he'd missed being apart from them.

"*We* don't need supplies," she said, looking at him. "We don't need anything from you. I appreciate all you've done, but this is where we part company."

Her wide blue eyes held his own. He studied the straight line of her nose, the shape of her mouth. She had the picture-perfect face of a model and the body to match. That was why she got to him. There was no other reason that being close to her made him want things. No other cause for his arousal. It wasn't her.

"What are you going to do?" he asked, resting his elbows on the table.

"I'll figure something out." She glanced at Bobby, then glared at Jeff. "Don't think I'm going to throw in with you, Rambo. You've made it perfectly clear what you think of me. Besides, I don't trust you."

"You don't have a choice." They were both speaking softly, whispering in the crowd of laughing tourists. "Besides, if you'd really wanted to get away from me, you would have brought your suitcase with you and slipped away in the crowd. I'm your only prayer of getting off of this damn island and we both know it."

Jeff looked at her son. Bobby was licking a rapidly melting strawberry ice-cream cone covered with chocolate sprinkles. Mrs. Coleman was making almost as much of a mess while her husband smiled indulgently at her.

"It'll take a couple of days, but I can get you safely away," he said, still watching Bobby.

He didn't want any part of this, but he didn't have a choice. His mission to take care of Kray took a back seat to a civilian's safety, even if that civilian was Kray's ex-wife. He didn't have to like Andie Cochran, but he did have to get her off the island. Only then would he be free to continue with his plan. With a little luck, by the time she arrived in Florida, Kray would be dead and her problems would be over.

"Why should I trust you?" Or like you? But she didn't have to say that part.

"Face it, Andie, I'm all you've got."

She sighed. "I know. If I'd planned better or been more lucky I wouldn't be stuck with you."

He turned toward her. She sat ramrod straight on the bench. Her mouth twisted with disgust.

"You're not my idea of a good time, either," he said. "But if you want me to help you, you have to do what I say. No surprises, no secrets. I can get you out of here, but if you don't cooperate with me, you're going to get us killed. You and me being dead doesn't help the kid.''

The afternoon sun beat down on them. Jeff removed his hat and wiped his arm across his sweaty forehead. He wanted a shower and a decent night's sleep. He could have the former as soon as they got back to the house, but he wouldn't be sleeping much until he'd finished what he'd come for.

Jeff knew he was just enough of a bastard to hope Andie turned him down flat. He even thought about making it easier on her by setting the Jeep key on the table between them. She could grab it and the kid and make a run for it. If he didn't follow too fast, he could let her get away.

The vision tempted him, but he squashed it. He couldn't afford to let Kray know he was on the island. Kray would catch her before sundown and force her to tell him what she knew. Bobby would be safe from his father's anger, but Andie would pay a high price.

She half rose from the bench, then sagged back down. Defeat slumped her shoulders. "You win," she said quietly, staring at her son. "I don't have another choice. I'll do anything for Bobby." She straightened. "No secrets, no surprises. I won't run away."

Despite their situation, he grinned.

"What's so funny?" she asked.

"At least you didn't promise not to be any trouble."

"Getting in trouble is what I do best, Rambo. I don't have to plan it. Things just seem to happen. You'll have to live with that."

She blinked several times, as if fighting tears. He didn't want to know she was afraid. It made it hard to hang on to his anger. He didn't want her to be a real person to him. He wanted her to be an object—Kray's wife. He could hate her then. It didn't matter that his body reacted to her closeness, as long as he could hold on to the hate. But the second she got vulnerable, he would start noticing things such as the bewildered innocence in her eyes. Such as the fact that she was in over her head and that if she really was a bitch, her kid wouldn't love her so much.

A single tear slipped down her cheek. "I'm sorry," she whispered, brushing it away. "I'm trying to keep it all together here, but I don't know if I can. I'm terrified. Of you, of Kray. What if I don't get Bobby away from him? Do you know what that man will do to my son?"

Jeff knew. Worse, he understood her fears. "It's going to be okay," he promised.

"How the hell do you know?" she asked, her anger chasing away the tears. "You don't have the slightest clue what I'm feeling."

"I know more than you think. I had a son once. I know what it's like to be afraid for your child."

"Are you divorced?" she asked.

"No. My wife and my son are dead." For a moment he thought about telling her the truth. Then he realized where they were. Bobby was almost done with his ice cream, and he and the Colemans would soon return to the table. "It was a car accident."

He spoke the lie he'd used many times before. Most people didn't need to know the truth. But the lie wasn't enough to keep him from seeing the bomb blast, hearing the explosion, feeling the heat or recalling the pain that had filled his broken body.

He'd long since realized he would never recover, never really be able to let go until Kray paid for what he'd done. He'd spent the past five years waiting to kill his enemy. Nothing was going to stop him now. Not circumstances, not even his enemy's wife.

Andie leaned forward and brushed her fingers against his arm. Her touch burned at him, hotter than the fires of the explosion. "I'm sorry," she said quietly.

He stood up, doing his damnedest to ignore the need that swept over him. He wanted to lash out at her, to make her suffer as he had. Compassion softened her expression, turning what was merely pretty into breath-stealing beauty. Despite the heat and the smudges of dirt on her shirt, de-

spite the fear and concern, she was lovely. At that moment
he hated her as much as he hated her husband.

"Stay here," he ordered. "Talk to the Colemans until I
get back. I'm going to buy you and the kid some clothes,
then get some food. If you're not here when I get back, I
won't bother looking for you. You understand?"

He didn't wait for an answer. He turned his back on her
and disappeared into the crowd.

Andie clutched the packages Jeff had thrust at her and
followed him down the narrow street. The new hat he'd
bought her to replace the one the man at the airport had
pulled off made her feel slightly more hidden. The crowds
in the shopping district were thinning as tourists made their
way back to the cruise ship.

It was nearly three. Her body ached from lack of sleep,
her nose was sunburned, her spirits sagged around her
knees. Bobby chattered away at her side. He hadn't wanted
to leave his new friends, although the three plastic action
figures Jeff had bought along with the other supplies helped
to ease the parting.

"I hated doing that," Andie said, moving closer to Jeff.
"They're going to wait for us after dinner tonight, only
we're not going to show up. I can see them sitting in the bar
wondering where we are."

"Get over it," Jeff growled, not even glancing back at
her. "Better for them to think we're rude than for you and
the kid to get caught."

He had a point there. But Andie had disliked deceiving
the older couple. They'd been so nice, sitting with her while
Jeff had gone shopping. It had been easy to pretend, just for
a few minutes, that everything was fine.

They reached the Jeep without incident. Within minutes,
they were speeding out of town, heading north along the
coastal road.

"Maybe in a few weeks I can drop them a note and explain," she said, half to herself.

Jeff shook his head in disgust. "You exchanged addresses?"

"I gave them a false one."

He mumbled something. She couldn't catch all the words, but had a feeling he wasn't praising her. "I'm sorry I'm not like you," she said, folding her arms over her chest. "Lies and deception aren't that easy for me. I haven't made a career of studying the tao of James Bond."

Jeff glared at her briefly before returning his attention to the road. "You've spent the last five years living a lie, babe."

She opened her mouth to protest her innocence, then closed it slowly. He was right. Everything about her life was pretend. She'd never told a soul about Kray, not even Bobby. She'd avoided friends and close relationships because she couldn't afford the questions.

"It must get boring always being right," she said.

He didn't answer.

Andie glanced at Bobby, but he was involved with his new toys, lost in a child's imaginary world. He didn't notice the tension in the Jeep or her own fragile hold on sanity. She felt that if one more thing went wrong, she was going to crack into a thousand pieces and never be whole again.

She shifted the bags in her arms. One of them held clothing and toiletries, the others were filled with food. Bread, fish wrapped in paper, vegetables, mangoes, bananas and a prickly yellow fruit she'd never seen before.

He'd thought of just about everything. She stared straight ahead, but could still see him out of the corner of her eye. He drove competently, turning on unmarked roads, keeping to the speed limit, constantly checking the mirrors. Had she made the right decision, or was this all an elaborate trick to hand her over to Kray?

Andie shook her head. She couldn't think like that. She didn't have the strength. She'd chosen to trust Jeff with-no-last-name, and by God, she would trust him. Second-guessing would only make her crazy.

"Where are we going?" she asked when the silence became unbearable.

"I've got a house. We'll stay there until I can make arrangements to get the two of you off the island."

A house. That sounded nice. Maybe she would sleep tonight. She hadn't slept much since Kray had stolen her son. He'd come in the early evening, barely knocking before his men had broken in the door.

She stiffened at the memory. "How do you know he won't find us? You said he owns the entire island."

Jeff surprised her by grinning. "We're safe there."

"But how do you know?"

His grin broadened. "Kray owns the house. He's given it to one of his trusted lieutenants who is currently living in the States. Mando, his associate, uses the house to reward faithful workers. A recent run-in with the law has detained Mando in a high-security facility. The man who had earned a couple of months in the sun has also been detained. They were nice enough to give our men the key. So don't worry. There's no leasing agent, no contracts, no way to trace the house to me."

"You must love the irony of the situation," she said leaning back in the seat.

"It has a certain appeal."

The road curved to the right, away from the ocean, then angled up hill. Jeff downshifted. The Jeep moved along the road. Through the tangle of trees and brush she could see the occasional narrow paths veering off. Without warning, he turned left and started down a narrow trail.

"We're here," he said.

Andie could feel the perspiration on her back and her neck. The moment of truth. What would be waiting at the end of the dirt road? There was barely enough room for the vehicle. Trees and vines grew together, making their route a tunnel. The temperature dropped slightly, but it was still humid.

She glanced at the back seat and saw Bobby had dozed off. His limp body didn't budge as the vehicle bounced over the rutted road.

"We're at the north end of the island," Jeff said. "The jungle comes right down to the ocean. This house sits in a cove protected by rocks. You can't get in from the water. Even a rubber raft would get chewed up. There's trees on both sides of the property and no one around for about three miles. The house can't be seen from the water unless the boat is directly in front of it. The locals know to avoid any land that belongs to Kray. Unless you plan on setting off fireworks, no one will know we're here."

"How comforting."

He ignored her sarcasm. "There's a pool. Don't let the kid swim in the ocean. The current is strong and the rocks are only about ten feet out. Stay near the house. The sandy areas are safe. The only variety of poisonous snake is pretty shy, but there are a couple of deadly lizards and spiders in the underbrush."

"I'm not sure if you're trying to make me feel better or frighten me."

"I'm telling you what you need to know to stay alive."

At that moment they broke through the tunnel of trees and vines and drove into the sunlight and onto the beach. A one-story house sat in front of a large oval pool. Beyond the sandy yard, blue ocean stretched on forever. The rocks jutted out of the water like ancient sentries guarding the property. It was a place for lovers. A haven. When Jeff stopped the Jeep, Andie scrambled out. Once again, she was a fraud.

The absence of motion woke Bobby. He sat up and stared at the pool. "Golly, Mom, can we go swimming?"

Jeff got out more slowly and stretched. "The pool's safe enough," he said. "Can you swim, partner?"

Bobby nodded vigorously. "I've had lessons," he said importantly.

"Good for you." Jeff picked up the shopping bags. "I bought him swimming trunks."

"Thanks." Being a good spy, he'd probably thought of everything. No doubt there was a shoe phone, as well.

Andie grabbed the bags he'd given her to carry, then reached for her purse. Together, the three of them walked toward the house.

The wood-and-stucco building was bigger than she'd first thought. There was a wide veranda all along the front with a swing half-hidden in the shade at the far end. Jeff unlocked the front door, then went inside. Andie followed more slowly.

Bobby ran around the porch, his arms held out from his sides. "I'm an airplane," he called loudly. "I can fly us back home, Mommy. Look at me."

"Fly yourself over here and let's go inside," she said.

Bobby swerved in front of her, stopping long enough to smile up at her, then stepped into the house. Considering all he'd been through, her son was holding up very well. That was something.

She stepped into the house, then paused as her eyes adjusted to the dimness. The entire front section was one large room. The furnishings were practical wicker and wood, with cloth cushions, but they were high quality. Several paintings filled the white walls. There was a bookshelf between the two side windows, and a view of the ocean. As Jeff moved around opening windows, she could hear the sound of the surf pounding on the sand.

"Groceries go in the kitchen," he said, pointing to her left.

She walked through an informal dining area, then into a spacious kitchen complete with a built-in grill and microwave. She set the bags on the counter.

"There's electricity," Jeff said, following her and setting down two bags of his own. "It's a little erratic, but there's also a generator out back." He dug through one of the bags, pulled out a papaya, then handed the bag to her. "I got a couple of things for you."

Before she could look inside, or thank him, he was moving away. "The bedrooms are down here," he said.

She went after him. Bobby trailed behind her. "The master suite," Jeff said, jerking his head toward a half-open door. She caught a glimpse of a king-size bed and more windows.

"Bathroom." He pointed to a door on the other side of the hall. "The last two bedrooms are down here. One has a king-size bed, the other has two doubles."

She poked her head in both rooms. "Bobby and I will sleep in here," she said, motioning to the one with two double beds. She wanted to be near her son. Just in case.

Jeff dumped the bags he was holding on the bed closest to the door, then left without saying a word.

Bobby flew in, arms wide. "I want to go swimming."

"I'll bet you do." She dug through the bags. Jeff *had* thought of everything. There was a pair of swim trunks, shorts, two T-shirts and underwear for Bobby. For herself, their host had bought a red one-piece swimsuit that looked a little large, but it would do, a romper in a pink-and-white print, a pair of shorts and a couple of oversize T-shirts. She tossed the softest one on the bed. She would sleep in that tonight. At the bottom of the bag was a large bottle of sunscreen.

When Bobby had his trunks on, she coated him with the sunscreen, then sent him into the main room. She quickly changed out of her clothes, then pulled the remaining T-shirt over her suit. She would have to remember to get her suitcase from the Jeep. It had all their toiletries in it.

She walked to the bedroom door, then hesitated before opening it. The hardwood floors under her feet, the smell of the ocean and the sunscreen, the sound of the waves and the birds made her feel as if she were on an exotic vacation. Or on her honeymoon again. A shudder raced through her. She didn't want to remember that time. She couldn't allow herself to dwell on the past or think about Kray. If she did, she would get scared. Right now, fear was her greatest enemy.

She could hear Bobby's excited chatter from the front of the house, then Jeff's low response. The sound of his voice made her insides quiver. She wasn't exactly sure from what.

Jeff was dangerous the same way Kray was dangerous. She could feel it. In a way, that made her feel better. At least she had someone strong on her side.

She wondered what had brought Jeff to the island. He must work for the government. Maybe...

A knock on the door jerked her out of her thoughts. "Bobby's still hungry," Jeff said. "I'm going to cut up a mango. You want one?"

"No, thanks."

She heard the sound of his footsteps fading as he walked away. Drawing in a deep breath, she opened the bedroom door and stepped into the hallway. She smoothed the front of her T-shirt. The price tag by the hem caught her eye. She'd almost forgotten. She had to pay Jeff for what he'd bought them.

She hurried into her room and grabbed her purse. After pulling out two twenties, she walked into the front room. Bobby was sitting on the front porch with a bowl resting on his lap. He picked up a piece of fruit with his fingers and stuck it in his mouth. Two gulls played in the surf. He watched them, mesmerized.

Jeff stood in the kitchen, slicing more fruit. "You sure you don't want some?" he asked without turning around.

"I'm sure." She moved closer to him and slid the money onto the counter. "Here. This should cover what you bought today."

"Keep it," he said.

She stared at his broad shoulders and back. The red tank shirt he wore accentuated his strength and maleness. The warm spring afternoon left a sheen of sweat on his thick muscles. He was long and lean. The proof of his strength made her shiver. She would never best him in a contest of physical strength. Pray God it never came to that.

"I can't let you pay for our things."

"You're going to need the money to stay away from Kray when you're back in the States. Keep it," he repeated, turning toward her.

She wished he was still wearing his hat or sunglasses. But there was nothing to shield his handsome face from her. Nothing to conceal his expressionless features or the blankness in his eyes. It was as if the man had disappeared and in his place was a machine without a soul. He frightened her.

She left the money where she'd placed it and started backing up toward the door.

"Stay out of the surf," he said, repeating his earlier warning. "Keep Bobby in the pool and close to the house."

"I understand."

"There's extra towels in the guest bathroom."

How incongruous that he should speak of towels when she wondered if he was going to kill them. "Thank you."

She collected the towels. When she came out of the bathroom, he was standing in the hallway. The light was behind him, leaving his features in shadows.

"I'm not the enemy," he said, obviously having figured out she was still scared of him. He folded his arms over his chest. "I'm going to get you out of here alive."

"I know," she said. "That doesn't make you any less frightening. That's what you want, isn't it? You want me to be afraid. Then you can be scornful, as well as dislike me. It's about Kray. That I married him. Therefore I must be like him."

"Yes."

"I'm not." She stared at the towels. "But why would you believe that? Sometimes I don't believe it, either. I should have known. That's the real kicker in all this. I should have been able to figure it out. Right?"

She looked up at him. He nodded slowly. But he would get her and Bobby off the island anyway. Personal feelings didn't enter into it. He didn't have to like her to help her.

As she brushed past him and tried to ignore the flicker of heat that ignited where their bare skin touched, as she told herself to forget he was handsome and sweet to her son, she wished he wouldn't despise her quite as much as he did.

Bobby was waiting for her on the porch. Her child was safe, as least. Kray would never get his hands on the boy again. She didn't care what she had to do to keep that promise. She didn't care if it killed her.

"Let's go swimming, Mom," Bobby said, heading for the pool.

"Good idea." She hurried after him, moving down the porch steps and into the sunlight. As the warmth touched her skin she stopped. "Wait a minute, Bobby. I was so busy putting sunscreen on you, I forgot to put some on myself."

Bobby laughed. "That's silly."

"I know, but come wait on the porch until I get back."

Her son trotted after her. "Hurry, Mommy. I want to swim."

"I'll be right back." She opened the front door and stepped into the house. Jeff was sitting at the table, bent over some piece of equipment. As she entered, he stood up and moved to shield it with his body.

He was too late. She stared at the metal pieces, not wanting to recognize them. Not wanting to know. But she couldn't escape the truth. She knew a long-range rifle when she saw one. She met Jeff's cold stare and wondered if that bit of knowledge was about to cost her her life.

Chapter 5

Jeff read the terror in Andie's expression. She started backing out of the room. Her hands rose to shoulder level as if she was unconsciously showing him she wasn't dangerous.

"I'm cleaning it," he said, motioning to the rifle on the table behind him. "It can't hurt you."

She nodded at his words, but her face was still pale and her eyes wide. At that moment he realized she wasn't afraid of the rifle. She was afraid of *him*.

"Look, I'm not going to hurt you, either," he said, moving a little closer to her.

She continued backing up. Her expression tightened into panic. She couldn't decide whether to trust him or simply run for cover. He didn't want her going off anywhere. The jungle around them wasn't safe. Besides, if she gave into the fear, Bobby would join right in. He could do without the hysterics.

"Andie, come on. It's okay."

Her gaze was unfocused. She opened her mouth to

scream. He lunged for her, grabbing her wrists and pulling her close.

"Don't hurt me," she pleaded, barely fighting. She trembled against him. "Don't hurt my son. I'll do anything."

She was tall for a woman, and strong. But she didn't try to attack him as she had in the jungle. It was as if the last of her strength had slipped away, leaving her completely defenseless. Big blue eyes stared into his.

A single tear clung to her lower lashes. She blinked several times and it slipped down her cheek. At that moment he became aware of her near-naked body pressed against his. The red bathing suit outlined her feminine curves. Her long bare legs brushed against him, her blond braid lay against his forearm. She smelled sweet, like a woman, and his body strained toward her.

In those few seconds before he released her, he felt the hunger fill him. The need was overwhelming, more powerful than the hatred or even his common sense. He wanted to kiss her hard until she forgot the fear and he forgot the pain. He wanted to bury himself inside of her until there was nothing but the glory of the present, of the pleasure, until the past faded to an insignificant recollection.

Instead he shook her slightly. "You're overreacting. No one is going to hurt you." He released her.

She stared at him, then at her wrists. Slowly she rubbed her left forearm with her right hand. "What are you going to do? Are you going to hold us for ransom?"

"I was checking out the rifle. Nothing more. I already told you, if I was going to kill you or turn you in, I would have done it already."

"I see." She nodded. "It makes perfect sense. Why go to all the trouble to keep us around? You could have gotten rid of us countless times." She lowered her arms to her side. "I just came in to get some sunscreen."

"Then go get it." He turned his back on her and returned to the table.

He heard the sound of her bare feet on the wooden floor. She moved down the hall, then was back in a few moments. He could smell the scent of the sunscreen, feel her standing in front of him, but he refused to look up at her. Instead, he touched the barrel of the rifle. He heard her breath catch in her throat.

"I don't suppose you've got any proof?" she asked.

"Of what?"

"That you won't hurt us."

He glared at her. "My membership in the 'Be kind to prisoners' club expired. You'll just have to take my word for it."

Her fear was a tangible thing, living and breathing in the room with them. She was all the more vulnerable for being almost naked. The bathing suit left little to the imagination. Her legs stretched on forever. He was a bastard for noticing.

He set the rifle barrel on the table, then braced his hands on the smooth surface and leaned toward her. "I can't give you proof. You'll get that when you're off this island. Until then, try to relax. You've been living on nerves since Kray took your kid. If you don't get your strength back, you won't have anything left when you're finally away from here."

"I know." She tossed her head, sending her braid over her shoulder. She folded her arms under her breasts. "Will you promise me something?"

"What?"

"Mo-om, I want to go in the pool," Bobby called from outside.

"I'll be right there," she answered, then returned her attention to the weapon on the table. "If something happens, if there's a choice between us, make sure Bobby gets away."

"Nothing's going to happen."

"You don't know that. Kray is dangerous. Promise me you'll get Bobby out, no matter what. I'd rather he was in a foster home than living with Kray. At least with strangers he would have a chance. If his father gets him, we both know what will happen.''

Jeff knew. If Kray got his hands on the boy, Bobby would become the heir apparent to his criminal empire. Her son would forever live in the shadows, outside the law. He would be hunted, not just by the police, but by other criminals.

''I trust you because I don't have a choice,'' she said, raising her gaze to meet his. ''So give me your word that you'll get Bobby away from here, no matter what happens.''

He didn't want to do that. It was the kind of commitment any decent field man avoided. Personally, Jeff didn't want to be responsible for his enemy's child. He knew there would come a time when he would regret what he was about to say. But he couldn't refuse her. Not because he liked her or because she had appealed to his honor, but because regardless of who his father was, no five-year-old child deserved a life with Kray.

''You have my word.''

She lowered her arms to her sides. ''Thank you.'' She turned to leave.

''It won't come to that,'' he said before she stepped out onto the porch. ''I'm going to get you both off of this damn island.''

She glanced at him over her shoulder. ''I hope so.'' The screen door slammed shut behind her.

Jeff sat down at the table, but he didn't pick up the rifle. Instead, he wondered if five years behind a desk had softened him too much. He didn't doubt his ability to pull the trigger and take Kray out, he just wondered how he was going to keep it from being personal.

''Hell, it *is* personal,'' he muttered.

From outside came the sound of splashing and childish squeals. He stood up and walked to the windows beside the front door. He could see the sun as it slipped toward the horizon, the darkening ocean and the pale sand. Closer to the house, he could see Andie and Bobby together in the pool. True to his word, the boy could swim. He shrieked with laughter, then dove under the clear surface.

Andie treaded water next to him. Her long braid floated behind her. The lapping waves distorted his view of her body, but it was still obvious she had the kind of female appearance that bordered on perfection. He'd never much cared what a woman looked like. Jeanne had been pretty, but nothing like Andie. It hadn't mattered, he thought remembering those first few months with his wife. He'd loved her as much as he'd ever loved anyone. She'd been his entire world. They'd been young and filled with the excitement of unlimited possibilities.

He wondered when that had started to change. When had being in love ceased to be enough? When had the marriage started to fall apart and how much of that was his fault?

He stared at the pair in the pool, seeing instead another woman with another child—his child. Jeff knew he'd spent too much time away from his family. He'd wanted to be in the field while Jeanne had pleaded with him to take a desk job. Even the birth of J.J. hadn't been enough to slow him down. Now, with the perfect vision of hindsight, he knew he'd paid a high price for his career. He'd lost his wife and son. Kray had won even without killing him in that car bomb.

Once Jeanne and J.J. were gone, Jeff had taken the desk job. At first because physically he couldn't be in the field and later because he'd come to see he could matter more behind the scenes. Jeanne had gotten her wish. Unfortunately it had been too late for her.

A soft feminine voice recalled him to the present. He stared at the pool, at the two people swimming together there. A wave of hatred swept over him, leaving him angry and his mouth filled with the flavor of resentment. How dare they be alive and his family dead?

Bobby bounded up the pool steps, raced around to the deep end and jumped in. Water splashed over the sides. He surfaced, laughing.

"Good for you," Andie called. She pulled herself out of the pool and was sitting on the edge. Her back was to Jeff. He could see the slender arms, narrow waist and curvy hips. He ignored the passion that flared, instead focusing on the hate, knowing he would trade them both for a moment with Jeanne and J.J.

Then he closed his eyes and leaned his forehead against the window frame. He didn't hate them, he didn't even wish them dead. Instead, he wanted a chance to make it all right. He knew the truth now. Time was precious. Every moment was to be savored because it could all be gone in a flash. He wanted to take the time to bring his wife flowers, he wanted to figure out how to fall back in love with her and recapture what they'd once had. He wanted to play ball with J.J. and teach him to ride a two-wheeler. He wanted them back.

But they wouldn't come back. They were gone and he was alone. All because he'd cared more about his career than his family. Because he wouldn't give in when Jeanne has asked him to come home. When he'd refused, she'd joined him in Lebanon. It had been a move designed to save their failing marriage. When he'd threatened to send her back to the States, she told him if she left it was over between them.

He raised his head and stared at the woman and child by the pool. Sadness replaced the hatred, leaving him feeling old and alone. It had ended anyway. All his hopes and plans for the future. Ended in one moment, in a fiery explosion that had filled a quiet afternoon with death.

"But I'm hungry now," Bobby said, leaning against the kitchen counter.

Andie stared at her son and counted to five. When that didn't work, she tried ten, then prayed for a miracle. "I'm cooking as fast as I can," she said, poking the fish on the indoor grill. "I know you're hungry, sweetie, but it will just be a few minutes."

Bobby's lower lip thrust out. His hazel eyes grew mutinous. Tantrum time. Andie looked around, searching for a diversion. The problem was they were both overtired. Plus she'd let him play too long in the pool. He was exhausted and that meant cranky was just around the corner.

"I'm hungry now!"

Jeff walked into the kitchen. "Come on, sport," he said, holding out his hand. "If you help me set the table, I'll tell you a story about a magical bird named Echo."

Bobby eyed him suspiciously. "I don't care about no dumb birds."

Jeff looked shocked. "You haven't heard about Echo?" He glanced at her. "Did you know your son hasn't heard of Echo?"

Andie stared at the handsome stranger in front of her. He was serious, but she could see the hint of a smile pulling at the corners of his mouth. He was relaxed and almost playful, very different from the man who had been cleaning a rifle just an hour ago. At the first hints of twilight closing in around them, she'd begun to feel uneasy. But now, with Jeff teasing her child, some of her concerns slipped away.

"Isn't it shameful," she said, going along with the game. "He's very stubborn sometimes. I would appreciate if you'd tell him—" She glanced down at a now-bewildered Bobby. "No, he's too hungry to want to listen to a story right now."

"Tell me," Bobby demanded. "I want to hear the story."

"All right, but you'll have to help me set the table."

"Okay." Bobby reached for the plates she'd left stacked on the counter.

Jeff took them from him and pulled open a drawer. "Why don't you be in charge of the spoons and forks, sport?"

Bobby grabbed a handful of each. As they moved toward the dining room table, Andie heard Jeff start to talk about a magical, sometime invisible bird named Echo. He spoke in the animated tones of a born storyteller. His voice was low and seductive. She could listen to it for hours. Instead, she forced her attention back to the fish on the grill.

While it continued to cook, she made a salad with the greens Jeff had bought, then fixed some rice. As she worked, she listened to the story of the bird, all the while trying not to think about the gun and why Jeff was here on the island. It was too late to worry about trusting and not trusting. She'd made her decision. Pray God she hadn't made a mistake.

When everything was ready, she brought it to the table, and they sat down. "Go on," Bobby said, staring up at Jeff and smiling. "How does the little boy get out of the evil emperor's castle?"

Jeff leaned toward the child. "Echo made himself very small and invisible, then flew through the bars in the window. Once he was inside the room, he returned to his regular size, then opened his mouth. Out dropped the key. The boy unlocked the door and was far away before the emperor even knew he'd escaped."

"Wow!" Bobby took a forkful of rice and stuffed it in his mouth. "I want a bird like that, Mom. Could we get a bird when we get home?"

"We'll see what they have in the pet store," she said. "But I doubt we'll be able to find a magical bird."

"If I was real good, would Echo come visit me?" he asked Jeff.

"Maybe. But birds like Echo usually only visit in our dreams."

"Oh." Bobby closed his eyes. "I can almost see him. Maybe he'll visit me tonight."

Andie listened as her son continued to talk about the bird. Jeff answered all his questions. She wondered where he got the patience, then remembered he'd had a child of his own. And a wife. How horrible to have lost them both in a car accident. She knew how that felt. She wondered if he would like her more if she explained she understood what he'd dealt with. She'd lost both her parents in a car accident.

She stared at him, at the way he thought about Bobby's questions before answering them. The overhead lamp highlighted the different shades of blond in his conservative haircut. She reached up and fingered her braid. They both had blond hair and blue eyes. They could probably pass for brother and sister. Except she didn't feel like Jeff's sister. He was too male, too frightening.

She didn't know exactly why he was here on the island, but she had a good idea. He was probably part of a team assigned to take Kray into custody. She hoped they got him and fast. She would sleep a lot better if she knew her ex-husband was safely behind bars.

As she ate her dinner and listened to the conversation between Bobby and Jeff, she wondered if it would end well for all of them. If they arrested Kray, would she be held responsible for anything? She'd seen him kill a man in cold blood and she'd never reported the murder. That had to be illegal. But surely the government would understand her fear. She'd been three months pregnant at the time. She couldn't risk her child.

When they finished the main course, she brought out a bowl of fruit. As she carried dirty plates to the sink, she could hear the soft rhythm of the surf on the shore and the call of some night creature. How would Jeff contact the other people in his team? How would he get them off the island?

The ever-present fear swelled up inside of her. She didn't want to think about it. She couldn't not. She of all people understood Kray's determination and his power. She was a fool to think she could outwit him.

From behind her came the sound of laughter. Bobby had told one of his silly knock-knock jokes and Jeff was pretending to be amused. She turned and looked at the two of them. Jeff glanced up and their eyes met. Behind the humor was wariness, and below that, the flicker of something that could only be pain. Being with Bobby would be difficult for him, she realized, then wondered how old his child had been when he'd been killed.

She was his enemy's ex-wife, and Bobby was Kray's heir. Yet Jeff was willing to get them off this island to safety. She wondered how she would ever be able to repay him.

Andie closed the bedroom door behind her and leaned against it. She could hear the faint sound of the baseball game and nothing else. She exhaled deeply and walked toward the kitchen.

"You were inspired," she said quietly, as she paused to pick up the last few dishes from the table. "He'll be asleep in no time."

She walked into the kitchen, then stopped dead.

Jeff stood beside the sink. He'd stripped off his tank shirt and was standing facing the counter wearing nothing but a pair of white shorts. He was tall, strong and disturbingly male.

"Inspired how?" he asked without turning around. He pulled a cloth from a bowl in the counter and squeezed it. Dark liquid ran down his hands. He took the cloth and wiped it against his left arm. Instantly his skin darkened several shades.

"Offering to let Bobby listen to the opening-night baseball game was a brilliant idea. He's finally stopped whining, and he'll be asleep in a couple of minutes."

"Most boys like baseball," he said, still not turning around. "He's a good kid. He's just tired."

"I know." She moved closer. "What are you doing?"

"Going native." He rubbed the cloth against his chest, then started on his other arm. "I need to make arrangements to get you off the island. I'll blend in better if I look like one of the locals." He stretched out his darkened hand in front of him. "I couldn't pass during the day, but at night I'll be fine."

She stared at the small bottle sitting on the counter, but there was no label, nothing to say what it was or where he'd gotten it.

"You have friends here?" she asked.

"One or two contacts."

"So you'll be going out?"

He glanced at her. His face was still its normal tanned color, but his chest and left arm were dark brown. He looked like an alien from a science fiction movie. "I'll be gone a few hours."

Irrationally, she was suddenly terrified at the thought of being alone. It didn't make any sense, she told herself. She was also nervous being around Jeff, so she should be glad he was leaving for a few hours. Bobby wasn't the only one who was overtired.

"You'll be fine," he said, then dipped his cloth in the bowl again.

She didn't know how he knew what she was thinking and she didn't care. "I have been up to now." She glanced around the kitchen. "This is all like a dream. Like your stories about that magical bird. I keep thinking I'm going to wake up in my own bed back in L.A. That I'll find out this is just the result of too much studying and not enough sleep."

"Don't get your hopes up. This is real."

"I know." She was too scared to be dreaming.

He finished his right arm, then reached for a small mirror. Quickly, as if he'd done it countless times before, he swept the dye over his face. She watched as he was transformed from a tanned surfer into a local.

"What if it rains?" she asked.

He grinned. His teeth flashed bright white against his now-dark skin. "It won't wash away. I have a neutralizer with me. If I forget it, or don't use it, the color fades in about a week."

"You came prepared."

The smile faded. "That's my job."

"Spy school must be an amazing place. The most exciting thing that's happened at law school is some student got thrown out for cheating."

Jeff raised his chin and colored the underside of his jaw, then started on his ears. "You really go to law school?"

His casual surprise irritated her. "Yes, Rambo, I have a brain and I've been known to use it a time or two. I'm even in the top ten percent of my class."

He raised still-blond eyebrows. "I wasn't implying you're dumb. I was wondering about Kray's ex-wife deciding to be a lawyer."

"Oh." She folded her arms over her chest. After swimming, she'd showered and changed into the shorts he'd bought her and one of her own T-shirts. The night air was balmy, the breeze from the open windows, seductive. "I suppose it is an interesting career choice."

He reached for a small brush and dipped it in the liquid. After blotting the extra, he stroked it carefully over his eyebrows. She stared. He gave her a quick glance. "Details are important. The people who forget them don't survive long in my business. Eyebrows are a dead giveaway."

She flinched. "Maybe we could avoid the word *dead* in our conversations."

He used the small brush to stroke the hairline around his face, then used a comb to darken his short hair.

"Make yourself useful," he said, tossing her the cloth. He bent over the counter, resting his weight on his forearms. "Do my back. Don't forget my neck and behind my ears."

She stared at the vast expanse of gleaming male skin, then at the dark rag in her hands. He wanted her to touch him?

He glanced at her impatiently. "I can't reach the middle of my back."

"I understand," she said, and stroked the long muscles by his shoulder.

His skin rippled under her touch. She could feel the warmth of him, as if his body were a degree or two hotter than hers. Part of her wanted to throw the cloth down and run for cover. Part of her wanted to step nearer and snuggle against his strength. She hadn't been this close to a man since her marriage, and that had been over six years ago. Not that she was attracted to Jeff. She refused to be. She didn't know anything about him except for the fact that he thought she was almost as bad as Kray.

The dye went on easily. It had little scent, although she could still smell the maleness of Jeff himself. He stood perfectly still, apparently unaffected by what she was doing. If she was honest with herself, he hadn't once looked at her as if he knew she was female. Better for both of them, she told herself, even as she felt a slight flicker of irritation.

She shook her head. She was crazy. One minute she was frightened of him, the next she was cranky because he hadn't made a pass at her. Obviously she'd spent too much time with her young child and not enough around other adults.

She worked down his broad back, to the waistband of his shorts. He didn't ask her to go lower and she didn't offer. She dipped the cloth in the bowl again, then wrung it out.

"You'll have to bend over more," she said, trying to reach his neck.

He hunched down. "So why'd you pick law school?"

She moved around him to his other side and completed darkening his skin. "I'm done." She handed him the cloth. "I didn't want anyone to take advantage of me again."

"How did Kray take advantage of you?"

The way he asked the question made her realize what he was thinking. "Oh, not that," she said, waving her hand at him. "He didn't attack me, or anything. I was just so innocent, and unaware of what was going on around me."

He straightened and stared down at her. His mouth twisted in disbelief. "Where did you think the money came from?"

"I thought he was a businessman. I never asked any questions, and he didn't tell me otherwise. I suppose you think I should have known."

He didn't answer. He didn't have to. The momentary truce between them ended. She felt the change as he shifted away from her. There was a tangible coldness between them.

She wanted to tell him it wasn't her fault. She'd been a fool, but that was her only crime. When she glanced up at him, she couldn't say it. He wouldn't believe her. Besides, she didn't need his approval to get on with her life.

"Great Halloween costume," she said. His blue eyes looked eerie, contrasting with his brown face. She took a step back.

"It gets better. Here." He handed her a plastic jar. "Use this to get the dye off your hands."

She glanced down at her fingers. They were brown. She opened the jar and scooped out a small amount. After rubbing for a few seconds, the dye faded. She rinsed her hands, then dried them on a clean towel. Jeff worked beside her, checking his face in the mirror. It was as if the moment of hostility had never been.

How did he do that? she wondered. Did his anger fade so quickly or was he better than her at concealing his emotions? She watched as he opened a small plastic case containing brown contact lenses. After putting them in his eyes, he slipped false teeth into his mouth. Next came a thin black mustache. He reached for a bundle of clothing on the counter. Within minutes, he was dressed in khaki trousers, an open short-sleeved shirt and worn athletic shoes. The California surfer was gone and in his place stood a dark-skinned stranger.

He was the same size, but with dyed skin, the shadows fell across him differently, making his bulk look unfamiliar. The false teeth changed the shape of his face; the mustache accented the differences. She fought the urge to move away from him.

"Don't be frightened, pretty lady," he said, then grinned. The accent was perfect, the smile frightening.

Yes, Jeff could easily conceal his emotions from her. She wasn't exactly sure what he did for the government, but she suspected it required skills she couldn't begin to imagine. No wonder he thought of her with contempt.

"I won't be gone long," he said, his voice now normal. He gathered up his supplies and put them in a small black suitcase. "Four or five hours at the most."

"What if you don't come back?"

He stared down at her, his expression unreadable. "I will."

She hoped he would promise to return, or tell her not to worry, but he didn't. He took his supplies to his bedroom, then left the house without looking back.

She stood in the kitchen, listening to the sounds of the surf and fighting the fear. Jeff with-no-last-name might not like her, but she didn't care about that. He was all that stood between her and Kray. If he didn't come back, she was on her own.

Chapter 6

Jeff has said he would be back in four or five hours. Andie tilted her wrist toward the light spilling from the living room window. She stared at the dial, not wanting to believe, not wanting to know her worst fears might, at this moment, be realized. Six hours and fifteen minutes. What would she do if he didn't come back?

She sat on the porch swing, curled up in the corner, waiting. A thousand images passed through her mind. All the things that could have gone wrong. All the legitimate problems that might have delayed him. She was too tired for anything to make sense, and too worried to sleep.

She'd tried. She'd gone to bed about an hour after Jeff had left, but she'd only tossed and turned. Even the sound of Bobby's regular breathing hadn't been enough to calm her. Yes, she had her son back and she was thrilled about that. But they were still stuck on Kray's island with no way out.

She leaned her head back against the wooden slat and stared up at the palm trees beyond the porch. They were still in the warm night, their fringed fronds blocking most of the brilliant stars. The sound of the surf provided a rhythmic counterpoint to her frantic thoughts. Would he come back? What would she do if he didn't? She would have to find another way off the island. Could she wire the nearest embassy? What about—

She closed her eyes and forced her thoughts to slow. She would face those questions in the morning. *If* Jeff didn't return. There were still several hours of darkness left.

Gradually her mind emptied until she focused on nothing but the sound of the sea and the scent of the land. Softly tropical, the fragrance was familiar. Too familiar. Her eyes opened. So much for relaxing. The last thing she wanted to do was remember her honeymoon here with Kray.

Before she could find a safer topic to occupy her mind, she heard the low rumble of a car engine. She slipped off the swing and moved into the corner shadows of the porch. Headlights swept across the pool area of the yard as the Jeep came down the dirt path and stopped next to the house.

Andie froze, not daring to breath. She waited until a tall man stepped out. Moonlight illuminated him. He'd removed his false teeth and mustache. She recognized the easy stride, even if his dark skin gave her pause. Yet she couldn't move away from the shadows. There was something about the way he walked, about his posture. The predator had returned from the kill.

Jeff paused at the porch stairs. "Everything all right?" he asked, staring right at her.

She moved toward the swing, stopping behind it. "How could you see me?"

"When you moved, the moonlight caught the white in your T-shirt."

She glanced down at the shirt, then back at him. "I wouldn't have thought of that."

He shrugged. "Dark clothes are better at night, but don't worry about it. It's not going to be on the bar exam."

"Good thing. I suspect I'll be a better lawyer than I would be a spy."

"You don't want to be a spy. Trust me on that." He lowered himself to the top step and stared out toward the ocean. "So, everything okay here?"

"Fine." She took a step closer. "Bobby's been asleep since you left."

"Why aren't you in bed?"

"I couldn't settle down. Not with you out there."

"I've made arrangements," he said, resting his forearms on his raised knees.

Relief swept over her. Thank the Lord. "That's great." She took another step toward him.

"You'll be getting out on a boat. It'll take you directly to Florida. From there you can take a plane anywhere you'd like. And stop hovering behind me. If you want to come and sit down here, just do it."

His tone of voice didn't change so it took her a moment to figure out what he'd said. She realized she *was* hovering. She thought about retreating to the swing, then decided she might as well continue to be brave. The worst wasn't over by a long shot.

She lowered herself to the top step, but kept as close to the railing as she could. The stairs were wide; there was at least a foot between them.

"When do we leave?" she asked.

"Forty-eight hours." He pushed a button on his watch and the dial lit up. "Make that forty-four hours from now. Just after midnight. I've worked with this man before. He can be trusted. He's probably one of about three people Kray doesn't own on the island."

She risked glancing at him. "I really appreciate this," she said.

"Don't thank me until you're safely away."

"Still, I'm grateful. How much is the boat going to cost?"

"Keep your money."

"I can't. Buying us T-shirts is one thing, but chartering a boat is another. That's got to be expensive."

He glanced at her. He was still wearing the contact lenses and his eyes were so dark, the irises looked black. The odd combination of familiar and unfamiliar startled her. Her heart began a funny sort of thumping in her chest and her palms were damp. It was just fear, she told herself. Fear and very natural apprehension about the future.

"Keep your money," he repeated. "I don't want it and I don't need it."

"But—"

He shifted suddenly, turning so he was facing her. "You're going to need it to stay alive once you're back in the States. Don't be a fool, Andie. Kray isn't going to let you and the kid go. We both know that. So quit worrying about how you're going to get off this island, keep your money and instead figure out how you're going to keep Bobby alive and away from his father once you're in the States."

She flinched as he spoke and clasped her hands together on her lap. He'd frightened her again. Jeff swore under his breath. He seemed able to do that without even trying. The worst of it was he might be scaring her for no reason. If he succeeded, she would be free.

He looked back at the dark ocean and the faint white froth of the waves against the shore. He was tired and he'd been on St. Lucas less than a week. Of course he'd been planning the mission for months, maybe even years. It had always been there in the back of his mind, he admitted to himself. He'd never not thought about revenge.

"You're right," Andie said quietly. "Thank you."

He didn't bother replying. Instead, he wished she would go inside, or at least move far enough away so that he didn't have to inhale the sweet scent of her body. The fragrance was subtle, blending with the tropical breeze and the heady perfume of the night. It made him wonder what she would feel like in his arms and how she would taste if he kissed her.

He shook his head. He didn't want to think about that. Not now; not with her. She was Kray's wife. That made her the enemy. He searched for his anger and hatred, but couldn't find either. Maybe it was because he was beginning to see her as a person. Maybe it was because her strength made him respect her.

There had been rumors about Kray's wife. He'd assumed they all were true, but now he wondered. Andie had the good looks of a model, but she didn't strike him as the party-girl type. She cared too much about her kid for one thing. For another, she wasn't that dumb.

He shifted on the hard porch. He hoped she was smart enough to keep clear of Kray. If that madman got a hold of her— Jeff didn't want to think about it. Andie had to know the danger she was in. She'd lived with Kray, she knew what he was capable of.

"What are you thinking?" she asked.

He searched for the closest thing to the truth he was willing to risk. "How did you meet Kray?" he asked, glancing at her.

She rolled her eyes. "Please. Give me some credit."

"What do you mean?"

"You've been wasting your time thinking about me and wondering how I met Kray? I don't think so. If you've thought about me at all, it's probably been ten different ways to get me as far away from you as possible."

Jeff stared at her. She didn't blink or look away. "You're some gutsy lady, you know that?"

"Yeah, I've got more courage than sense. Don't rub it in." She sighed. "It's okay that you don't like me, Jeff. Just get Bobby safely away from his father. That's all I care about."

It was the first time she'd used his name instead of "Rambo." That was surprising, but not nearly as startling as the realization that she could read his emotions. Either she was a hell of lot more insightful than he'd given her credit for, or his five years behind a desk had left him dangerously vulnerable. He had a bad feeling it was a combination of the two. Or maybe, he thought, being completely honest with himself, he'd been acting like a macho jerk from the moment he met her. He wasn't usually like that. Of course he didn't usually run into his enemy's ex-wife in the middle of a tropical jungle.

"I still want to know how you met Kray," he said.

"How did a small-town girl from Nowhere U.S.A. get involved with a notorious crime lord?"

"Uh-huh."

She pulled her knees close to her chest and wrapped her arms around them. "It's a long, boring story."

"Neither of us seem to be sleepy."

"I guess you're right." She sighed again.

The sound came to him, like a whisper of the wind. In the faint light of the moon and the glow from the windows, her long hair gleamed like pale gold. She was too far away for him to feel the heat of her body, but he knew she was there. Just out of reach. A temptation.

He hadn't been with a woman since Jeanne died. Sometimes that surprised him, if he bothered to think about it at all. He hadn't set out to avoid women, it just sort of happened. The invitations that came his way hadn't been intriguing enough to make him forget the pain and guilt. Now, without warning, he wanted again. His mind might hate Andie for who and what she was, but his body didn't give a damn about anything but being with her.

The hell of it was, despite the erection straining against the fly of his trousers, this wasn't all about sex. Sure he wanted to bury himself inside of her and get lost in the passion, but it was more than that. He wanted to hold and be held, to whisper in the middle of the night, to sleep in a sweet tangle of arms and legs. He missed more than the sex. He missed the closeness of living with someone. He missed being married.

He studied Andie's profile, but instead of seeing her as she sat next to him, he saw the photographs taken with telephoto lenses, blown up until everything was grainy. He remembered her in short tight dresses and cropped red hair. He remembered her clinging to Kray's arm and laughing.

Even while his body ached for her, even while he felt guilty for being a jerk and judging her, even while he acknowledged she was brave and smart, with a strong sense of survival, he hated her. Not for marrying Kray, but for being alive when Jeanne wasn't.

"Once upon a time there was a tall gangling fifteen-year-old, with big eyes and skinny legs." Andie glanced at him. "I was *not* popular in high school."

"I'm surprised."

"No, you're not." She tucked a loose strand of hair behind her ear and continued. "We lived in a small town in central California. You wouldn't have heard of it. Anyway, one weekend my mom took me to the mall. There was a big model search. We didn't know anything about it until we got inside. There were all these really beautiful girls there. I'd never seen so many. I was standing there watching when one of the photographers saw me. He wanted to take my picture."

She smiled at the memory. "I don't know who was more surprised. Me or my mom. I let him take a bunch of photos, then I gave him my name. Three weeks later I got a call from an agency in New York. They wanted me to come see them. If I looked anything like the photos, they were going to send me to Europe to do some print work and model for the spring collection. I thought it was joke."

"Did you go?"

She shook her head. "I was only fifteen. The farthest I'd been from home was the weekend I went with my parents to San Francisco. I was going to finish high school and become a veterinary assistant." Her smile faded. "Such lofty goals."

"What happened?"

"When I was a senior in high school, my parents were killed in a car accident."

She paused, then looked at him. For a moment he didn't understand what she was waiting for. Then he remembered. The lie. That Jeanne and J.J. had died in a car accident, as well. It was something they had in common.

The explosion of rage surprised him. He wanted to stand up and tell her they had nothing common, nothing except the fact that her husband had murdered his family. He wanted to destroy her world, as his had been destroyed. He wanted to see her suffering and in pain.

He did nothing. He didn't move, didn't speak, didn't look away. Finally she realized he wasn't going to respond, so she went on with her story.

"By that time I'd done some local modeling. I'd just turned eighteen. Their estate was small, but it was enough to get me to New York. From there the agency took over. I was sent to Europe. It was a huge mistake."

He'd calmed down enough to speak normally. "Weren't you successful?"

She rested her chin on her knees. "I made a lot of money, if that's what you're asking. But I was kid. I'd never traveled, had never been on my own. Suddenly I was thrust in this high-powered existence. I had more money than I knew what to do with. Everywhere I went, men wanted to be with me, take me places. I missed my parents, my home and my friends, but I couldn't go back. I remember that the most. Thinking I couldn't go back. I was never clear why I couldn't." She took a deep breath. "Now I know I wanted desperately to fit in, to belong somewhere. I was trying to replace my family. I fell in and out of love a lot. Or at least I thought it was love. There were a lot of strange people around."

She stared at the ocean. "I know what they said about me. About the parties and the men. I had a reputation for being wild." She smiled. "I was so happy to be notorious. The truth was I was a terrible drinker. After one glass of wine I felt like I was going to throw up. I'd always felt awkward about my body, so I'd never been free with men. Then I got involved with a dashing Frenchman." She shivered slightly. "Very handsome, very suave. Elegant dresser. He was my first—" She cleared her throat. "Anyway, I fell in love, for real, I thought. We got engaged. Two weeks later I found him in bed with my best friend. I was stunned. I ran off to Monte Carlo." Her half laugh sounded sad. "Isn't that dramatic? I ran off to Monte Carlo. To lick my wounds and salvage my pride."

He didn't want to feel sorry for her, and he didn't want to know she might have been one of the innocents. It was easier to hate her if he thought of her simply as Kray's wife.

"Yeah, you had it real hard."

She glanced at him. "You're consistent, Rambo. I'll give you that. While I was staying with a friend in her rather small but exclusive apartment, I met Kray." Her bravado slipped a little. "I didn't know. I swear I didn't know. I was young and stupid, but I would have run in the other direction if I'd had a clue about who he was."

She paused as if waiting for him to yell at her. When he didn't, she straightened and stretched out her long, bare legs. "He was older, very charming. He knows women. I didn't have a prayer. Within the first hour, I'd told him everything about myself, including the experience with the Frenchman. By the end of the week I had a private suite in the hotel where he was staying. I thought he was a good man. I thought he cared about me. It wasn't until later that I put it all together. I can't be sure of course, but I've always wondered."

"What?"

"There was a car accident. I didn't find out about it until we were married. The Frenchman I'd been engaged to had been hit by a car about a week after I met Kray. He died instantly. I think it's because of me. Isn't that awful? I'm afraid to face the truth, yet there it sits for everyone to see. How am I supposed to live with that?"

He wasn't surprised by what Kray had done. A twisted form of justice had always been the crime lord's calling card. He protected what he owned and that protection would extend to the woman he planned to marry. In a single, large explosion Kray had stolen Jeff's ability to protect those *he* loved. He wondered what Andie would think if she knew the truth.

She blinked several times before continuing. "I didn't want to know, you see. I didn't want to have made a mistake. I was looking for a place to belong. No, that's not right. I wanted to belong to someone. I was a child inside, but no one knew that. Not even me. I just wanted to love someone and have him love me back. I wanted what everyone else has and takes for granted—a normal life. Is that so awful?''

She turned toward him. The moonlight filtered through the palm fronds and highlighted her high cheekbones and full mouth. Her skin glowed.

The question hung between them. Was it so awful? Was it her fault? Did he have the right to keep on hating her for being alive?

He wanted to shout *yes*. She deserved what she got, and more. Except it wasn't that simple anymore. He could feel her confusion and her pain. The first twinges of compassion surprised and irritated him. The need within him was overwhelming. Not just to touch her, but to comfort her. To hold her until the wounds had closed and begun to heal.

Who was he to heal anyone?

She glanced back at the ocean and raised her chin slightly. He realized she fought against her emotions and the tears they produced. She looked fragile, sitting there alone in the dark. She waited for him to pass judgment. To continue to hate her. He did hate her. Almost as much as he wanted her.

Without stopping to think why he risked it, he slid toward her. Her lower lip quivered.

''No, it's not so awful,'' he said, reaching his arm around her shoulder and drawing her close.

He was ten different kinds of a fool. Worse, he was crossing the line and once on the other side, he might never find his way back.

Before he could pull away, Andie threw herself against him. She wrapped her arms around his waist and pressed her face against his chest.

''I know you hate me,'' she said, her voice broken and contrite. ''I'm sorry I'm in the way. I'm sorry I married him. I just want everything to be okay and it's not. It's never going to be okay. What if I can't do it? What if I can't keep my son safe? I'm so afraid.''

''It'll be all right,'' he said automatically.

"You don't know that."

She raised her head and looked up at him. Her blue eyes glistened with unshed tears. He should shove her away from him. He should tell her the truth about what Kray did. He should remember his wife and the explosion that took her life.

But all he could see was Andie. She was close, too close. Too real. In his arms, trembling. She was alive and made him realize how he'd missed the living. He studied her perfect features. Her eyes. Her mouth. God, he couldn't look at anything but her mouth. There, for the taking. Then the wanting overwhelmed him with unexpected force. He had to taste her or perish.

He hesitated that last moment. Fighting the need, the pain, the desire and the past. Her gaze locked with his. He read uncertainty, then an answering flare. He brushed his lips against hers.

It had been so long, he wasn't sure what the kiss would feel like. He'd forgotten about the rush of desire, the passion that flooded his body. She was soft and hot, her sweet lips trembling slightly under his.

He gripped her shoulders tightly, wanting to thrust her away. Instead, his eyes closed and he hauled her against him.

She made a small sound, surprise and encouragement, as if she, too, needed this moment of holding and touching. He felt a flash of sympathy, of connection; then it was lost, burned away by the fire that engulfed him.

He pressed hard against her mouth, wanting to feel every part of her. So smooth and soft, so willing. As he increased the pressure, her lips clung to his, as if afraid he would leave too soon. Her fingers brushed against his sides; then she leaned against him. Her breasts flattened against his chest, her thighs bumped his knees. The warmth of her, the scent, the need surrounded him in a woven net of desire.

He parted his mouth. She responded in kind, opening for him. He swept his tongue inside. She was hotter there, sweeter. Oh, the taste of her. He'd forgotten about the forbidden flavor of a woman. His breathing deepened.

Between his thighs, need pulsed in time with his quickening heartbeat. His muscles tensed, his blood heated. He was harder than he ever remembered being, the passion was stronger, the hunger deeper. He raised his hands from her shoulders to her neck. How slender she was. Her skin felt like rose petals, cool and smooth. He touched her hair, the liquid satin, then fingered the long rope of her braid.

She clutched at his back. Her fingers branded him, as did her breasts. He moved his chest back and forth. Through the layer of her T-shirt and bra, he felt her breasts swell and tighten.

He wanted her naked. He wanted to touch her and taste her—all of her. He wanted to explore every inch, to discover secret freckles, the feminine dips and hollows, the shape of her hips, her ribs. He wanted to trace the long lines of her legs, her arms, her hands. He wanted to bring her pleasure in his arms, see her shudder, hear his name spoken in passionate surrender.

The need overwhelmed him. He cupped his fingers along her jaw, holding her still. He tilted his head so he could go deeper inside of her mouth. She met his assault, matching him thrust for thrust. There was a fire between them. He could feel it licking along his body, consuming him. There was nothing but the moment and how she made him feel. Long-denied hunger exploded into a beast he couldn't control. There was only this woman in his arms and the night. Nothing else mattered.

He pulled back slightly so he could kiss her face. She laughed softly as he nipped at her nose, then gently traced an outline of her mouth. She was different. He liked the differences. They—

Jeff stiffened. His muscles tightened with shock, as if he'd plunged into icy water. He opened his eyes to find Andie looking up at her. Wide blue eyes darkened with confusion. Different. She was different from Jeanne. Different hair color, different features, different shape.

"Jeff?"

Even her voice was different. Even the question, the slight flicker of pain, the shifting of her against him was different.

He stood up and crossed the porch to the corner opposite the swing. He stared out at the night. Instead of seeing the surf or the stars, he tried to picture his wife. The image wouldn't come to him.

Instead, he saw Andie's face. The faint glistening of tears, the slight quiver of her mouth. Had Kray also fallen for tears in the moonlight?

He needed to know more about her. More about her marriage so his hatred could strengthen him. For despite the pain and the loss, he still wanted her.

"So you met Kray in Monte Carlo and he fixed your broken heart," he said harshly. "Then what?"

Andie stood up. She leaned against the porch railing and stared at him. "You still want to hear about my past?"

"Yes."

She touched her fingers to her mouth as if she didn't believe what they'd just done. Or how he was acting. He didn't care about that. He had to know more. "Tell me everything. You must have married pretty quickly."

"We did," she said slowly. "We were engaged within the month and married a few weeks after that. Are you all right?"

"I'm fine." She flinched at his harsh tone. He hated that he noticed the way her hands trembled slightly. "Go on. When did you first figure out the truth about him?"

"There were clues before we were married, but I didn't put them together until after. I suppose I began to wonder on our honeymoon. At first it was just the two of us." She folded her arms over her chest and looked out at the sea. "At first it was exactly what I thought it would be. Then things began to change. More and more people flew in to meet with him. There was always something odd about the way he did business. I couldn't put my finger on it, but I was uncomfortable around his associates. Unfortunately they were staying with us at the villa, so I couldn't escape them."

Jeff heard the words, but he didn't want to believe her. "At the villa? Here? You honeymooned on St. Lucas with Kray?"

She stared at him. Slowly she lowered her arms to her side, then stiffened her spine. She walked toward him, stopping when she was two steps away. The light from the living room spilled onto her face. "Yes. What did you think?"

"You've been here before?"

"For six weeks. I left him a few months later, so I never came back. The honeymoon is the reason I knew about the island in the first place. That's why I knew where he would take Bobby."

He could still taste her sweetness. He wanted to scrub the flavor away. He glared at her, despising her, despising himself. She'd been with Kray on this island. She'd touched him and loved him. Jeff clutched the railing, squeezing until his fingers ached. How could he have been so blind? How could he have kissed her?

"Jeff, what's wrong?" She placed her hand on his arm.

He jerked away. "Go inside."

"What?"

"Go inside," he repeated slowly. "Get some rest. We'll be leaving soon. In the meantime, just stay out of my way."

"Stay out of *your* way? You're the one who—"

"Don't say it," he growled, glaring at her. "Damn you, don't you say it."

She stared at him as if he'd gone crazy. Perhaps he had. He'd also hurt her. He read that in the slight slump of her shoulders as she turned away and walked into the house.

Jeff closed his eyes against the memories, but that didn't help. He could still see her and taste her. His body was still hard from wanting her. It didn't matter that she'd screwed his wife's killer. It didn't matter that she'd borne Kray's son.

"I'm sorry," he whispered to the night. "Jeanne, I'm so sorry."

He wasn't sure what he apologized for. The kiss? Or not being the kind of husband she'd needed. Did he wish to atone for a moment of passion, or all the years he'd loved his job more?

But it wasn't enough. He still couldn't recall her face. The exact sound of her voice, of her laugh, eluded him, like the echo of a dream he couldn't recall. He could see J.J. easily. The boy lived on in his heart. But Jeanne had faded.

It was a punishment. Once again Kray had won. Jeff wondered what Kray would say if he knew the truth. That Jeff lusted after his woman.

Chapter 7

It was another perfect day in paradise. Andie glanced up at the brilliant blue sky, at the bright sun, and frowned. How did the locals stand so much happy weather? Right now she wanted the climate to match her mood. That meant it should be cold, gray and rainy. Instead she was stuck here on St. Lucas, basking in the tropics.

She reached down and splashed water onto the inflatable raft she and Bobby had found in a nearby storage shed that morning. While her son sat on the steps in the shallow end of the pool and played with his now-amphibious action figures, she pressed her sunglasses more firmly on her face and closed her eyes to block out the sun.

She wished she could sleep. Last night, after she'd fled the porch and Jeff's odd behavior, she'd lain in bed staring at the ceiling. The sound of the surf and her son's even breathing hadn't been enough to block out Jeff's pacing. He'd walked back and forth on the porch for hours. She'd been torn between wondering what he was thinking about, wanting to go and ask if she could help, and staying out of his way. He was the most confusing and exasperating man she'd ever met.

Did he worry about getting them off the island? Was it concerns about his secret mission that kept him awake? Or was it the kiss?

Andie sighed and opened her eyes. Better to stare at the sparkling pool water and the white sand than to relive that kiss again. She didn't want to remember how it had felt to be in Jeff's arms. It had been so long since someone had held her. She could have wept with happiness, not that she'd had a chance to do more than absorb his strength and maleness. It had almost felt foreign. Dormant sensations had awakened painfully. She hadn't felt desire or need in years. She hadn't had the time or even been willing to risk those feelings. They would have meant she was close to someone. Letting a man into her life had been too risky. She'd never known when Kray was going to return, but she'd always known he would. He wasn't the type to let his possessions go, even one he didn't want anymore.

So she'd stayed on her own, because it was safer. She'd been determined not to let anyone past the barriers. With Jeff she hadn't had a choice. He'd surprised her, sweeping her up in a maelstrom of need, touching her, not just physically, but inside. Then he'd pushed her away.

She knew why. It even made sense in a twisted way. Jeff despised her because of Kray. Because of who her ex-husband was. Jeff didn't know her, but that didn't matter. He judged her by the company she'd kept. He judged her by Bobby's father. He'd probably been on Kray's trail for years.

"Mommy, I want to swim to the deep end," Bobby announced, standing up on the second step.

"Okay, honey. I'll watch."

She sat up, straddling the floating raft. Her legs dangled in the warm pool water. Bobby raised his arms above his head and made an exaggerated dive from the step. He splashed around for a couple of seconds, then found his stroke and started for the far end of the pool.

Andie watched him swim. Her son was a physical creature, preferring to run rather than walk, to bounce instead of sit. At least with the nice weather and having access to a pool, she didn't have to worry about him being bored. He was used to playing by himself. She allowed him to have as many friends as he wanted but somehow he understood her need for them to stand alone against the world. He went to other people's houses for play and parties, but he didn't stay late. He sensed her fear. She hated that. Hated what Kray had reduced them to.

Bobby reached the far end of the pool. He grabbed the side with one hand. "Look at me."

"I see. You're doing great with your swimming. I'll bet Coach Earnhart will move you up to the red team this summer."

Bobby's hazel eyes widened. "Wow, really? The red team?"

He grinned showing white teeth almost the same color as the zinc oxide she'd put on his nose. Sunscreen wasn't always enough to protect him from sunburn. She'd rubbed the same cream on her own nose. They must look like clowns.

"I think so," she said. "Tryouts are next month. You've really improved a lot. You've been working hard, haven't you?"

Bobby nodded, then puffed out his thin chest. "Watch how fast I swim back!"

He threw himself in the water and paddled toward the shallow end. Andie kept her eye on him, staying upright on the raft until he'd returned to the steps in the shallow end. He picked up his action figures and immediately began a competition with them. She smiled and leaned back. She splashed water up onto her legs to keep herself cool. It would be terrific if Bobby made the red team. She wasn't like some mothers—she didn't care if Bobby came in first or last when the swim team competed. All that mattered to her was that her son was having fun and that he tried. Bobby had been working hard all winter, swimming several times a week. The lesson and membership dues were one of her few indulgences. It was worth it to see him so happy and successful. If Coach Earnhart agreed with her and—

Andie stopped splashing the water. She raised her head slightly and gazed at her son playing happily. A band tightened around her chest. She didn't know if Bobby was ever going to see his coach or his friends again. For a few moments she'd forgotten that they were on the run. Unless Kray was somehow caught and put away, they wouldn't be able to return to their old life. Nothing was ever going to be the same for them again.

Sometimes she thought she was living in a dream. This couldn't be happening to her. It wasn't real. Nothing had been normal or sane since her parents had been killed in the car crash. The months following the accident were like an old home movie. The memories ran through her brain without sound. Some things she could see clearly, others were foggy with whole sections missing. She didn't remember very much clearly until she met Kray. Those memories were vivid, almost frightening in their intensity. She'd been so sure, so convinced he was the one. She's squashed any doubts until it was too late. On her honeymoon, she'd had vague feelings of uneasiness, but she'd ignored them. She hadn't wanted to know the truth. Until that afternoon when she'd been unable to deny what had happened.

Andie bit down hard on her lower lip. She didn't want to remember. She didn't want to see it again. But she couldn't stop the past from intruding. She clutched the raft as if she were afraid of being swept up in the storm. The plastic seemed to dissolve beneath her fingers. The water, the bright sunshine, everything faded until she was once again in a long corridor, listening to the *tap tap* of her high heeled shoes on the wooden floor.

Two fifty-eight. That time stood out in her mind because she'd just glanced at her watch. A slim gold timepiece. Expensive, elegant. Only one of the dozens of gifts Kray had showered her with. She'd been to lunch with an acquaintance. Afterward she was supposed to get her hair styled for a party that night. At the last minute she'd decided to wear a different dress that had a matching hat. She'd canceled her hair appointment from the restaurant and had come back to the apartment.

She remembered the silence, broken only by her shoes. It was as if even the walls paused to listen. Then she'd heard low voices. Men having a conversation. The tone had changed. To anger. They spoke in a language she didn't know, although she recognized Kray's voice. She hurried to tell him she was home.

The door to the drawing room was open. She remembered laughing at him when he'd called it a drawing room, teasing him for speaking as if they were Victorian aristocracy. Kray had pulled her close, whispering she was his lady of the manor. They'd made love on the elegant gold-and-cream settee. Since then she'd always had a fondness for that room.

A length of Oriental carpet covered the hallway floor, muffling the sound of her approaching steps. She moved closer, wishing they would speak in English so she would know what they were saying.

Then the voices got louder, harsher, and she hesitated. It was the sudden silence that drew her closer. She took that last step to the open doorway.

Her husband stood with his back to her. A man she'd never seen before knelt on the floor in front of him. Two of Kray's bodyguards stood a few feet away.

The stranger raised his head and begged. She didn't have to understand the language to recognize pleading. Her husband shook his head.

"You betrayed me," he said in English. "You stole from me."

"I have paid it back with interest," the man answered in the same language. "It was a momentary lapse. A present for my child. Forgive me, I beg you. Forgive me. Until that moment, I had been the most loyal—"

The single gunshot cut the man off. His eyes widened in surprise as blood blossomed on the front of his white shirt. He continued to stare up at Kray for several seconds before slumping to the floor. Andie bit back a scream as her stomach started to heave. She backed up from the room, slipped off her shoes and ran down the hall to their bedroom. Once there, she locked herself in the bathroom and, with a towel pressed against her mouth, gave in to the hysteria.

After some time has passed, perhaps a few minutes, perhaps an hour, she left the bathroom. Kray was waiting for her in the bedroom. His expressionless face told her all she needed to know. Somehow he'd sensed her presence. Would he kill her now, or would he wait?

"The man was disloyal to me," he said, watching her as a predator watched a potential victim, gauging her strength, her ability to fight back.

"I see." Her voice was calm. Did he know how much that cost her?

"I'm sorry you had to witness his punishment."

Punishment? Kray had shot someone in cold blood. In the same room where he'd made love to her. Didn't any of that matter?

She stared at the man she'd married and realized she'd never known him at all. So many oddities from their honeymoon suddenly made sense. He wasn't a successful businessman, he was a criminal. A murderer. God knows what other crimes he'd committed.

She kept her gaze locked with his, her body straight, her hands still. She said little as he explained. When he held out his arms, she went to him. When he touched her body, she forced herself to sigh with pleasure.

For the first time her skin crawled when he caressed her nakedness. For the first time, she pretended to reach ecstasy. For the first time her soft words of love were bitter-tasting lies. She played the game as if her life depended on it, for it did. And not just *her* life.

Later, when Kray left her to dress for their evening out, she stared at her naked body in the mirror. She touched her still-flat belly and was grateful she'd never mentioned her suspicions. She didn't want him to know. If he did, he wouldn't let her go.

She waited a month, wondering each day if it would be her last. But he seemed to believe her when she expressed contentment. He never showed any doubt of her loyalty. And when she left him, he didn't come after her.

The memories faded as quickly as they'd come. Andie stared at the blue sky, at the palm trees and the sand. Despite the warm afternoon, she shuddered. Bobby spoke to her and she replied automatically, but she couldn't shake the feeling of dread. She knew what would happen if Kray caught them. She knew her ex-husband would reclaim her child and kill her as easily as he'd killed that man six and a half years ago.

The scents of the island mocked her, reminding her of her honeymoon. How foolish she'd been, how willing to believe the best. Now she hated everything about the island, especially the fact that she was trapped here. She was a fool. No wonder Jeff despised her.

She turned her thoughts to him because anything was better than thinking about the past. She glanced toward the house. She could see Jeff sitting in the shadow of the porch. He'd still been in his room when Bobby had dragged her out of bed. So far they'd managed to avoid each other. With luck, they could spend the next day and a half living in the same house without having any contact at all.

Who was this stranger who protected her and her son? She was grateful he'd rescued her. If he hadn't been with her, she would have been caught at the airport for sure. Was he really a spy? He had to work for the government in some way, but how? She told herself to stop asking questions. She didn't need to know anything about him.

But that didn't stop her from wondering about his late wife. He still mourned her. He must have loved her very much. Andie was willing to bet he hadn't been with another woman since her death. He hadn't kissed her like a man who'd been keeping company with a lot of woman. His kiss had been hungry, as if he'd been starving and she was the first meal he'd had in who knows how long.

It was the circumstances, she told herself, not wanting to remember the kiss and her reaction to it. Not wanting to recall her need and the powerful attraction that had swept her away, even when she'd known better. It wasn't just that her life was in danger and she had to get her son off the island. It was that she didn't know anything about Jeff. All the romantic relationships in her life had been impulsive. She'd never met someone, sort of liked him, then gradually, slowly, built a bond. She immediately jumped into the fire. Look where that had gotten her. Married to a murderer, and now, on the run from him.

She adjusted her sunglasses and splashed more water on her legs and torso. She envied Jeff. Envied him the love he'd shared with his wife before she'd been taken from him. Andie had wanted that for herself once. She'd believed she'd found it with Kray. When those dreams had shattered, she'd known she would spend the rest of her life alone. She couldn't trust herself to fall for the right kind of man and she couldn't risk letting someone learn too much about her. It could endanger both their lives.

She glanced at her son. "You're turning into a prune, Bobby. Let's get out for a little while and dry off."

"Ah, Mo-om."

He was only five, but already had the "ah, Mo-om" down perfectly. She smiled. "The pool will still be here in an hour or so. Besides, I want to freshen your sunscreen."

Bobby poked at his arm, then grinned at her. "I'm not burned." He wrinkled his white zinc-oxide-covered nose.

"Let's keep it that way." She took off her sunglasses and tossed them onto the cement edging the pool. There was no graceful way on or off a raft. After taking a deep breath, she rolled off the side and into the water. She stood up and pushed a few loose strands of hair out of her face. Her now-wet braid hung down her back. "Come on, sport. Let's find something fun to do."

A quick glance told her Jeff was still sitting on the porch. Andie snagged her sunglasses and the T-shirts she and Bobby had worn over their swimsuits. She tossed him his, then slipped her own on. They could walk by the ocean, she thought, not wanting to deal with Jeff. He'd said the rocks were dangerous but if they stayed on the shore it should be fine.

"Want to play baseball?" Jeff asked.

She turned toward him. He was walking down the stairs carrying a plastic bat in one hand and three plastic balls in the other.

Bobby finished wiggling into his T-shirt and raced over to Jeff. "Can I hit first?"

"Sure," Jeff answered, but he was looking at her. Waiting. "We need three to make a team."

Andie slipped on her sunglasses. He'd washed away the dyes from the previous night. His hair was once again blond, his skin tanned, but not dark. His T-shirt advertised a local fishing cove. His shorts were well-worn and exposed long, powerful thighs. Blue eyes held her gaze. Blue eyes almost the same color as her own. Despite their outward similarities, tall, lean, blond, they were nothing alike. There was a hardness to Jeff, an edge she didn't understand. They both lived on the fringes, but for different reasons and in different worlds. Yet last night . . .

Her gaze dropped to his mouth. He stiffened as if he knew what she was thinking. He couldn't, she told herself even as she flushed. He couldn't see through her sunglasses. But she still took a step back. She still winced when he glared at her as if he hated her.

"You gonna play, Mom?" Bobby asked.

She glanced at her son. He grinned in anticipation. He liked Jeff and the man was good to her son. That's all that mattered. "Sure, I'll play."

"Why don't you be in the outfield," he said, motioning to an area close to the Jeep. They used towels to mark the bases.

By the time Bobby was bent over, ready to hit, the dangerous man who'd kissed her last night and still hated her this morning was gone. In his place was a handsome but distant stranger. Better for both of them to keep it that way.

Jeff moved close to where Bobby was standing. He pitched gently. The boy swung and missed.

"Look at the ball," Jeff said. "Don't turn away when I pitch it. I won't hit you."

"Okay."

Bobby bent over and clutched the bat tightly. Jeff pitched again. This time her son connected with the ball. It arced about ten feet in the air before falling to the ground about a yard from where Jeff was standing.

Bobby dropped the bat and yelled. "I hit it Mommy, did you see? I hit it!"

"Good for you. Now run to first base."

Bobby took off as fast as he could. His small feet dug into the sand. He laughed when he reached the base, then looked at her. She glanced at Jeff, but he'd made no move to pick up the ball.

"Keep going," she called.

Bobby started to second. He said something, but she didn't hear it. She was staring at Jeff. He looked at her son with such an expression of longing, she thought her heart might crack in two. As her child ran the bases, Jeff watched the boy. She knew he wasn't seeing Bobby at all, but was instead picturing the child he'd lost. The tragedy of it all made her want to cry out against the unfairness. Being with Bobby was hard on Jeff, yet he never let the child know. He was patient and gentle, even thoughtful, bringing back toys from his nocturnal excursion.

Bobby jumped on the towel that was home base. "I went all the way around," he said proudly.

"Good for you," Andie called, clapping at his accomplishment.

Jeff shook himself slightly. "Let's try it again." When Bobby picked up the bat, Jeff pitched. The boy missed.

Andie watched Jeff coaching her son. She couldn't hear anything in his voice or see anything in his expression. He didn't give away his pain, but he must be feeling it. He hated her, yet took time with her son. He risked his life to get them off the island. He would risk it again, when they were gone, to capture Kray. To bring an evil man to justice. How many times had he faced death for his country?

Bobby swung and missed again. He didn't let the boy get frustrated; instead he moved closer and showed him how to swing the bat.

Andie recognized the feeling that swept over her. Admiration for the man and his courage. If only they'd met under other circumstances. If only he didn't dislike her quite so much.

Bobby swung again and missed. "That's three," he said and set the bat down. "Mommy, are you going to hit?"

"Sure." Andie moved toward the towel that marked home plate. She turned toward Jeff. He stared at her for a long time.

"Why don't you pitch to your mom?" he said, handing Bobby the ball.

Her son grinned and took his place. Jeff moved to the outfield. Andie pushed her glasses up her nose, then picked up the bat.

"Come on, Bobby," she called. "Over the plate. Gimme a good one and I'll hit it clear to the other side of the island."

The first pitch was so low, it hit her in the ankle. She jumped, then chased the ball toward the palm trees by the surf. When she grabbed it, she threw it back to Bobby.

The warm sun felt good on her back. She dug her toes into the sand and bent over the plate. In the background she could hear the humming of insects and the faint call of birds. The pounding of the waves added rhythm to the noises. Bobby pitched again.

This time the plastic ball came directly toward her. She swung and hit it, sending it over her son's head toward their imaginary outfield. Jeff took off after the ball. Andie dropped the bat and started for first base.

"Run, Mom," Bobby yelled, jumping up and down. "Run fast."

She reached the base, then tried to judge the distance to second. Jeff had already collected the ball and was heading toward her. But there was no one for him to throw the ball to. She started running.

He picked up his pace and angled toward her. They were both aiming for the faded red towel lying in the pale sand. She laughed out loud, wondering how long it had been since she'd just plain had fun.

"Run, Mom. Catch her, Jeff!"

Andie stuck her tongue out at her son. "Make up your mind who you're rooting for."

Bobby grinned back.

Jeff was gaining. He raced toward her, the ball held in his right hand. She thought about diving for the base, then slowed suddenly when Jeff's expression changed. He stopped running, as if giving her the chance to get to the base first. She didn't understand why. Then she saw his eyes and the fire flaring there. She became conscious of wearing only a T-shirt over her bathing suit. Her legs were exposed to his hungry gaze. An answering need flickered inside of her.

His mouth twisted with disgust. She didn't know if it was at him or herself and she didn't want to know. The only thing that was clear was that he didn't want to touch her if he could avoid it.

"Tag her, Jeff," Bobby said.

Jeff took a step toward her, then reached out and brushed her forearm with the ball. She looked down and saw his arousal straining at the front of his shorts. He wanted her. Her thighs quivered with anticipation. She wanted him, too.

"Jeff?" she whispered.

"No." His voice was a low growl. He dropped the ball on the sand. "The last one in the pool has to clean up after dinner."

He raced toward the pool, tearing off his T-shirt as he went. Bobby ran after him and jumped in. Her son's laughter filled the afternoon. She watched them wrestle and play for a while, then went inside. Her body still hummed with awareness. Her skin was hypersensitive, her movements restless. But she would gladly ignore the passion, she thought as she sat in the house alone. The bigger need was for someone to talk to. She was more lonely than she was aroused. She would trade all the desire, even their kiss from the night before, if only Jeff would like her half as much as he wanted her.

Clouds rolled in through the early evening. By the time the sun set, they obscured the colors on the horizon. Jeff sat on the porch railing, staring out into the darkness. There would be no stars tonight. According to the weather report, the squall would be over quickly. Good news because they would need the light of the moon and the stars tomorrow when they went to meet the boat.

In just a little over twenty-four hours, Andie and Bobby would be gone. He would be free to get on with his mission. He'd survived worse than this for much longer. He would endure her presence while she was here.

Through the open windows he could hear muffled conversation, then the faint *click* as the bedroom door closed. Bobby had been sleepy during dinner, exhausted from his day spent in the pool and playing baseball. Andie walked into the living room, but didn't join him on the porch. He was grateful. He needed his time in the shadows. Often he dreaded night, knowing the ghosts would join him, but this evening he welcomed their company. He needed them to help him remember.

He closed his eyes to recall his wife's face. He could see J.J. laughing, playing, struggling over a big word in the books he was just beginning to read. His son still lived. But Jeanne was gone.

He thought about their wedding day and how she'd looked in her beautiful long white dress. He could see the shape, but her individual features blurred. He called on other memories—their honeymoon, the time they spent three weeks in London. Buildings, other people, half bits of conversation came into focus, but not her. He'd lost her by betraying her memory. After he'd spent five solitary years mourning her, she was gone.

He stared at the ocean, comforting himself with the thought that if he survived, he would go home and see her pictures. Then he would remember. He hadn't brought any with him; he couldn't risk it. He had no ID, nothing to link him with his real identity. Safer for him if he was caught.

He grimaced. If he was caught after he killed Kray, he would be shot on the spot and no one would give a damn about who he was. If he was caught before taking care of his enemy, Kray would recognize him instantly and the game would be up. Still, the precautions made him feel better. As if he had a chance.

"Mommy, I want a glass of water."

He heard Andie's bare feet slap against the wooden floor. "Bobby, it's late. Go to sleep."

"But I want Jeff to tell me a story about Echo. I didn't dream about him last night and I want to. Can we get a bird when we go home?"

She laughed softly. "What on earth would you do with a bird?"

"Teach him to talk."

"I think you talk enough for yourself and any three pets. Come on back to bed and I'll tell you one more story, but that's all."

Their voices faded as they walked down the hallway. Andie Cochran wasn't anything he'd expected. The flashy bimbo with an eye for wealth didn't exist. In her place was an intelligent, brave woman who loved her child with all her heart. Despite her fear, she was doing everything she could to bring her kid up safely, without letting the trauma damage him. She had guts. He would give her that. If only she didn't turn him on.

He listened to the faint whispers of her story about Echo. Bobby's questions became fewer, his voice slurred as he drifted off to sleep. Andie returned to the living room. She walked to the front door and paused.

"Is he asleep?" he asked.

She stepped outside. "Finally. I don't know how he can be so tired and still keep on going. I guess he's afraid of missing something. This is all an exciting adventure to him."

"Now that he's with you."

She settled on the swing. He heard the creak of the wooden slats, then the faint brush of her foot on the porch as she pushed off. "Yes, being with me makes a difference." She sighed. "He won't talk about what happened with his father. I'm afraid to push him."

"Is he acting normal?"

"Pretty much. I'm hoping all he's suffered from is homesickness and being scared about being away from me."

"Kray's an animal, but he wouldn't hurt his heir."

"I hope you're right," Andie said.

Jeff shifted on the railing. The porch swing was behind him on his left. If he turned, he would be able to see her. The light from the living room spilled out the windows and would illuminate her face. But he didn't want to see her. Looking at her would make him think about touching her and being close to her. He would remember last night and their kiss. He would want to apologize for being a jerk. She would touch him then, and he would lose even more of his past. The pain and the memories were all he had left.

He shouldn't have kissed her. He shouldn't have thought about the kiss today when they'd been playing ball. He hadn't been able to help himself. There was something about her that drew him. He'd never experienced that reaction before. Of course he'd wanted women before, but never to the exclusion of everything else. Never to the point of endangering his sanity and putting the mission in jeopardy. He'd been a faithful husband, if not an especially loving one. Why did this have to be happening now?

"It looks like it might rain," she said.

"It will."

"Did you listen to the weather on the radio?"

He shook his head. "I can smell it."

She took a deep breath. "What do you smell?"

"Moisture."

She laughed. "What on earth does moisture smell like? And if you say, 'Something wet,' I'll have to push you off the railing and into the bushes."

"You'll have to trust me on the rain, then."

"Okay. How long will the storm last?"

"It will be gone by morning. Tomorrow night should be clear."

"You can tell all that from a smell?"

He smiled in the darkness. "No, I listened to the radio, too."

She shifted on the seat. The chains clinked together. "I'll be glad to get going," she said. "This waiting is hard. Yet a part of me wants to just hide out here. I suppose I'm afraid of the unknown."

"You'll be fine."

"You don't know that."

He risked glancing at her. She was curled up in a corner of the swing. She'd pulled her knees to her chest. For once, her hair was loose around her shoulders. The long blond strands shimmered in the darkness; the waves from the braids she'd worn caught the living room light. She looked small and defenseless. He wanted to go to her and protect her. Instead, he stayed in place.

"You're smart," he said. "You've done as much as you can. With a little luck, you'll be able to stay hidden."

"We're due for some luck." She raised her head and stared at him. "I'm sorry about your men."

"What men?"

"The ones you're with. I'm sure they don't appreciate having their leader tied up with my problems. Once Bobby and I are gone, you can get on with your mission."

"Is that what you think?"

She nodded. "I know you're with the government somehow. I don't want to know anything more, you know, in case I get caught."

"You've watched too many movies."

"You're *not* here to arrest Kray?"

Not exactly. But he couldn't tell her that. Better if she did think he was part of some secret armed force invading St. Lucas to take her husband away in chains. It was slightly dramatic, but if it helped her sleep at night, she could think what she wanted. He slid off the railing and stood up. He rested one shoulder and hip on the support beam. She was directly in front of him. He couldn't avoid looking at her, and he didn't want to.

She tilted her head and the light caught the side of her face. He could see the first faint lines around her eyes and the perfect arc of her cheekbones. What would she think if she knew the truth? That he was a task force of one. His mission wasn't to arrest her husband, but to assassinate him. What would she say if she knew he was willing to die to see Kray dead? Would she be relieved, or would she fear him? He was surprised to find he could accept her fears but not her disdain. He'd gotten soft, no doubt about that.

"I'll get the job done," he said at last. "You've delayed what needs doing, but that's all. In the end it won't make any difference."

"I'm glad." She gave him a half smile. "Isn't that awful? I want my ex-husband in prison. Not just because he deserves it, but because then Bobby and I will have a chance at life. Have you been after him for a long time?"

"Years."

"So you'll feel good when the job is finished."

Their definitions of "finished" were different. She meant arrested and he meant dead. "Yeah, I'll be glad."

"This is very surreal to me," she said. "We're talking about spies and arresting criminals. A month ago my biggest worry was keeping my grades up in law school."

He told himself to keep his mouth shut. She didn't have to know. He opened his mouth to ask about her classes, but instead blurted out, "I might not be here to arrest him."

She lowered her feet to the floor and folded her hands on her lap. "I've thought of that, too," she said quietly. "A part of me wants him dead. Now you know the worst there is about me. I wouldn't be happy if he was killed, but I wouldn't mourn him.''

If this was the worst she had to tell him, he *had* misjudged her. If she was who and what she appeared to be, then she'd been caught up in Kray's world by mistake. The stories of wild parties, of alcohol and drugs, of using her money from modeling to attract the world's elite made no sense when he stared at the woman in front of him. Last night she'd implied that the Frenchman who'd betrayed her had been her first lover.

Jeff had gone through her things while she'd been in the pool with Bobby. She had nothing with her—no prescription drugs, no mysterious bottles. She was too healthy to be living on the edge. His gut told him the truth. He didn't want to listen, he didn't want to believe she was other than what he'd been told. Yet he knew. Andie Cochran had been an innocent in a den of wolves.

''I saw him kill a man,'' she said.

Jeff stared at her. ''What?''

''He shot him, in our apartment in Paris. It was the middle of the afternoon. A Wednesday.'' She shook her head. ''I remember what I was wearing. Isn't that the oddest thing? It was a blue suit. Silk, with my pearls. And there wasn't very much blood. I thought there would be more. I remember thinking the rug would be ruined. But when I finally made myself go in the room later, it was fine. There was only a damp spot, where the stain had been scrubbed away.''

She spoke the words without feeling, as if she were describing a picture in a book. Her expression was calm. Only her hands gave her away. Her fingers twisted together so tightly, he could see her knuckles getting white.

Jeff could fill in the details she left out. She must have been horrified. People who lived normal lives couldn't imagine what went on in the shadows. Violence, fear, cold-blooded reprisals for disobedience. That was Kray's world.

''Did he know?'' he asked.

"Yes. We never talked of it, but he knew. I was afraid to leave right away. I thought he would kill me, too. So I stayed for a month. I pretended everything was fine." She shuddered. "I hated it. Being with him, having him touch me. At night—" She stopped and looked away. "It was difficult."

"But he let you go."

"I never understood why. I finally gathered my courage and told him I really missed living in the States. It was obvious I wasn't the right kind of wife for him. I wasn't ornamental enough. I said it would be best if I went home. He agreed."

"Just like that?"

She nodded slowly. Her long blond hair slipped over her shoulders and concealed her expression. "I spent the first month waiting for a bullet in my back. I figured he had people watching me. I wanted to go to the police and tell them about the man I'd seen shot. But I was afraid."

"That's understandable."

"It's because of Bobby." She brushed her hair away from her face and looked at him. Her eyes were wide and dark, her mouth trembling. "I knew I was pregnant. My child mattered more than justice. So I kept quiet and Kray let us live."

She was asking if she'd done the right thing. Not in so many words, but in the way she stared at him. He didn't want to get suckered into this. He was having enough trouble maintaining his distance. Still, it wouldn't hurt to give her a pat on the back. She'd been through a hell of a lot.

"Bobby's a great kid," he said.

"You think so?"

"Yeah."

She smiled. His gut clenched tight. Before he could recover, she rose to her feet and approached him. He'd thought he would be safe by the railing, but he was wrong. She moved close to him. Her scent surrounded him. Sweet, tempting. When he'd gone through her things, he hadn't seen any perfume, so the fragrance was uniquely hers.

"You're a good man, Jeff."

He folded his arms over his chest. "Not everyone would agree with you."

"They don't matter."

She touched his forearm. Fire singed his skin. Why was she doing this? Why was she tempting him?

"I know what you're going through," she said.

He doubted that. Andie didn't have a clue as to his real mission. He was going to kill her ex-husband, no matter what it cost him. She wouldn't understand that. She would understand it even less if she knew the circumstances that had brought him here.

"I saw it today," she said. "When we were playing ball. I lost my parents when I was eighteen. I was devastated. I can't imagine what it must be like to lose a child."

Compassion softened her features. He stiffened. He didn't need her feeling sorry for him, or offering her brand of sympathy. His temper flared. He forced the anger down. It wouldn't accomplish anything.

"In time . . ." she started.

"What do you know about time?" he asked, his voice low and harsh. "Leave it alone."

She was standing too close. He tried to conjure up Jeanne to protect him, but he still couldn't recall what she looked like. All he could see was Andie.

"You're right, I don't know exactly what you're going through. But I understand part of it. I was in the car when my parents were killed. I saw them die. I know it's hard." Her fingers pressed against his skin. She stared up at him. "I just wanted to thank you for taking the time with Bobby. I know he reminds you of your son. I know—"

"Lady, you don't know anything." Jeff wrenched his arm free of her. His hands curled into fists. The anger burned hotter and became rage. She wanted to care and he wanted her to leave him the hell alone. She was too much. Too feminine, too alive. He couldn't resist her. He hated them both for that. Guilt swelled inside of him. Not just because it had been his fault his family had been killed but because she was helping him forget. He didn't want to forget. He wanted to remember forever. If he forgot, they would be truly gone.

"Jeff."

Her beautiful face, her tempting curves all taunted him. She made him want things he'd done without for five years. Not her. Anyone but Kray's ex-wife.

"They didn't die in a car accident," he said slowly. "It was a car bomb."

She stared up at him. "How horrible. I'm so sorry."

"Are you?" He grabbed her upper arms and shook her. "Are you really sorry? I'm sure they'll be grateful to know that. Andie Cochran is sorry. Let's all give thanks."

"Stop it," she commanded.

He stopped shaking her, but didn't let her go. "There's more. Do you want more to be sorry about?"

She swallowed. "Let me go."

"Not yet." He moved his head down until their faces were inches apart. "I'd been working on a case. Chasing a criminal. I'd gotten too close. The car bomb was meant for me."

She paled under her tan. "No," she said, trying to pull free. He held on tighter. "No, don't say that. Don't tell me that."

"It's true," he growled.

She jerked free and covered her ears with her hands. "No," she said, louder. "Dammit, not that."

"Yes, that." He glared at her. She lowered her hands to her sides. "Kray set the car bomb. Kray killed my wife and child."

Chapter 8

Andie stared at him. The words washed over her, but she didn't hear them. No, that wasn't true. She didn't *want* to hear them.

Kray set the car bomb. Kray killed my wife and child.

She moaned low in her throat. She refused to believe it was true. Not even Kray would be so cruel. Yet, even as she formed the thought, she knew he could and he had. Her ex-husband. The man she'd married. Bobby's father.

She turned quickly and stepped off the porch. She walked away from the house and circled around the pool. She moved faster until she was jogging, then running. The clouds were low, the air thick with humidity. There was no-where to go. Bushes and trees crowded in on both sides. She tripped over something sticking out of the sand and fell to her knees. A sob tore at her.

"No," she cried. "Dear God, no."

Up ahead she could hear the sound of the waves as they crashed against the shore. The tide was in. She staggered to her feet and ran into the surf.

Water swirled around her ankles, then up to her calves. It was warm. The white foam clung to her skin. As she sank down, she felt the first drops of rain on her face. She reached up to brush them away and was surprised to feel tears on her cheek.

Crying would do no good, she told herself, even as the sobs came faster. She caught her breath, trying to stay calm. It was too late. The tears wouldn't erase the past, but she couldn't control them anymore. Her stomach heaved. She coughed, then dropped her chin to her chest. The waves slipped over her thighs and her hands.

The pain started in her chest. She squeezed her eyes tight, but that didn't stop her from imagining the moment. The flare of the bomb. The small pieces of the car littering the sidewalk. The dead body of a child. Jeff's son.

How old had he been when his life had been cut short? What about Jeff's wife? Had their last words been loving? Had she smiled, knowing she would see her husband soon? Had she died instantly or had she had time to know she would die and her child with her?

Kray had done it. Andie clutched her hands to her stomach and rocked back and forth. She could see his face. The handsome lines. The brown hair and eyes. He dressed well, walked like an aristocrat, yet he had the soul of the devil.

Murderer! her mind screamed. Killer of children. Husband. Father. Dear God, she'd made love with a madman. She'd held him and promised to love him forever. She was as guilty as he. The sin was just as much hers. Innocence and foolishness weren't excuses. She should have known. She should have seen the truth.

The rain fell harder. She raised her head toward the murky night sky, letting the drops wash away her tears.

What did the explosion sound like? Did Jeff hear it night after night in his dreams? Did he feel the heat of the fire? Did he hear their screams?

More tears, more sobs. She cried until she was empty and shaking. She cried until her throat was raw. The guilt, the pain. She would never forget. Never forgive. No wonder he hated her. She was alive, and his wife was dead.

She rocked back and forth in the surf, holding in the pain. In time it would fade. Even if she held on to it, eventually the edges would be blunted. But she would never forget. Not even after Kray was gone.

No wonder Jeff had been sent in to capture Kray. He was the best man to lead the team. He wouldn't let anything get in the way. She stopped moving and stared into the darkness. Only, she'd gotten in the way. She'd interfered when he'd tried to take Kray. Oh, God, why?

She closed her mind to the questions. It was going to end soon. That was Jeff's job. It was past time for the killing to stop. She drew in a deep breath and wondered how she would explain this to her son. Bobby hadn't asked many questions about his father, but he would. How was she supposed to tell him the truth? How was she supposed to tell him about Jeff's wife and son? What about the other people Kray had murdered? How many families had been destroyed? How many souls waited for revenge?

She wasn't sure how long she knelt in the surf. The waves continued to wash over her, the rain fell lightly. Eventually she felt a slight prickling along the back of her neck. She turned and saw Jeff standing by the edge of the sea. It was too dark to see his individual features, but he seemed to be waiting.

"You all right?" he asked.

She nodded, then slowly rose to her feet. The white-and-pink romper was wet and clinging to her. The damp edges of her hair stuck to her arms and back. She felt drained.

She walked toward Jeff. He waited. No wonder he stared at her with contempt. No wonder it hurt him to watch her son laugh and play. What strange twist of fate had brought them together? If there was one woman in the world most wrong for him, it was her. Yet he'd promised to get them off the island. He was their only hope.

When she reached the soft dry sand, she stopped and turned toward him. The faint light from the house didn't reach this far. She still couldn't see his face.

"I'm sorry," she said. Her voice was low and raspy from her tears. She cleared her throat.

He didn't answer. She wanted to touch him and offer comfort, but she had none to give. None that would matter to him, anyway. She understood why he was contemptuous of her. It would have been so easy for him to walk away and leave her on her own. But he hadn't.

"I know my apology doesn't mean anything to you. It can't bring your wife and son back." She glanced down, then squeezed the hem of her romper. The wind blew harder now, the rain was more insistent, although still warm. "It must be difficult for you to be with us, knowing we're alive and they're not."

In the distance came a faint rumble. Jeff turned toward the sound. "The storm is going to get worse," he said. "We'd better get inside."

She didn't move. "You're so honorable and good. You probably don't understand about not recognizing evil until it's too late." There were more tears. She hadn't thought she had any left to cry. She brushed her fingers against her cheeks. "I never meant to be one of the bad guys."

"It's not your fault."

He grabbed her arm and started toward the house. She let him pull her along. When they reached the porch, she climbed the stairs with him. Once under the protection of the overhead covering, he released her. She stared up at him.

Now she could see his features. The light from the living room exposed the starkness of his expression and the grim line of his mouth. Something dark and ugly hid in his eyes.

"If it's not my fault, why do you blame me?" she asked softly.

"Because you married him."

"I didn't know."

"You should have. You should have made it your business to know."

"I just wanted to belong. I just wanted someone to care for me."

"You wanted to be taken care of. You wanted the easy way out and you took it. Now you're paying the price."

She struggled hard for control. "No, it wasn't like that. I really believed I'd found someone I could care about."

"That doesn't say a whole lot about your judgment, does it?"

"I swear I didn't know," she repeated, knowing she would never convince him. "I met him and he was so overwhelming. I didn't have time to think."

"You didn't want to think."

He had her there. "Yes," she whispered. She brushed her wet hair off of her face. "I wanted to be protected."

"We all pay a price for what we want."

But he wasn't looking at her anymore. He was staring past her, toward the storm. She wondered what he saw, what he was thinking, then decided it was best if she didn't know.

"If I could change things . . ." she started.

"What would you change?" he asked. "What would be different this time?"

"I would question. I wouldn't let it happen so fast. I wouldn't just react to what I was feeling." Like now. Only, she didn't say that. She didn't speak, didn't dare to breathe. Because, once again, she could feel the heat. The need between them. It frightened her, because he frightened her. He hated her, yet he wanted her.

Jeff tilted his head back and stepped away from her. Every line of his body screamed his contempt. But that didn't erase the desire. His gaze narrowed.

"No," he growled. "Never."

He turned on his heel and walked into the house. Andie stared after him. When he went into his bedroom and closed the door, she leaned against the railing and watched the storm. The rumbles of thunder grew louder. Soon lightning filled the sky. She had to check on her son. If the storm woke him, he would be frightened.

She went inside. As she walked past Jeff's closed door, she paused long enough to touch it with her fingertips. He'd risked his life for his enemy's wife and son. Despite the disdain and the hostile remarks, he was a good man. In the end, it was actions that counted, not words. The measure of a man could be found in what he did, not what he said. Jeff was one of the best.

She continued down the hall, then peeked into the bedroom. Bobby lay sleeping, unaware of the storm swirling around him. She watched him, praying for his safety. If they could just get off the island, they would have a chance. If...

As she listened to the thunder and the rain on the roof, she felt strangely calm. They would succeed, because Jeff wasn't the kind of man who failed. They would escape. She felt it deep inside. For the first time since Kray had stolen her son, she felt hope. And bittersweet longing. After six years of watching her back, after Kray had destroyed her life and her ability to believe, she'd finally found a man worth trusting. A man who made her want what she'd long ago decided she could never have. A man she could care about.

And for what? He would never look at her with anything but contempt. He would never forgive her for a crime she didn't commit.

The deafening blast of the explosion knocked Jeff off his feet. He tried to stand, tried to crawl, but he couldn't move. It was as if the concussion of the blast had sucked away his mobility along with the air. His chest was tight, his lungs empty. He opened his mouth to scream, but there was no sound. Nothing but the flickering of the flames and the pain.

He stared at the wreckage, at the burning hulk of metal that had, moments before, held his wife and child. He opened his mouth and this time the scream of pain echoed across time.

"No!"

He sat up in bed. Sweat coated his body. He was breathing heavily, his pulse racing. It was just a nightmare. He hadn't had one in over a year. He knew why it had come back tonight. It was there to punish him for giving in to temptation, for wanting Andie when he should have been mourning his wife.

He took several deep breaths to calm himself. The storm had abated. The thunder and lightning were gone. All that was left was the gentle rhythm of rain on the roof. He leaned back against the headboard and listened to the sound. Slowly his body returned to normal. Only when his heartbeat slowed did he realize someone was hovering in the hallway.

In one quick, fluid movement, he reached for the pistol he kept on the nightstand. As he went to grab it, the door opened. He saw the faint gleam of long blond hair. He left the gun in place and rolled back into the center of the bed.

"What do you want?" he asked coldly.

She jumped, as if she hadn't expected him to speak. "I was checking on you. You've been having nightmares. I heard you cry out a couple of times."

"I'm fine."

"Do you want a glass of water or something?"

"I'm not Bobby."

"I know, I just thought—"

She stood partway in the room, yet poised to flee. He knew he was being a jerk, but he couldn't seem to help himself. The memories of their last conversation crowded around them, filling the room. The harsh words, the ugly truth, her sorrow and apologies.

In the deepest part of his soul, he knew it wasn't her fault Jeanne and J.J. were dead. Yet it was easy to blame her. It saved him from blaming himself.

"What did I say?" he asked.

She took a step closer. There were a couple of night lights in the hallway. They allowed him to see her shape. She wore an oversize T-shirt that hung to midthigh. He wondered if she wore anything underneath.

"You called out a few things I couldn't understand. And a woman's name." She hesitated.

"Jeanne," he said, then pulled the pillows up behind him and leaned once more against the headboard.

"Yes, that was it." Andie folded her arms over her chest. "Is she— Was she your wife?"

He couldn't remember her face when he was awake, but he called out her name when he was asleep. "Yes."

"I'm sorry."

"It's not your fault."

She sighed. "You said that before, but I'm still . . . I feel responsible somehow. As if I should have been able to prevent it or have known it happened." She waved one hand in the air. "*Sorry* is such an inadequate word. There should be a different one for greater tragedies."

He understood that. He remembered after the explosion, when he'd finally gone home to the States. His family and Jeanne's had wanted to talk about what had happened. They'd wanted to hear the details. He'd refused to talk with them about it. He couldn't bear to remember. They'd all been sorry. He remembered thinking he would be happy never to hear that damn word again.

"It's not you," he said, then wondered why he bothered lying. Some of it *was* her. Or maybe it was just him. The guilt wasn't her fault. He was the weak one. He was the one who was having trouble holding on to the past. "It's this place and the situation."

He could lash out and say something ugly, but he didn't care enough to continue hurting her. Or maybe he cared too much. Maybe her courage and intelligence deserved more. If he believed her, and he had a bad feeling he did, her only crime was that of being young and foolish. She'd married the wrong man. Not for his money or power, but out of ignorance. She'd paid a big price for that already. Maybe he should let it go.

Even if she wasn't perfect, she was hardly in Kray's league. After all, she thought he, Jeff, was here as part of a team to take her ex-husband in. That he was part of a noble, well-thought-out act. Killing someone was never noble. It was ugly and difficult.

He had no right to judge her, not without first looking at his own situation. If she knew the truth about him, she would take off running in the opposite direction.

He leaned over and flipped on the small lamp on the nightstand. He squinted against the light. Andie stood just inside the door. She still had her arms folded over her chest. With her short T-shirt exposing her long legs, and her loose hair spilling over her shoulders, she looked like someone posing for a men's magazine. All soft curves and temptation. Her full mouth was straight, her eyes wide, her expression wary. If she smiled, if she tilted her head and whispered an invitation, there wasn't a man alive who could resist her.

"Go to bed," he ordered.

"I can't sleep."

"Well, I'm tired."

She shook her head slowly. Blond hair drifted back and forth in lazy counterpoint. "You're afraid the nightmare will come back if you go to sleep now." She shifted slightly, then dropped her arms to her sides. "Will it go well tonight?"

The mission. He'd almost forgotten. In less than twenty-four hours she would be on her way to Florida. Then he could get on with what he'd come for. With a little luck, Kray would be dead soon.

"My man is trustworthy, if that's what you're asking."

"I wasn't worried about that. I just wondered if there was anything that could go wrong."

There were a thousand things, but he knew she didn't want to hear about them. "You and Bobby will be fine."

She gave him a half smile. As if she weren't quite sure she believed him, but she appreciated the effort on her behalf.

"When we're gone, will you kill Kray?" she asked.

He raised his eyebrows.

"I know you're going to. I mean, not just because of what you said before, but because of the rifle I saw. I understand that waiting for him to make a mistake is taking too long. He's very smart and he's very lucky." She twisted her hands together, lacing and unlacing her fingers. "He's a bad man. That's sounds simplistic, but it's true."

"And that justifies killing?"

She stared at him. "No, it doesn't. But I don't think there's another solution. He's a murderer. Not just what I saw, but others we'll never know about, and your family..." Her voice trailed off.

She looked around the room. There was a single straight-back chair in the corner. She walked over to it and perched on the edge. "I don't know what's right anymore. When he came into my condo to steal Bobby, if I'd had a way to hurt him, I would have done it. I'd do anything to protect my child. But shooting someone deliberately is different. Not necessarily wrong, just hard to understand." She shook her head. "I'm not making any sense."

Jeff leaned back against the headboard and closed his eyes. "You'd be amazed how much sense you're making."

"How do you do this for a living?"

He smiled slightly. "I'm not a paid assassin, if that's what you mean."

"Good."

He opened his eyes and glanced at her. She sat straight in the chair, with both feet on the ground. Prim and proper. If he hadn't been sure she wore almost nothing under her nightshirt, it wouldn't have been provocative at all. Or it shouldn't have been. He had a bad feeling everything Andie did would turn him on. He shifted on the bed and was grateful the white sheet bunched around his waist hid his arousal from her.

"Sometimes the lines are gray," he admitted. "I don't always know what the right thing is, but that's my goal. To stay on this side of the line."

Except for this mission, he admitted. This time he'd crossed the line. There was no going back.

"Do you spend a lot of time out—" She waved her hand around them. "What's the technical term? In the field?"

"Most of the time I'm stuck behind a desk in Washington."

"Really? So you're not Rambo Two?"

"No." He smiled. "I'm just an ordinary man trying to take care of business."

"Only, Bobby and I got in the way," she said softly. "No wonder you were so angry at us that first day and angry at me ever since. I don't blame you."

Big eyes met his own. Sorrow and compassion darkened her irises to the color of a stormy sky. She was beautiful. Not a flashy look-at-me kind of woman, but someone who would always have classic features. In time her face would change. The skin would draw tighter, wrinkles would deepen around her eyes. Yet she would age with elegance. He could imagine her in forty years. That should have scared the hell out of him.

He didn't want to like her. He wanted everything to be her fault. "Andie, I—"

"No, really," she interrupted. "It makes sense. Besides, I trust your temper."

"You're crazy."

"No, I'm not. The fact that you haven't wanted me around is sort of comforting. If you'd been nice to me from the beginning I would have wondered what you wanted from me. By making me stand up to you, you've forced me to keep being strong. I'm scared of the future but I think I have a chance at keeping Bobby safe."

"I hope so," he said, and meant it. He wanted her and the kid to get away.

She tilted her head slightly and smiled. His groin tightened. "You're the closest thing I've had to a friend in years."

"You've got to be kidding."

"I'm not. Think about it, Jeff. I left Kray in Europe six years ago. I didn't expect him to let me go, let alone live without him. I kept waiting for him to come and get me." She grimaced. "It was like waiting for the other shoe to drop all the time. I hated it. I didn't dare tell anyone. I was afraid they wouldn't believe me."

"Or that they would."

She nodded. "Exactly. My whole life was tenuous. I was afraid to get close, afraid to connect with anyone. I wanted to belong somewhere, but it wasn't safe. So there was only ever Bobby and me." She leaned forward. "In my heart, I knew he'd come back. Leaving had been too easy for it to be real."

"I understand." And he did. She'd lived in the shadows, too. Not because she was a criminal or on assignment, but because of Kray. More than most civilians, she would understand about the frayed edges of life, of being just short of fitting in. Jeanne had never been able to relate to what he was talking about.

He grimaced. The disloyal thought annoyed him. He had no right to think less of Jeanne. Her only crime had been to try and save their marriage. She'd paid for it with her life.

"I know I've followed you around like a puppy," she said. She brushed her hair off of her face. "You keep kicking me and I keep coming back wagging my tail. You're the only person I can be honest with. This time tomorrow, we'll be on our way to Florida. The lies will start again. We'll be hiding out from Kray. I'm going to spend the rest of my life looking over my shoulder. But for these few days, I haven't had to do that. I haven't had to pretend to be other than I am. You know the worst about me. In a way, it's almost a relief to have you dislike me. I know that sounds strange. But you're the only person who knows everything."

"Not everything," he said.

"Okay." She grinned. "I have a couple of secrets. But you know the bad stuff. It's very freeing not to pretend."

She was making him feel worse by the minute. "Andie, don't make me a hero in all this."

"I'm not."

She laughed. Her long hair caught the lamplight. She looked young and happy in that moment. He saw her as she must have been when Kray first met her. Alive. Charming. Funny. He didn't want to be drawn to her, but he didn't have a choice in the matter.

"I prefer my white knights to be in literature, not in life."
Her humor faded. "I don't really believe in white knights
anymore. Although Rambo is a close second."

"You're not so bad yourself."

She lowered her head and started pleating the hem of her
T-shirt. "Most of the time I'm terrified. The only thing that
keeps me going is trying to keep the truth from Bobby. I
don't want him to grow up scarred by this experience."

"You've come this far on your own. I'll tell you a secret." He lowered his voice. "You're doing better than most
of my field agents would, and they have the benefit of experience."

He thought she might laugh again, but instead she smiled
slowly. She straightened her shoulders. He saw the faint
movement of her bare breasts under her shirt. Need flared
brighter as his blood heated. He admired her strength and
he wanted her. It was a deadly combination.

He tried to grab hold of the anger to help him resist her.
He thought of a half-dozen cruel things he could say to drive
her from the room. Instead, he watched her, wishing he was
strong enough to ignore her, or weak enough to invite her
into his bed.

"I appreciate your understanding," she said.

He raised his eyebrows. She couldn't possibly know what
he was thinking. "Of what?"

"Me. My situation. You're a decent kind of guy. You've
probably never done a bad thing in your life."

"Get real, Andie. Everyone does things they regret." He
could fill pages with lists of his. It wasn't just Jeanne and
J.J., although God knows he had plenty of regrets with
them. "I've made bad decisions. I've sent agents into impossible situations."

She shifted on the chair, stretching her long legs out in
front of her. The need became unbearable. He had to have
her or explode. He thought about asking her to join him in
his bed. He could just throw back the covers and expose his
nakedness. She would know right away what he wanted.
They could both escape into the passion.

But no matter how much he might admire her courage and the way she'd raised her kid, he couldn't forget she'd once belonged to Kray. He couldn't do that to Jeanne. He owed her. Bad enough not to have loved her in life, the least he could do was mourn her in death.

"Do you think—"

"Go to bed," he said abruptly, cutting her off. She opened her mouth to speak, then closed it.

"We both need to get some sleep," he continued. "You'll be up all of tomorrow night."

"Of course."

She rose slowly and walked to the doorway. He'd hurt her feelings. He could tell by the stiff set of her shoulders. He watched her move, her hips swaying under the thin T-shirt. His body throbbed painfully. She closed the door behind her without once looking back.

When he was alone, Jeff turned off the lamp, got out of bed and stood in front of the open window. The hardness between his legs throbbed in time with his heartbeat. It would have been so easy to bury himself inside her and forget. Easy but wrong. He owed Jeanne more.

Maybe he owed Andie more, too.

Chapter 9

Andie folded the last of Bobby's T-shirts and slipped it in her soft-sided carry-on bag. She'd only brought a few pieces of clothing with her, but when combined with Jeff's purchases, they filled out the bag. Still, she wouldn't have to worry about shopping when they arrived in Florida. They could go directly to the airport and take the first plane out of town. Staying away from Kray was her main objective.

She glanced around the now-bare room. Their towels were folded neatly on the single dresser. Everything else had been packed. Bobby had a plastic shopping bag filled with his new toys. They would keep him busy on the boat.

It was a simple enough plan, she thought as she sat down on the edge of the bed. Yet a thousand things could go wrong. Kray could be waiting at the dock. The captain, whom Jeff trusted, could turn them in. Kray's men could catch them before they arrived in Florida, or they could be waiting at the airport there. A storm could knock them off course, causing them to—

She covered her face with her hands. "Stop thinking about it," she said out loud. She was only making herself crazy. She was nervous enough without imagining trouble that hadn't even happened yet.

She stood up and walked toward the dresser. She pulled a brush from her purse and began to stroke it through her hair. When she was done, she divided the strands into three sections and quickly wove a braid. Jeff had given her a dark baseball hat to keep any light from reflecting off her blond hair. When she finished, she glanced at her clothing. She wore jeans and a dark blue long-sleeved shirt, fastened at her wrists. Her athletic shoes were white, but that couldn't be helped. She'd dressed Bobby in dark colors, as well. They were doing all they could. She would have to pray for a little luck to help them survive the rest of it.

The sounds of the night surrounded her. She could hear the cheeps and whistles of the insects, the faint rustlings of the night creatures. The waves provided a familiar counterpoint. Bobby was asleep on Jeff's bed. They would wake him up right before they left. Andie had also convinced her son to take a nap that afternoon, so he wouldn't be too exhausted for their boat trip. She had enough problems without adding a cranky child to the mix.

She pressed her hand against her stomach and drew in a deep breath. Nerves made her jumpy. She wanted it over with now. She wanted to never leave the house.

She set the hat on her head, then stared at her reflection. Fear pulled her mouth straight. If she was honest with herself, she would admit that she was terrified of being solely responsible again. For these last few days, she'd had someone else to depend on. It had been nice to lean on Jeff, even for a little while. It didn't matter that he didn't like her. He'd been there and he'd kept them safe. Once she was on the boat, she would be on her own. What if she couldn't do it?

That line of thought was too dangerous. She turned away from the mirror and quickly checked the room for the last time. She bent down and looked under the beds to make sure Bobby hadn't accidentally kicked something under there. The floor was dusty but bare.

She knelt on the floor and rested her forearms on the mattress. She hadn't slept much last night. If only she could close her eyes for a few hours and make this all go away. But she couldn't. She fingered the cotton bedspread and closed her eyes. Instead of this room, she pictured Jeff's room and how it had looked last night.

If she hadn't heard Jeff call out, she would never have dared go into his room. Despite what people said about her, she wasn't bold around men. While she'd been a model, she'd had a reputation of being a party girl. If only they knew the truth. She'd never done drugs, hadn't been able to handle liquor well so she didn't drink and she'd made love to exactly two men in her life. She'd been engaged to one and had married the other. Not exactly the shocking lifestyle most people assumed she'd led.

She knew what Jeff thought of her. She'd seen it in his eyes when he'd stared at her. She'd heard it in the contempt in his voice. Now that she knew the truth about what Kray had done, she didn't blame Jeff. She despised herself for being so stupid.

So last night, when she'd felt so alone and afraid, she'd foolishly been tempted when she'd seen Jeff in his bed. His broad chest had been bare, his skin tanned, his muscles strong. She'd wanted to crawl in next to him. It would have been wonderful to make love. Not just because she was afraid she was going to die, but because she liked him. And trusted him. She hadn't been able to trust anyone in a long time.

She thought she might have seen desire in his eyes, but she wasn't sure. Besides, how exactly was a woman supposed to bring up the subject? She'd been too embarrassed and ashamed to ask him to hold her. She reminded him of all he'd lost. How he must hate her every breath. But she needed holding desperately. Not just because she was lonely and afraid but because she cared about him. He was the sort of man she dreamed about giving her heart to.

On those lonely nights when Bobby had been a baby, when she'd stayed awake waiting for Kray to return and destroy her life, she'd imagined a world where she could meet someone and risk caring again. She'd thought about being normal, of waking up next to someone, of raising children together, arguing over money or visits from in-laws, then making up with a quick laugh and slow lovemaking. Her imaginary mate had no face. She didn't care what he looked like as long as he was honorable, patient and kind. A good man. Like Jeff.

She walked to the window and stared out at the night. He made her think of her foolish dreams for a life that would never be. He made her long for a man to care about. He made her think about love.

She inhaled the scent of the island. At first, the tropical breezes, the exotic flowers and the salt of the sea had reminded her of Kray. But not anymore. Now, when she remembered St. Lucas, she would think of Jeff. Of these few days of feeling safe, of her wish that she was anyone but Kray's ex-wife.

The sound of footsteps in the hall made her move away from the window. By the time Jeff knocked on the door, she was sitting on the bed, checking the suitcase for the last time.

"Come in," she called.

He opened the door. "You almost ready?" he asked, stepping into the room.

"Yes." She zipped the case shut.

He closed the door behind him and approached the bed. He, too, had dressed for their escape, although instead of dark clothes, he wore the camouflage uniform she'd first seen him in. His short blond hair gleamed in the overhead light. Blue eyes met her own. She studied his face, memorizing individual features so that years from now she would be able to recall what he looked like.

"I appreciate everything you've done," she said as he sat on the other side of the suitcase.

"Save your thanks until you're off the island," he said, then handed her a pistol. "I want you to take this."

She stared at the handgun. Except for when Kray had shot that man, and the one Jeff had pulled on them when they'd first run into him in the jungle, she'd never seen a pistol close up.

"No." She shook her head. "I can't."

"You won't. There's a difference."

He grabbed her hand and forced her to take the gun. It was heavier than it looked. Instinctively her fingers closed around the steel. "Do you expect me to shoot someone?"

"If you have to."

She glanced up at him. He was serious. "That's ridiculous. I've never fired a gun in my life. I don't know how to use it and I don't want to know."

He took the gun back from her. "It's simple to use. Here's the safety." He flicked a small lever on the left side of the gun, just above the grips. "If you don't release the safety the gun won't fire. This button here drops the magazine." He pushed the button. The clip fell out onto the suitcase. "It holds fourteen rounds. Pop it in like this." He pushed it back in place, then handed her the gun. "Now you do it."

"I can't," she said. "This is too scary. I don't want a gun."

He leaned close and took her face in his hand. His expression was hard, his eyes glinted like ice. "Kray wants you dead. I'm going to do my damnedest to get you off this island, but I need your cooperation. If something happens, you may need to protect yourself and Bobby. If you don't care about yourself, at least think of the boy."

Her son. She would do anything for her son. Slowly she took the pistol, then wrapped her fingers around the handle. She pushed the button and the clip dropped onto her lap. She replaced it.

He showed her how to work the action, then explained which position activated the safety. When she understood everything, he handed her a second clip of ammunition.

"Just in case," he said.

"I feel like you expect me to take out an entire regiment."

He smiled. "It won't come to that. Stand up." She did. He rose also and pulled the hem of her shirt out of her jeans. "You're going to have to sacrifice fashion for safety. This is the best place to keep your pistol." He moved behind her and raised her shirt, then slid the gun into the waistband of her jeans, against the small of her back.

The pistol was cold and hard against her skin. He dropped the shirt back in place. "No one can see it," he said. "You've got easy access to it. Keep the spare clip in your front pocket."

She did as he asked, then looked up at him. The handsome man who'd listened while she'd confessed her secrets last night was gone. The passionate stranger who'd kissed her, the friendly guy who'd played ball with Bobby, all those men disappeared. In their place stood a warrior. Emotionless, unafraid, determined.

"What else do I need to do?" she asked.

"When you dock in Miami, leave the gun and the extra magazine on the boat. Take a cab to this street." He handed her a small piece of paper. "There are about two dozen small hotels and motels stretched for a mile. Pick one and register under a false name. Don't use Smith or Jones, though. It's too obvious."

She frowned. "You want me to *stay* in Miami? Isn't that going to be the first place he'll look for me?"

"Yes. But he won't know when you're arriving and he'll check the large hotels first. He can't be everywhere. It's just for one night. You leave Miami on Saturday."

"Why?"

"The cruise ships dock then and the airport is jammed. Take any flight going to a major city. Change planes. About three flights should be enough. Wait about four days, then do it again, but this time go to smaller cities."

The pistol poked into her back. Her heart was beating quickly and they hadn't even left her bedroom. It was overwhelming. "I don't know if I can do this," she said. She regretted the confession as soon as she'd made it and waited for Jeff to make some snide remark.

Instead, he placed his hands on her shoulders. "I know," he said. "Worry about one step at a time. Don't think about too much at once, or you'll go crazy."

His voice was gentle and encouraging. She wanted to throw herself against him and cling forever. Instead, she forced herself to smile and step back. "Good advice."

"One more thing," he said, reaching in his front pocket. "You'll need this." He pulled out a wad of bills.

"I can't take your money."

"You're going to need it to stay away from Kray. Hiding is expensive. Believe me, I know."

She shook her head. "I don't need it. I got a large settlement when Kray and I divorced. I've never been one to spend lavishly, so Bobby and I have been living off the interest. I've got cash stashed in safety-deposit boxes all over the country. We'll be fine."

He thrust the bills at her. "Just in case. You can pay me back later."

He waited. Finally she took the money. The bills were all hundreds and fifties. There had to be at least five thousand dollars there. "How am I supposed to pay you back? I don't even know your last name."

He smiled. "I'll find you."

She hoped he would, when this was all over. Maybe they could have a second chance. "I wish we'd met under other circumstances," she said, then cleared her throat and stuffed the money in her jeans pocket, the one without the extra ammunition clip. "That is, I wish I was someone else so you wouldn't—" That wasn't right, either. "What I'm trying to say is—"

"Hush," he said, then touched her face. The brush of his fingers against her cheek was gentle. "I know what you're saying, Andie."

His blue eyes were dark and unreadable. She wanted to see a flame of desire flickering there. She hoped he would kiss her, but in the end, all he did was tap the brim of her baseball cap and step away.

That was it then. This was goodbye. No mention of missing her, or the fact that he didn't really mind who her ex-husband was. Nothing about forgiving or liking her. Jeff would get them off the island, then go back to his men and his mission. It made sense, she told herself. She didn't really matter to him—not like he mattered to her.

She pushed away the "if onlys" and forced herself to concentrate on the moment. A quick glance at her watch told her time was slipping away from them.

"We have to leave," Jeff said, confirming her thoughts.

She picked up her purse and slipped it over her head so it hung across her chest. She wanted her arms free. Jeff grabbed the suitcase and walked to the door.

"Wait," she called.

He paused, then turned toward her. He raised his eyebrows expectantly.

"If anything happens to me, you've given your word to look after Bobby."

"I haven't forgotten."

"I want to be sure. Please get him back to the States. Give him a false name and put him into a child-services department somewhere. Any foster home would be better than being with Kray."

"I agree. I've already given you my word, but if you need to hear it again, I swear I'll take care of your son. Kray will have to come through me to get to the kid. But you're not going to die."

The fear was growing. She knew she could handle it, although she wondered how much faster her heart could beat and still stay in her chest. "I know. I just want to be sure."

He grabbed the door handle, then released it. "While we're making promises, I want you to make me one."

"Which is?"

"No heroics. If something happens to me tonight, get the hell out of there. Take the Jeep and drive back to this house.

You'll be safe here for a couple of weeks. Once Kray knows we're together, he'll start searching the island inch by inch.''

"You're saying you're expendable?"

"Exactly."

"All right, I promise."

Jeff stared at her. "If they get me and Bobby, leave him with his father and get the hell away."

"What?"

"If you're alive, you can hire someone to kidnap him back. If you're dead, Bobby is stuck with his father and no one is going to come looking for him."

"I couldn't." Leave her son with that murderer?

"You don't have another choice."

She didn't like what Jeff was saying, but she couldn't deny he made sense. Better to live to fight for her son, than to die in some useless act, abandoning him forever.

Oh, God, she couldn't do this. She didn't have the strength. She pictured Bobby's smiling face. "So, neither of us can be caught," she said.

"That would be best," he admitted. "You ready?"

No, she wasn't ready. She would never be ready. But she didn't have a choice. Until she was off the island, she was playing on Kray's terms. She trusted Jeff. He was risking his life for her.

"I'm ready," she said, and followed him out into the hall.

Jeff drove through the empty streets of St. Lucas. They didn't have to go through town. The route he'd chosen to the public dock on the far side of the island was indirect and took them on narrow, ill-kept roads.

The storm from the night before had moved on, leaving behind brilliant clear skies and millions of stars. It had also washed mud onto the streets. Jeff drove slowly, trying to avoid most of it. He didn't want to come this far only to be late because they got trapped in some dirt road.

There weren't any streetlights at this end of the island, and very few houses. They didn't pass any other cars. Of course it was late and a weeknight. Most people were already home in bed. He wondered how many of Kray's men still roamed, looking for their employer's son.

The crawling sensation at the back of his neck refused to go away. He told himself it was nerves and nothing else. He wasn't used to being in the field anymore. He'd gotten soft.

"Five years is too damn long," he muttered.

"What?" Andie asked from the seat beside him.

He glanced at her, then at the boy curled up in the back seat. The strangeness of leaving the house in the middle of the night had kept Bobby up and bouncing for about the first fifteen minutes. Then even his nap that afternoon hadn't been enough to keep him awake. He'd gotten more and more quiet before finally collapsing in the corner.

"I was just thinking out loud," he said, keeping his voice low so it wouldn't carry and wake up the kid. "It's been five years since I've been in the field."

"Are you nervous?"

"A little."

"This probably sounds dumb, but I'm glad I'm not the only one." She gave him a quick smile.

"It's going to be okay," he said.

"Are you trying to make me feel better, or is this some gut instinct?"

He didn't think she would want to know that he had no instincts about this mission. Reactions like that came from training and detachment. He had neither. He was rusty as hell and far too personally involved to have a sense of anything. Two things were certain though. First, he would risk it all to get Andie off this island, and second, he still wanted Kray dead.

"It's going to be all right because we're willing to pay a higher price than they are," he said.

"That makes sense."

She shifted in her seat. She hadn't been able to find a comfortable spot since they'd left the house. He figured the gun was digging into her back.

"Why are you leading this mission if you haven't been in the field for so long?" she asked.

"I volunteered," he said. A committee of one. He wondered what she would say if she knew the truth. Just as well she didn't. He wanted her to think of him as one of the good guys. Stupid. He wasn't, of course. The second he pulled the trigger on Kray, he crossed the line. This time he wouldn't be able to find his way back.

"Will it be in the papers?" she asked. "Will I know, or will it be hushed up?"

He thought about the headline. Rogue U.S. Government Agent Murders Crime Lord. "I think it'll make a paper or two."

"Good. I'll check. I hope..." She paused and drew in a breath. He glanced at her. She was staring straight ahead. "You probably think this is horrible, but I hope you're successful. I hope you do what you came to do and I hope you get away. Maybe you could make sure they put that in the papers, too."

She wanted to know that he was okay. Despite his attitude, despite the fact that he'd been a complete ass around her. She thought he was some good guy, wearing a white hat, riding in to save the day.

Now that she was leaving, now that the dock was less than five miles away and he could begin to believe she was going to get out, he could admit the truth to himself. He claimed to hate her because she was once married to Kray and because she made him forget, but the only person he hated was himself. Andie was what she said she was—an innocent, caught up in a frightening world. She had neither the temperament nor the training to survive there, yet she'd hung on. She'd escaped and made a life for herself. She had grit and backbone. More courage than any five men he knew. She was sweet and funny, and God help him, she got to him. Not just her body or the thought of making love with her. This wasn't just about sex. The sex was easy. It was the feelings that were difficult. He didn't want to think that he would miss her.

But he would.

From the corner of his eye, he saw her shiver slightly and fold her arms over her chest. He could smell her fear. He reached out and placed his hand on her thigh. "Hang in there."

She nodded. "I will."

He withdrew his hand. At least she was leaving. If she wasn't, he would start to worry about himself. He couldn't afford to care anymore. Not just because of what was going to happen after he shot Kray, but because he couldn't handle the emotions. He could spend the rest of his life in mourning for his wife and son and it would never be enough. He would never be able to make up for what he did to them. Nothing, certainly not caring about someone else, could distract him from his penance.

They rounded a bend in the road. Once again Jeff could smell the sea. He forced all personal thoughts from his mind, mentally shutting down. From now on there was only instinct and survival. No distractions.

The dock was up ahead. He'd chosen it specifically. It was public, but closed at dusk. Because of its out-of-the-way location, it wasn't used much during the week. There were no guards, no fences, no gate.

He slowed the Jeep. The crawling sensation on the back of his neck continued. He adjusted his hat. Would the boat be there? Were Kray's men waiting? He pulled his pistol from its holster and set it on his lap. Beside him, Andie stiffened. He didn't spare her a glance.

Three hundred yards from the dock, he turned off his lights and stopped the Jeep. The air was still around them.

"There's a dirt parking lot on the side of the road," he said quietly. "From there, a footbridge takes you out to the boats. Ours should be the only one there. I'm going to park and leave you while I go check things out. Any questions?"

"No."

Her voice was low and tight. Fearful. He didn't spare her a glance. He pressed on the accelerator. They drove down the road. Once in the parking lot, Jeff turned the Jeep so it was pointing the way they'd come, then backed it under several low tree branches.

"Stay here," he said. "At the first sign of trouble, get the hell out of here. If it's a false alarm, I'll find my own way back to the house. You understand?"

"Yes."

Without glancing at her, he grabbed his pistol and climbed out. The low rumble of the engine disguised the sounds of the night.

"Get behind the wheel," he said, then turned and disappeared into the brush.

Slowly he inched his way closer to the bridge. There were a few faint lights along the dock. They cast murky pools that couldn't penetrate the jungle undergrowth. He moved steadily toward the sea, stopping every few seconds to listen. Gradually the sound of the engine faded behind him. He could hear the surf, some insects and the local variety of frog. The night noises told him he was alone.

He continued to walk through the brush, breaking free of the plants about twenty feet south of the dock. He could see the cabin cruiser rocking in the ocean. The starboard light had been broken, so there was only a bare bulb burning in the darkness. Just like he'd arranged.

From where he was standing, he could see down to the beach. Nothing stirred. At the sea end, the bridge was tall enough for a man to walk under. It dropped lower as it neared the shore. The incoming tide swirled around the rocks. Nothing looked out of place.

He hurried back to the Jeep. Andie was sitting in the driver's seat, her hands clutching the wheel. When he came up the path from the bridge, she turned toward him.

"Everything looks fine," he said.

"Thank God."

"Don't relax yet. You're not on the boat. I want to go down and check it before you board."

She frowned. "I thought that's what you did."

"You can't see the boat from here. I want you and Bobby to stand at the top of the path. I'll go down to the dock. If everything's okay, you follow me. If it isn't, I want to be able to signal you to get the hell out of here."

"I don't like this."

He reached past her and turned off the ignition. "I know."

She scrambled out of the vehicle, then leaned in the back and shook her son. "Bobby, honey, wake up. We've got to go."

"Huh?" The boy squirmed. "I don't wanna wake up."

"I know, honey, but we're going to ride on a boat."

That got the kid's attention. His eyes opened and he grinned. "Now?"

"Yes, now. Come on, get up."

He sat up sleepily, rubbing his eyes. When he stood up, she lifted him over the side of the vehicle and set him on the ground. Jeff opened the trunk and pulled out their suitcase and Bobby's bag of toys.

"I want you two to wait up there," he said, pointing to the top of the path.

Andie nodded. She adjusted her purse, then the weapon at the small of her back. She handed her son his toys, then took the suitcase. "We're ready."

Jeff led the way. There was a large sign at the end of the parking lot. In the dim light he couldn't read what it said. He paused there.

"Can you see the boat?" he asked.

"Sure. It's not very big."

He grinned. "Big enough to get you to Florida. The captain will have motion-sickness medicine on board, just in case."

"Great. I hadn't even thought of that."

He felt a tugging at his pant legs and he looked down. Bobby was staring up at him.

"Aren't you coming with us?" the boy asked.

"Sorry, sport. I've got to stay here and take care of some business." His stomach clenched. He was going to kill the kid's father. That was his business. But he wouldn't think about that now.

"I thought you were coming with us."

"We'll be fine, Bobby," Andie said, then touched her son's shoulder. "We're going on an adventure."

"But I want Jeff to come, too."

"He can't."

Jeff squatted down so he was close to eye level. "You're going to have to be real brave for your mom. Can you do that?"

Bobby nodded solemnly.

"Good." Jeff held out his arms. "Why don't you give me a hug?"

The child dropped his bag of toys and flew into his arms. Jeff stood frozen for a moment, unable to respond. He hadn't thought, he'd just reacted. He was being assaulted by a battalion of memories. Bobby was bigger than J.J. had been when he'd died but the little-boy hug was almost the same. Thin arms pressing so hard, the narrow back, the scent and sounds. Jeff's heart ached. Slowly he wrapped his arms around Bobby. They clung to each other. He hadn't expected to care. He hadn't expected to miss the kid.

Bobby sniffed once, then stepped back. Jeff didn't want to let him go, but he released him. "I'll be good," the child promised, then picked up his toys.

Jeff stood up. Andie tried to smile. "I still don't know your last name."

"I know."

"I wish—" She shook her head. "It doesn't matter."

He stared at her, at her perfect face. He wished it, too. That it could have been different. That she could have been someone else. He thought about kissing her, but he was afraid of what they would feel and say. Better to just move on.

"I'm going down to the boat," he said, stepping away from them. "If everything's all right, I'll click on my flashlight three times. Walk quickly to the boat. Don't run on the dock. Once you're there, get on and get down. Is that clear?"

"Yes," Andie said, and took her son's hand.

Jeff hurried down the long bridge. The hairs on the back of his neck prickled. He didn't like being that exposed, but there wasn't another way to the boat without swimming.

When he was close to the craft, he paused and whistled twice. There wasn't any response. He whistled again, low and clear.

Silence.

He swore under his breath. Not now, not when he was so damn close to getting her off the island. He ran the last ten feet and boarded the vessel. It rocked slightly under his feet. The light didn't reach here; everything was in shadow.

"Daniel," he called and took a step forward. "Where—"

His toe hit something soft. He bent over and touched a man's arm. Squatting down, he turned on his powerful, thin flashlight. Daniel's open eyes stared up lifelessly. His throat had been cut. The job was professional. No one on the island would dare kill someone without Kray's permission.

Jeff stayed crouched down, trying to figure out if they would jump him here or wait until he left the boat. He drew in a deep breath and smelled it. Gasoline. The boat's engine was diesel.

From under the deck came a faint scratching sound, like a sparking device. He sprang to his feet and jumped out of the boat. He started up the dock. He could see Andie and Bobby standing where he'd left them.

"Get out of here," he screamed. "Go! Now!"

She started to move away.

"Run!" he called. If she left now she might have a chance. She might—

The explosion was louder than he'd expected. The sound convulsed around him. It shook the dock beneath his feet and buffeted his body. The wooden support beams buckled. The bridge cracked. He was caught in the second blast and thrown high into the air. The world spun into blackness. He knew he was going to die and Andie would be left alone. His last conscious thought was one of bitter regret.

Chapter 10

The blackness was complete. Some still-functioning part of his brain acknowledged that. Then he landed and instantly began to sink. The sensation of regaining consciousness combined with the terrifying reality of saltwater filling his lungs.

Jeff fought against the instinct to panic. He opened his eyes but it was dark. He had no idea where he was or what had happened. His chest tightened. He had to breathe, cough, choke—anything. The band of pressure increased. Instead, he relaxed, allowing his body to float. He hung suspended in the salty depths. Every cell of his being screamed for air, for life. Training battled instinct. He knew this time, under these conditions, instinct would kill him.

Slowly, so slowly he almost didn't notice, he began to move. His body floated up, through the darkness, toward the surface and life-giving air. When he had broken free of the water, he gasped in a breath, then choked on the saltwater he'd swallowed. He treaded water while he cleared his lungs and tried to figure out where he was and what had just happened.

His arms and legs felt bruised. His head was light, his memory fuzzy. But even if he couldn't remember, something inside drove him on. Even as he was still catching his breath, he began to move toward the shore. In the faint lights up ahead, he could see the foamy surf slapping against the sand. His shoulders ached as he moved his arms. What the hell had happened?

To his left the end of the dock burned. A piece of wood floated by. Jeff grabbed it. He looked around. There were more pieces. A boat maybe? An explosion?

Then the memories returned. Andie—was she safe? Daniel was dead. Kray knew about Jeff hiring the boat. Did he know his old enemy was helping his ex-wife escape?

Ignoring the throbbing pain in his body, he continued for shore. Dear God, just let her have followed his instructions. If she had, she would long gone by now. It would take her a while to find her way back to the house, but when she made it she would be safe for several more days. By then, he could get back to her and—

His foot touched the sandy bottom. He gathered his fading strength and staggered onto the shore. His legs were shaking. The concussion from the explosion had hit him like a brick wall. He wanted to lie down and rest but there was no time. He had to be sure Andie and Bobby had gotten away. He had to know they were safe.

But despite his good intentions, his knees buckled and he went down. He crawled out of the surf, cursing Kray and his efficiency, the bad luck—or bad timing—that had brought him to this. Jeff's arms shook from the effort, then he groaned once and collapsed.

He wasn't sure how long he was out. One minute he surrendered to the darkness, the next, something hard was poking his side.

"You think he's dead?" a male voice asked.

Jeff came awake instantly. He didn't move.

"I saw him breathing. He's not dead." The hard poke came again, this time bruising his ribs. "Time to wake up."

There was the distinctive *click* of an automatic weapon's safety being released. "Or not. It's up to you."

Jeff rolled over and opened his eyes. Two men stared down at him. Their clothes and coloring indicated they were locals, the well-cared-for, expensive weapons told him they worked for Kray.

"Who is he?" the first man asked. He was short and young.

His companion reached in his baggy trouser pocket and pulled out a flashlight. He punched a button. Jeff flinched against the intense beam.

"He looks familiar," the second man said. The light danced over Jeff's face, then was shut off. "What's your name?" he asked, punctuating the question with a jab from his automatic rifle.

"John Doe," Jeff said, his voice scratchy from the saltwater.

"We got us a smart one," the second man said. "He probably works for the United States government." He laughed. "You wanted to go fishing tonight, Monty, but this catch will be our best yet." His grin broadened. Dark eyes stared down at Jeff. "You're a fool, American. Why are you here? You want to capture Kray on his own island?"

"I was on vacation," Jeff said. "Working on my tan."

"You've come a long way to see Kray, and now you'll get your wish."

"I didn't come here to capture him," he said in a spurt of temper.

"No? To kill him, then?" Now both men laughed. "You and what army?" The man looked around. "I don't see anyone else. Your men seemed to have abandoned you, American. And now you die."

Jeff closed his eyes briefly. He sent up a quick prayer that Andie was gone. He knew they hadn't got a hold of her yet. From the sound of things, these two men were alone on the beach. That gave her a fighting chance. If only she had the good sense to take it.

"Get up," Monty, the younger man, said.

Jeff raised himself to his knees. He thought about making a run for it. His body still ached, but his strength was returning. Not that he could outrun fire from an automatic weapon. As he rose to his feet, he strained to listen to the silence around them. Was she already gone? If she wasn't, the men with him would hear the Jeep start up. She'd had time right after the explosion. If she'd started running right away, she would have reached the Jeep while the boat was still in flames. No one would have seen her leave then. But if she'd waited— He shook his head. He didn't want to think about that.

Jeff stood between the two men. Monty was facing him. Now they would start, he told himself. He shut down his mind and his fears for Andie's safety. He thought of nothing. Slowly all feeling fled. He relaxed. He was ready.

Even so, the first blow to his kidneys caught him off guard. The older man hadn't hit him himself; instead, he'd used the butt of the automatic. The unyielding surface slammed into his back, driving him to his knees. He exhaled sharply. Pain exploded at the point of impact, then radiated out in all directions.

The second blow almost dislocated his left shoulder. He braced himself with his right hand to keep from going down. He'd known he would pay a high price if he was caught. His only regret was that he hadn't had a second chance at Kray.

"How many men are with you?" the older man asked.

Jeff didn't answer.

"How many?"

The butt of the rifle swung down and slammed into his ribs. All the air rushed out of his chest and he felt himself falling into the sand. If he'd had any breath left, he would have laughed. Even if he told them the truth, they wouldn't believe him. No way one man would be crazy enough to go up against Kray alone. He could lie, but he wouldn't. Once he gave in to the pain, they would have won. It was better to disconnect. Eventually he would fall into unconsciousness. Eventually they would kill him. Then, as he'd promised five years ago, he would wait for Kray in hell and have his revenge there.

"Can I hit him?" Monty asked.

"No, you'll kill him like you did the last one. We need him alive." The older man stepped back. Jeff knew it was to give him a moment to regain his strength. It was more fun to bring a man to his knees than to keep hitting him while he was down. If they would let him rest there for about a week, he would be ready to take them both on.

"Stand up, American," the young man ordered.

Jeff forced himself to his knees. There was too much pain for him to locate any one place that hurt more than another. Every breath was agony, although he didn't think his ribs were broken.

"I said get up!"

Jeff braced his hands on his thigh and started to push up. When a bullet hit the sand next to him, he was so startled he almost collapsed.

"Thank goodness," Andie breathed. She'd figured out how to use the pistol after all. Now she had to distract the men holding Jeff without hitting any of them. She pointed the muzzle toward the sand just to the left of them and fired again. The recoil didn't surprise her as much this time and she was able to keep her arms out in front of her.

She felt foolish, standing there, legs spread, knees bent, her arms stretched out like some actress playing a cop in a low-budget movie. All she needed was to yell some tacky line of dialogue like "Freeze, sucker, or I'll blow your head off."

Only, this wasn't a movie, it was frighteningly real. Her heart was pounding too hard, her palms were damp, the fear so overwhelming, she could taste it.

The men on the beach peered in her direction. She stood in the shadows of a large bush, next to a tree. If they started to fire back at her, she wanted to be able to duck. She didn't dare call out. She didn't want them to know who she was. Otherwise she would have ordered them to drop their weapons. She wondered if they would have listened to a woman, then thought the gun in her hand was a pretty decent equalizer.

"Where'd that shot come from?" one of the men asked the other.

"Hell if I know. How many are there?"

At least they thought she was dangerous. That was something. She knew how many bullets she had in her clip. She didn't want to waste any more than she had to. She might need them later. Or Jeff might.

Jeff. The light from the parking lot didn't reach onto the beach. She couldn't see much more than vague shapes. She prayed he was all right. She wanted him to be healthy enough to be able to yell at her when they got out of this trouble.

She should have run, she thought, even as she prepared to fire again. When he screamed her name, she'd grabbed Bobby and headed back for the Jeep. The explosion had knocked them both to their knees, but otherwise they'd been unhurt. She'd hidden her son in the back of the vehicle, but she couldn't leave. Not without knowing if Jeff had survived. She told herself it was because she was afraid they couldn't make it without him. Her heart told her her reasons for worrying about him were much more personal.

She saw the men moving. They'd separated. She took aim between them, closed her eyes and squeezed.

"*Damn,* that was close," one of them called out, sounding slightly panicked.

She smiled briefly, then sobered as she wondered how they were going to get out of this. She hadn't seen Jeff crawl out of the ocean. She hadn't been able to see anything until one of Kray's men had turned on his flashlight. She'd been standing on the dock staring into the blackness, praying for a sign. When it came, she'd been so startled, she'd almost cried out. Almost.

The men on the beach moved again. She took aim between them and fired.

"Got 'em," one of the men called.

A bright light hit her full in the face, blinding her. Instinctively she turned away, but she couldn't see anything. She stumbled over something on the ground, then dropped down so she wouldn't be a target. She listened, wondering how long it would take them to find her. And where was Jeff in all this?

Someone swore. "It's that woman. The one who took the kid. This is our lucky night, Monty." She heard a metallic click. "Damn fool, put your gun down. We can't shoot her. She's got his kid."

"I don't see a kid."

"That doesn't mean he's not there. If we hurt him, Kray will kill us himself."

Andie kept blinking, trying to see something, anything. The bright light had blinded her. She could hear the men starting up after her. She turned and fired toward the noise. One of them yelped.

"The bitch winged me. Monty, get your butt over here."

Slowly, shapes began to emerge from the muddy darkness. She could see the foamy surf, the lights from the parking lot. Andie peered around the brush. She could see the two men moving toward the broken bridge, but not a third. Where was Jeff?

She didn't ask her question aloud, but one of them read her mind.

"He's gone," the one she'd shot said suddenly. "The American. He got away."

"We're in trouble," Monty said.

She hoped so. If Jeff had a chance to get away, then he would—

From behind her she heard the sound of an engine starting up.

"What's that?" Monty asked.

"Run," Jeff ordered.

Andie took off toward the sound of his voice. As she reached the end of the broken bridge, the Jeep roared across the parking lot, slowing slightly so she could jump in.

"Mommy!"

"Get down," Jeff said, his voice harsh. As Andie threw herself in the seat, Jeff stuck his hand in the back and pressed her son's head toward the floorboards. "You, too."

She heard cries from behind them. She dropped her head to her knees. Automatic gunfire hit the dirt parking lot around them.

"Are you crazy, Monty? You'll kill the kid."

"They're getting away."

"Let 'em go. Kray will find 'em soon enough."

Jeff hit the gas and they sped out of the parking lot and onto the road. He slowed as they rounded the first curve, then stomped on the brakes. As the Jeep jerked to a stop, he grabbed her pistol and aimed it out the side. She looked up in time to see him firing into a vehicle's tires. The worn pickup truck shifted and settled onto the rims. Jeff handed her back the pistol, then pressed the gas. Gravel and dirt sprayed out behind them. Within minutes the beach was behind them and they were swallowed up in the night.

Andie sat in a corner of the sofa. The lamp in the corner cast a soft pool of light over half the long room. The rest was in shadows. Overhead, the ceiling fan circled lazily, stirring the tropical night air. She wrapped her arms around her waist and rocked slightly. There was no sound save for the faint crash of the waves and the steady footsteps of Jeff pacing back and forth on the front porch. He was furious at her. But at least they'd all made it back alive.

Images sprang to her mind. The fireball of the explosion, the complete darkness and silence afterward. The men on the beach. The spotlight they'd flashed in her eyes. She recalled her terror when she'd first thought Jeff was dead. She hadn't known what to do. He'd told her to run, to get Bobby away from there. She'd known he was right. She was no use to her son dead. And yet she'd stayed.

Because she couldn't stand to face it all alone. Without Jeff she had no way off the island. He was her only hope. She'd also stayed because the thought of leaving him behind had been unbearable. It wasn't just fear that had made her wait, it was her heart.

A tremor shook her. She clasped her waist more firmly, hunching her shoulders down and staring at her lap. The fear was still inside, a living being that sucked up her air, leaving her gasping and terrified.

What now? The question repeated itself. What now? What now? Kray's men had seen her. They knew she was still on the island and they knew she was with Jeff. Kray would be looking for them. When would he find them? What would he do to Jeff when he found him? She knew her own fate and refused to think about it. But she might be responsible for Jeff's death.

The front door opened. She glanced up and saw him standing in the doorway. "Is Bobby asleep?" he asked.

She nodded. "He finally calmed down." They'd both been terrified. She'd stayed in the darkness listening to his steady breathing until her shaking had gotten so bad, she'd been afraid she couldn't stand upright.

Jeff stalked closer to her. He'd removed his cap, but he was still dressed in camouflage. The military clothing made him look dangerous. She didn't dare stare at his face. Instead, she kept her gaze on his broad chest.

"What the hell were you thinking?" he asked. "You could have been killed. I told you to get yourself and Bobby out. If you can't follow orders you're not going to stay alive very long." Anger filled every word. His hands curled into fists as if he would like to strangle her himself.

"I know," she whispered, barely able to force the words past her trembling lips.

"You know? The hell you do, lady. Do you know who those men work for? They thought I was part of a military operation. But no, that was too simple. You had to go and show yourself to them. Now they know you and I are together. Have you thought about that?"

"Yes, I have. It doesn't change anything." The last statement was said hopefully. She wanted him to confirm that Kray knowing the truth wouldn't endanger them more.

Jeff laughed harshly, shattering her brief illusion. "It changes *everything*. He knows you're still on the island. Now they'll be looking for the three of us. His men can describe me, and Kray will be able to identify me from the description."

"I'm sorry."

"Sorry? That's the best you can do? What if Kray's men had caught you, or shot you? What if they'd shot Bobby?"

She jerked her head up and stared at him. The anger in his eyes made her flinch, but she didn't look away. "Bobby was safe in the Jeep. I had him tucked down between the front and back seats."

"What if there had been a third man?"

She opened her mouth, but no sound came. A third man? She hadn't thought of that. "I couldn't let them kill you."

"They weren't going to. Not without Kray's direct orders."

"They were hurting you. I had to make them stop."

"If you act like a civilian, you're going to die and Kray's going to get your son."

The shaking increased. She bit down hard on her lower lip to hold back the tears. She didn't want to know that. She didn't want to have to think about the danger or what disasters had been narrowly avoided.

"Stop trying to scare me," she said. "Nothing bad happened. We're all fine and Kray didn't get us."

"The man I hired to get you to Florida is dead."

She'd forgotten about him. Her stomach lurched. She turned away from him, toward the arm of the sofa. She pulled her knees up toward her chest. Her skin was cold and clammy. Her pulse increased.

"I'm sorry," she whispered. "I'm sorry. It's all my fault. I should have listened. I should have taken Bobby and left. No, I should never have married Kray in the first place. That was the first mistake." She squeezed her eyes shut, trying not to remember that time. "No, not the first mistake, but the biggest. But I couldn't leave. Don't you see? I thought they were going to kill you. I couldn't bear to watch another man die. Especially not you. But a man is dead anyway. Because of me. I killed him. Oh, God, the explosion.''

"Andie.'' She felt Jeff settle on the sofa next to her.

"No, it's true. If it wasn't for me, he would be alive right now. Why did he have to die? Why did I have to marry Kray? How could I have been so stupid? I didn't know. I swear I didn't know."

She felt a hand on her shoulder. She jerked away from him, burrowing in the corner of the sofa. The thick cotton was smooth against her cheek. Expensive. Only the best for Kray and his man. She almost laughed, but was afraid she would sound hysterical.

"I understand,'' he said quietly.

"I doubt that. You blame me as much as anyone. I deserve it. I know that. I should have seen the truth." She opened her eyes and stared at the wall next to the fireplace. She blinked several times, surprised to find her eyes filled with tears. "My first stupid decision was to become a model after my parents died. My second was going to Europe. It was no place for an innocent teenage girl. I had no direction, no one to tell me what I should do. No one to give me advice. Kray was the first person to really listen to me." She drew in a deep breath. "He was intrigued."

This time the laughter did escape. "Intrigued. Can you imagine anything so ridiculous?''

"Andie, it's okay.''

She turned on him. "It's not okay,'' she said angrily. "You've just finished explaining how not okay it is. We're going to die on this island. Kray is going to take my son from me, then he's going to kill us both."

Steel blue eyes stared into her own. "I'm not going to let that happen."

He reached up and pulled off her baseball cap. Several strands of hair drifted across her cheek. Slowly he brushed them away. His fingers were slightly rough and callused against her skin.

"Don't," she whispered. His rage frightened her, but his gentleness would destroy her. She would be left vulnerable, with no way to protect herself from him.

He ignored her request and continued to stroke her face. She didn't know she was crying until he cupped his palm against her jaw and wiped the tears away with his thumb.

"You're shaking," he said.

"What did you expect?"

"Sometimes I forget you're not an experienced field person. I shouldn't have yelled at you. I'm sorry."

"Don't be. You were right. I wasn't thinking. I was just so afraid of being alone with Bobby. I wasn't sure I could keep him safe on my own."

He smiled at her. "Either way, you managed to save my hide. You were very brave."

"I didn't feel brave. I was terrified."

His eyes darkened to the color of a midnight sky. His jaw tightened. He was fighting some powerful emotion, but she didn't know what. She didn't know anything anymore except that she was cold inside. It was as if the fear leeched the very life from her bones. The only warm place on her body was where his hand touched her face.

"How long is it going to be like this?" she asked. "How long do I have to be afraid? How long until he catches us? How long until we're both dead and Kray has Bobby?"

"Hush." He reached for her and pulled her close.

She didn't want to go into his arms. She didn't want to be close to him. Not because she didn't care but because she did. He would make her feel things and want things. She would start to believe and she'd long ago learned believing was deadly. Nothing had changed between them. He was still on the island with his men, sent here to capture Kray, perhaps even to kill him. She was still his enemy's ex-wife—despised, disdained, unworthy.

Yet she couldn't deny his touch or his warmth. He angled toward her on the sofa and pulled her into the shelter of his heat. He stroked her head and her back. He murmured promises that it would be all right. She knew he lied.

He couldn't know that. But for this moment, she chose to believe him. The alternative was to surrender to the despair, and she couldn't do that. Not until her son was safe.

She wrapped her arms around his waist, clinging to him. He was warm and alive. His chest rose and fell in time with his steady breathing. She could hear the thudding of his heart under her ear. His muscles bunched and released against her cheek. His scent, faint fragrances from the night and the maleness that was his alone, surrounded her. She would remember these moments. Later, when she was alone and afraid, she would call on the memories to keep her strong.

"I'm sorry for yelling at you," he said. "You're probably in shock."

"I'm okay," she whispered, snuggling closer. His shirt was surprisingly soft against her skin. "What about you? I heard them hitting you."

"Just a few bumps and bruises."

She raised her head and looked up at him. "Are you sure? Nothing's broken?"

He reached down and felt his left side, then rotated his shoulder. "I'm bruised up pretty good, but it's all still working."

His face was so close to hers. The angle of his jaw caught her attention. Strong, clean lines. She could see the beginnings of stubble shadowing his features. His mouth was straight and well shaped. She remembered the feel of it against her own, then quickly closed her eyes. She didn't want to remember that right now. She didn't want the moment spoiled by fantasies of what could never be. Jeff was still very much in love with his late wife. She was the last woman he would ever want to be with.

She forced herself to think of other things. Of the sound of the sea and the stillness of the night. She relaxed against him, letting the soothing stroking of his hand against her back lull her fears.

Without warning she saw the explosion, heard the deafening blast and felt the concussion. She stiffened and pushed away from him. Her eyes flew open.

"What's wrong?" he asked.

She caught her breath. "Nothing. I just—" She shook her head.

"Andie, what?" He touched a finger to her chin, forcing her to look at him. "Tell me."

"When I closed my eyes, I saw the explosion again. I could hear it in my head. I'm afraid I'm going to have nightmares for a long time."

"You will, but they'll fade."

She wanted to ask how long that would take, then remembered he wouldn't be able to tell her. After all, just a couple of nights ago *he'd* had nightmares about his wife and had called out Jeanne's name. Andie wondered if she would call out Jeff's name when she dreamed of the boat exploding. She'd stood there, terrified, not knowing if he was dead. She hadn't been able to see anything.

"Don't think about it," he said.

"I can't think about anything else."

"I know."

She glanced up at him.

His expression was resigned. "I want to tell you it gets better, that you'll learn to live with it," he said.

"But it doesn't get better, does it?"

He pressed his hand against her head then, urging her to relax against him. She wanted to protest, but she couldn't. It felt right to be with him like this. His strength offered her the illusion of safety, the feeling that as long as she was with him, everything would be all right. It wasn't true, of course. But for a while she would pretend. Pretend that he liked her, that her admiration was nothing more than a fleeting well of gratitude. That she didn't really care for him specifically. She tried to gather the strength to move away. She told herself to be strong, not to be a fool.

"You're so damn beautiful."

His words shocked her. She looked up and found him staring down at her. His eyes were hungry, filled with a fire that kindled instant heat inside of her. He didn't move, yet he seemed to strain toward her. His muscles tensed, his heartbeat increased.

"Jeff?"

"I know, I'm a complete bastard." He pulled away from her, shifting on the sofa so he faced forward. "You need rest, Andie. Go to bed."

Did he want her? It seemed impossible to believe. She stared at him, at the way the lamplight caught the gold blond of his hair. At the breadth of his shoulders, at his strength. She needed him, she cared about him and she wanted him. Perhaps more than he could imagine. It had been so long since she'd been with a man, been touched intimately. She wanted to be held and loved. She wanted to be cherished, caressed, healed. She wanted to borrow his strength.

"Jeff?"

"Stop saying my name," he demanded. "You don't know what it does it me."

His hands clenched into fists. Did she really affect him? She sat up on her knees, not sure she was willing to believe what was happening. All this time she'd thought he despised her. Was it possible he thought of being with her as she'd thought of being with him? Was it possible he cared? Did his anger come from guilt? Not just because she was Kray's ex-wife but because he hadn't been with another woman since Jeanne's death?

He'd said she was beautiful. So often her physical body was merely a hindrance. Something people had to get past to see the real person inside. She was assumed to be stupid, or stuck-up, or superior, when in fact she was just like everyone else, with flaws and good points.

But at this moment, she was glad he liked the way she looked. She reached behind her and pulled her braid over her shoulder. She unfastened the tie at the end, then finger-combed the strands free. When her hair was loose, she moved closer to him. She touched his shoulder.

He turned toward her. He breathed her name, then slipped his hands through her hair. "You're incredible," he said.

She smiled. It wasn't love, but it was about her, and that was enough for now. She hadn't felt special to a man in a very long time. Perhaps not ever.

"I want you," he said.

She placed her hands on his shoulders and leaned toward him. Her lips brushed his. She touched him with the faintest pressure, more teasing than passionate, more playful than arousing.

The fingers in her hair twisted, holding her in place. He angled his head and opened his mouth. At the first touch of his tongue, fire raced through her. The flames ignited her skin, her breasts and the sweet waiting place between her thighs.

She slipped forward, falling across his lap. He released her hair and gathered her close to him. They never broke the kiss. Even as he picked her up in his arms. Even as she wiggled to get closer and held on to his neck. Even as he walked down the hallway and into his bedroom. Even when he kicked the door closed behind them, shutting out the rest of the world.

Chapter 11

Jeff carried Andie to the king-size bed in the center of the room, then bent over and placed her on the mattress. His muscles protested, especially his shoulder where Kray's man had hit him with the rifle butt. He ignored the pain and concentrated only on the need flooding through him. It had been too long.

Andie stared up at him with wide blue eyes. Her perfect features, her smooth skin and pouty mouth, all fueled his desire. She was every man's fantasy. The kind of woman who would stop traffic wherever she went. Yet she stared up at him as if he were all she'd ever dreamed of. Her body quivered. He could feel the slight tremors.

"Jeff," she breathed. Her voice was low and husky, as if desire had forced her to say his name.

He'd been hard from the moment he'd sat next to her on the sofa and pulled her close. He'd managed to control himself until she'd taken her hair down and touched him. Now there was no going back.

He taunted himself. Instead of letting the fire consume them both, he waited until the heat was unbearable. He stared at her, at her long jean-clad legs, at her hair spilling over the pillow. She studied him in return, looking at his face, then his chest. Her gaze dipped lower. She flushed slightly when she saw his erection straining against his trousers, but she didn't look away. Her lips parted and her breathing increased.

He reached for the belt buckle at his waist. After unfastening it, he set it and his holster on the nightstand. Next, he pulled his shirt free of his trousers. His boots hit the floor, followed by his socks. Only then did he sit on the bed next to her.

He placed one hand on her thigh. Her jeans were soft from many washings. He could feel the heat of her body and the rippling of her muscles as he ran his palm down her long, lean leg to her ankle. He stroked her calf, her knee, then the outside of her thigh. As his fingers crossed her belly, she caught her breath. He slipped over her ribs to her shoulder, then down her right arm to her hand.

Capturing her wrist, he brought it toward his mouth. Their gazes locked. Watching her watch him, he pressed his lips against the sensitive skin of her inner wrist. He felt the rapid flutter of her pulse. He opened his mouth and tasted her. Her eyes widened. She was sweet and salty. The combination made him realize how long he'd been starving for a woman's flavor. He held in a groan.

Desire swelled in his chest and groin. The fire burned hotter. Yet he held back. He knew what would happen when he gave in. He knew they would both eventually succumb to the flames. But not yet. Anticipation would intensify the act.

Still holding her wrist, he moved his mouth to her palm and nibbled her sensitive skin. Her fingers brushed against his cheek. He circled her palm, tracing life lines, touching each of her fingertips with his tongue, memorizing the taste and feel of her. Beyond the room were the muted sounds of the night. He could hear the surf through the open window, the faint rustle of a night breeze. The scent of exotic, tropical flowers carried to him, yet no fragrance was sweeter than her.

She continued to watch him. Her eyes darkened with smoky desire. She moved her free hand to his thigh and gently squeezed his tight muscles. The silence in the room hummed in expectation. Through her shirt, he could see the faint puckering of her nipples. Her hips began to move slightly, offering him paradise. His blood boiled through him—faster, hotter, urging him on. Yet he continued to hold back, not ready to take or give. In the back of his mind, a voice whispered of fear. There hadn't been anyone for so long. He wanted her, and yet...

She slipped her hand free of his hold and grabbed his wrist. Before he could stop her, she pulled his fingers to her mouth and touched the tips with her tongue. Electricity shot up his arm, through his chest to his groin. She drew his index finger into her mouth and suckled him. His arousal flexed hard against his belly. Had she touched him there, he would have exploded in her hand.

He growled low in his throat and reached for her. Sliding one hand behind her shoulders and the other around her waist, he hauled her up against him. She reached for his arms and clung to him. He pressed his mouth to hers.

She was already waiting for him. Her lips parted instantly, urging him to sup his fill. Moist heat surrounded him, urging him deeper, farther. He explored her mouth. Her sweet taste made him hungry for more. Even as his tongue traced hers, touched tip to tip, retreated and waited for her to follow, his hands were everywhere. He rubbed along her back and her hips. He moved his palms against her legs, up her hips over her belly to her breasts. Through the layer of her shirt and bra, he cupped the full curves and squeezed her taut nipples.

She moaned low in her throat. Her body arched toward him as if she, too, were as needy, as ready, as hungry for love. He angled slightly so she could recline on his lap. He buried his fingers in her long hair. It was gold silk, cool and sexy. He wanted to feel it trickling against his chest. He wanted her to stroke it around the hardest part of him. He wanted her to be over him, kissing him, her hair providing a sensual curtain of privacy.

He moved his hand from her breast to the buttons along the front of her shirt. They opened easily, exposing her pale skin. He raised his head and looked at her. Her bra was white cotton. Somehow he'd assumed she would wear black satin. The plain white bra made her vulnerable. Innocent.

She rolled away from him and sat up, then shrugged out of her shirt. Her pale midsection contrasted with the faint tan on her arms and chest. Despite her slender body, her breasts were full. He wanted to see them bare and taste them. But before he could reach for her, she touched him.

He sat still as she unbuttoned his shirt and drew it over his shoulders. Her movements were slow and sensual. Her fingers trailed over him, leaving him unable to do anything but feel. Her eyes—

"Oh, Jeff," she whispered, staring at him.

He glanced down and saw she was looking at the bruise on his ribs. His swollen skin had darkened, clearly showing the imprint of where he'd been hit.

"You said you were okay."

"I'm fine. Just a few bruises."

"A few? Where else did they hurt you?"

She quickly studied his chest, then checked both arms. She winced when she saw the mark on his upper back from the blow that had almost dislocated his shoulder. Her smooth hand brushed around the tender area. She slipped off the bed and found the swelling by the waistband of his trousers, to the right of his spine.

"Oh, Jeff, they could have killed you."

"They didn't."

"I know, but—" Instead of speaking, she pressed her mouth against his back. Soft lips replaced her fingers as she soothed his wounds.

"I'm so sorry," she whispered. She pressed herself against him. Her full breasts seemed to burn into his skin. She kissed his shoulders, then the back of his neck. "So sorry."

"It's not your fault." He turned suddenly and grabbed her arms. "Listen to me," he said, staring into her eyes. "It's not anyone's fault."

Guilt flickered across her face, then a fierce desire to believe him. He wondered how long she'd carried the shame and how much he'd contributed to the feeling.

Before he could consider the question, she touched her hands to his chest. Her palms grazed his flat nipples. Fire shot down to his groin. Need swelled there. He was tired of thinking, of having conversations. He only wanted to feel. She needed that, too. Getting lost in the passion was the only escape for both of them.

He pulled her up onto the bed. Even as he lowered his mouth to hers, he reached behind her and unfastened her bra. Her lips parted, accepting him, pleasuring him. She let her bra slip down her arms onto the bed, then raised her hands to his shoulders and clung to him.

Her breasts flattened against his chest. He could feel her rounded softness brushing back and forth as she moved against him. He rested his hands on her waist, then moved them higher until he cupped her feminine curves. She filled his palms, spilling over. His greedy fingers reached for her nipples. As she nipped at his lower lip, he brushed his thumbs over her taut peaks. She caught her breath.

The fire between them grew rapidly. There was no time to think or question. He could only react. To the feel of her next to him, to her heat and her passion.

He pushed her onto her back, then knelt over her. Even as he kissed her neck and her throat, then trailed lower to her straining breasts, he reached for the button of her jeans. As he drew a pink nipple into his mouth and tasted her exquisite flavor, he lowered the zipper. His fingers slipped past her panties, to the waiting curls. She was already wet. As he probed her secrets, his own need ached.

He found her place of desire. With two quick circles of his fingertip, he had her writhing. Her hips arched toward him, her eyes fluttered closed and her breathing increased.

He withdrew his hand and she whimpered a protest. He grinned at her impatience. With one quick jerk, he pulled off her tennis shoes and socks, then pulled down her jeans. Her panties came with them, leaving her bare to his gaze.

She was more beautiful than he'd imagined. Pale belly and breasts, the faint honeyed tan on her arms and legs. Her blond hair shimmered in the lamplight. He wanted to stare at her forever. Then she parted her legs, exposing her most secret place to him. He swallowed against the overwhelming need to take her. He had to pleasure her gently. He had to—

He swore silently and quickly tore off his clothes. He knelt between her welcoming thighs and touched his hand to her dampness. She smiled.

He bent over her belly and kissed her firm skin. Even as his fingers moved faster, he tickled and teased her midsection, then moved higher to suckle her breasts. She writhed beneath him. He brought her close to release, then slowed, taunting her. She tossed her head back and forth, straining closer. Her hips arched and he felt her moistness brush against his engorged organ.

"Yes," she whispered, drawing her legs back.

He sat up. His fingers continued to move against her. He could feel her muscles tightening as she neared her moment of pleasure. He wanted to wait until she had her release, but she arched closer, tempting him. He caught his breath. It would be so easy to plunge inside. Get lost in her. He probed her, pushing in slightly. So tight and wet. He swallowed hard, wanting to hold back. Usually he was able to hold off until he'd pleased—

No, he told himself. He wouldn't think about Jeanne. Not now. Not while he was making love with another woman.

The emotions crashed in on him. Guilt, anger, desire. They swelled together, filling him, erasing all from his mind. His self-control snapped and his body reacted. With one long smooth push, he entered her.

Instantly his entire being focused on the moist heat caressing him. He tried to call back the anger, but it was gone. There was nothing but the need to plunge into her again and again. He hated himself even as he withdrew slightly, then arched forward. She drew her knees back, taking him deeper. He moved his fingers faster. She whimpered and trembled beneath him.

Not this way, he pleaded. He was losing every part of himself inside of Andie. She was consuming him. He couldn't remember anything, feel anything except this moment.

And then it didn't matter. Her muscles tightened around him as she prepared for her climax. He moved his fingers faster, liking the slick feel of her most sensitive place. Her breasts quivered with each movement of her body. Her neck stretched back, her mouth parted. She was consumed by the sensations he created.

Or was she? Jeff tried to push the question away. Not now. He didn't want to know that Kray had done this before. That she had held his enemy, loved him, given to him even as she was now giving to Jeff. The unwelcome thought could not be banished. Did she think of her husband?

"Look at me," he commanded, feeling her soar even closer to release. He wanted her to know who was in her bed and in her. He moved deeper inside, faster, as if the act would brand her.

"Jeff," she whispered, then opened her eyes and stared at him. Passion glazed her irises, darkening them. Her mouth curved sweetly in a smile. She whispered his name again, as if she'd had no other thought.

He was a fool, he thought as shame filled him. Worse than that, he'd assumed her betrayal. He felt his expression changing. He tightened his features, but it was too late. She saw the truth.

"You thought—"

Then her body reacted to the pleasure. He felt her tense. Her eyes closed. The tremors began in her center and worked out. Strong muscles rippled around his arousal, forcing him to the edge, then flinging him off the side. He tried to hold back. He had no right. Not only had he hurt her, he feared getting lost inside of her and never finding his way back.

It wasn't supposed to be like this, he thought, even as the explosion built between his legs. It wasn't supposed to hurt them. It wasn't supposed to—

He shuddered with his release. It swept through him, over him, leaving every part of him sated. It went on forever, until he'd been wrung dry and left broken.

Only when they were both still, did he raise his head and look at her. She was staring at him. For once he couldn't read her emotions. Just as well. He didn't want to know what she was thinking. It would make it easier for him to apologize.

He moved away from her. She sat up and swung her legs over the bed, then stood up.

"Where are you going?" he asked as she gathered her clothes and clutched them to her midsection.

She walked to the door. He thought she was going to leave without saying anything, but she paused and looked back at him. She was still naked. Her long hair hung down, partially concealing her round breasts. She looked like a pagan princess—except for the stark pain in her eyes.

"Andie, look, I'm—"

She shook her head. "Don't say you're sorry. It's too late." She opened and door and stepped into the hall. "I have to go take a shower."

The door closed behind her. Jeff rolled onto his back and closed his eyes. He'd made her feel dirty. He'd taken her and used her. He was as much of a bastard as Kray had ever been.

Andie sat in a chaise lounge by the pool and watched the sun rise over the jungle. The sky lightened, changing from gray to almost white, to pale blue. There weren't any clouds. Nothing disturbed the beauty of the morning, except perhaps her mood.

She rubbed her eyes. They were dry and they burned. It had been another night without sleep. She was so exhausted, she'd passed tired days ago. Now she was just numb. She felt as if she were moving through thick water all the time.

The first rays of sunlight poked over the trees and slanted down by the pool. She pulled her legs up close to her chest. She wasn't out here to tan. She'd come outside because she couldn't stand to be in the house anymore. She was afraid of what would happen when Jeff left his room. She didn't want to think about last night, yet she couldn't think about anything else.

She closed her eyes against the memories, fighting them, trying to focus her attention on something else. It didn't matter. They returned. Reminding her of the magic she'd felt in his arms. The tenderness. He'd touched her as if she were a fragile piece of porcelain, as if she were beautiful. Right up to the end she'd thought he was thinking about her, caring for her. Instead, he'd been hiding anger at who she was and what she'd done. An act of love had turned into a violation. It didn't matter how long she'd stood in the shower or how much she'd scrubbed, she couldn't wash away the feeling of being dirty.

She'd cried then. Cried until there were no tears left. She'd lain down in the bed next to her son's and listened to his breathing. Over and over again, she'd relived her time with Jeff. She'd wondered what she'd done wrong. Was it something she'd said? Had it been how she'd touched him? In the end she'd realized it was nothing that specific. It was just her.

He judged her. Not by her actions, but by association. His reaction last night was one of the reasons she'd avoided getting involved with a man after leaving Kray. She didn't want to have to explain herself or justify her past. She knew she had to pay for her mistakes. Foolishly she'd thought at some point she would be able to put them behind her.

If only she'd never met Kray. Except she couldn't wish that. Without Kray she wouldn't have Bobby, and her son meant everything to her. Ironically without Kray she would never have met Jeff, either.

If only Jeff was another kind of man. Not quite so good or honorable. Maybe a little less kind to her son, a little less faithful to the memory of his late wife. But if Jeff was different, she wouldn't care about him so much. His opinion of her wouldn't matter. She'd hoped he would help her put the past in its place. Instead, he'd brought it to life.

She told herself it didn't matter what he thought of her. He was just one man. There were plenty of others out there. But that wasn't true. He wasn't just one man—she'd hoped he was the man for her. Someone she could freely give her heart to. Someone she could risk caring about. She'd been wrong.

The front door opened. She grabbed hold of the arms of the chair and held on tightly. She wasn't ready to face him, but he didn't have to know that. She'd bluffed her way out of more difficult situations; she would do it again in this one. He mustn't know how much he'd hurt her.

He walked barefoot across the porch and down the stairs. His hair was damp from a recent shower, his face freshly shaved. Despite the shadows under his eyes, he was handsome enough to make her heart pound faster and her palms sweat.

His stride was long and easy as he moved toward her. His open shirt flapped against his sides, exposing his bare chest. Baggy blue shorts sat low on his hips.

She expected him to take the chair across the pool, or at the very least, the one next to her. Instead, he got closer and closer until he perched on the foot of her chaise lounge. She drew her legs closer to her body, angling away from him. Her hair was loose. She tilted her head forward, using the long strands to shield her expression. He stared at her.

"You look like hell," he said, after a while. "Didn't you sleep?"

"You look like hell, too, and I'd like you to keep your opinions to yourself from now on."

The muscles in his jaw tightened briefly, then he nodded. "I will."

"Cheap talk," she snapped, allowing the rush of unexpected anger to give her strength. "How long will that promise last? Until you're ready to explain exactly what's wrong with me? Who do you think you are, judging me all the time? Who gave you the right?"

His steady gaze never left hers. "I don't have the right, Andie. I'm sorry. I know you don't want to hear that, but it's true. As for judging you—" He looked away. "It's a joke. As if I'm any kind of a standard. Compared to me, you're a saint." He rubbed the bridge of his nose. "But what you think of me isn't our biggest problem. I still have to get you and Bobby off the island."

In the pain of his rejection, she'd almost forgotten they were stuck here. "Can you still help us?"

He stretched his long legs out in front of him. "Yes. It'll take some doing, but I can get you two away from here. I have a friend who will help us."

"How do you know he's willing to get involved?"

"He just is. I trust him with my life. More important, I trust him with yours."

"Oh, please, don't waste your time with lines like that. You trust him with my life. As if my life has any value to you." She leaned forward slightly and poked him in the arm. "I was there last night, Mr. Jeff whoever-the-hell-you-are. You looked at me as if I was dirt. No better than some whore."

"I didn't mean—"

"I don't care what you meant, I care about what you did." She scrambled past him and stood up. "I'm just Kray's ex-wife. Not good for anything, except maybe a fast, easy way to get off. I'm still good enough for that I guess."

He glared up at her. "It wasn't like that."

"Oh? How was it? Look me in the eye and tell me you didn't once think about my being with Kray. Tell me you didn't try to stop, that you wanted to get away from me, but it was too late."

He turned away. The silence was deafening.

It wasn't until that moment that she'd realized how much she'd wanted him to deny the truth. She was bruised enough that she would have been willing to accept a halfway decent lie. At least she would have tried to. She didn't want to know the truth. It hurt too much. She wanted Jeff to like her, to care about her the way she cared about him. She wanted him to admire her. But that would never happen. It was too late for them. No—they would never have found a right time. It wasn't meant to be.

"You used me," she said, speaking slowly so her voice wouldn't crack. Sadness and shame filled her, but she wouldn't give in to the emotion. "You took my body, you made me think I mattered, then you used me. You didn't care. Not even a little. And because I was once married to Kray, it was all right. You could be contemptuous and disdainful. I'm hardly human, right? My feelings don't matter. If you started to feel guilty, all you had to tell yourself was that I'd earned it."

He stood up. She didn't move back. She let him tower over her. "I didn't mean to hurt you," he said.

"Yes, you did."

He reached out toward her. She stayed in place until his hand was inches from her face, then she ducked away. He curled his fingers into his palm and dropped his arm to his side.

"I thought you at least liked me," she said. "The worst of it is, I was foolish enough to care about you and admire you for being strong and honorable. All the things Kray had never been. I thought—"

"Dammit, stop thinking," he ground out. "Don't care about me. You hear me? Don't care. I don't want that. I don't want—"

You. He didn't say the word, but she heard it. She took a step back.

"No." He grabbed her arm and held her in place. "That's not what I meant. I can't—" His eyes darkened with anguish.

She wanted to go to him and offer comfort, but she knew better. He was dangerous, and her heart was already close to breaking.

He released her. "Just don't care about me."

"Don't worry. Your attitude is rapidly curing me of any gentle feelings I might have left. I'll leave you alone to your mourning. Your precious memories of Jeanne are safe."

He sank back on the chaise and rested his elbows on his knees. He dropped his head to his hands. "They're gone."

She didn't know what he was talking about. Despite the need to protect herself, she took a step closer to him. "You still remember her. I heard you call out her name while you were sleeping."

"It wasn't her. It was the car bomb. The memories are fading faster and faster. I can't hold on to them. They've been fading for while, but since I've met you, they're slipping away even more."

Since he'd met her? She didn't want to hope. And yet . . . How much of Jeff's attitude and anger was really at himself? Was it easier to get mad at her rather than face the truth? Was she simply convenient? "Maybe it's time to let them go."

He raised his head and stared at her. His face was drawn, his mouth a straight line. "I can't. They're all I have left."

"Such a perfect love will surely live forever," she said, tasting bitterness. Jeanne must have been an incredible woman to inspire Jeff to such loyalty. She couldn't imagine a man feeling that way about her. What magical powers did Jeanne possess? What were her secrets?

"It wasn't perfect," Jeff said tonelessly. "Not even close."

That made it worse, Andie decided. She brushed her hair out of her face. Bad enough to have a man mourn a perfect love, but to know he continued to mourn an imperfect one meant there was no hope. If Jeanne was the ultimate woman, she, Andie, couldn't be expected to compete against her. But if Jeanne was flawed, then Andie simply didn't measure up.

"It's not what you think," Jeff said.

She stared at the palm trees overhead. The air was warming and a slight breeze tugged at her T-shirt. "How do you know what I'm thinking?"

"You think this is because of you, but it isn't."

She stared at him. "Is it because of Kray?"

Jeff nodded. "Some of it. I know it's not your fault. I understand that in my head, but my gut isn't so willing to believe. I keep thinking you should have known somehow. It's not fair."

"You're breaking my heart," she said sarcastically, wondering why she was bothering to listen to him. Did it really matter why he'd done it? The reasons didn't affect his actions. He'd treated her badly last night and now he was trying to justify it.

He laced his hands together. "Some of it is me. I don't want to like you. It makes me forget."

His words tore at her protective defenses. "How do you keep doing that?" she asked. "I make up my mind that you're the bad guy, then you twist everything around so I'm supposed to be on your side again. Stop toying with me."

"I'm being honest. You want to believe the best about me. That I'm some heroic warrior here to rescue you." He laughed, but the sound had no humor. "If you only knew the truth." He shook his head and rose to his feet. "It doesn't matter. I have to make arrangements to get you off the island."

He started to walk away. She told herself to let him go. It would be better for both of them if she just put the whole thing behind her. It hadn't worked out. She would survive. She'd survived much worse in her life. Besides, she had to focus on keeping Bobby safe. And yet—

"What's the truth?" she asked before she could stop herself.

He'd already walked past her. He slowed, then turned to look at her. In that moment when their eyes met, she knew down in her soul she didn't want to hear what he had to say. His expression didn't change—it was still unreadable. His gaze gave nothing away, his posture didn't change. But a soft voice whispered this was trouble. She wanted to run in the opposite direction. She wanted to call back the question.

The faint breeze teased at his short blond hair and whipped open his shirt. His bare chest and the dark shading of his bruises reminded her of the danger and passion they'd shared, before he'd recalled the past and destroyed everything.

"I thought you might have guessed," he said.

"That you're here on a mission to arrest, or maybe kill Kray? Yes, I've figured that much out."

"When are you going to get it? I'm not some white knight, Andie. I'm just a bastard with a grudge."

"What? I don't understand."

He took a step toward her. "Then let me make it clear. I'm not on a mission. There's no *team* waiting for me to be done helping you. This isn't a sanctioned killing."

Her chest felt as if a band were being tightened around her ribs. Her breath caught in her throat. "What are you saying?"

"Officially I'm on a six-week leave of absence from my job in Washington. I got tired of waiting for Kray to make a mistake and get caught. I'm going to take care of him myself. I'm here on St. Lucas to kill your ex-husband."

Chapter 12

She physically recoiled from him. Jeff watched as Andie took a step back and folded her arms over her chest. She drew her delicate eyebrows together as if she hadn't understood what he was saying.

"You can't mean that," she said, disbelieving.

"Every word."

She shook her head slowly. Maybe she thought her denial would change the truth. "You're going to kill Kray in cold blood? You're going to murder him?"

It was like watching something from a distance. A play or a movie, maybe. Nothing felt real. "Yes."

"I don't understand. Is this to repay him for what he did to Jeanne and your son?"

"In part. But most of the reason is that Kray's evil. I'm tired of waiting for him to make a mistake. It's been five years and nothing has happened. At least this way he'll be gone."

"Gone? Don't you mean dead?"

He shrugged. "Whatever. He needs to be stopped."

"Not like this." Her eyes widened and she stared at him as if she'd never seen him before. "You can't do this. It's not right."

"Whatever's right isn't working."

"But if you do this…" She turned away and stared at the ocean. "You can't. I thought you were different from Kray. You're supposed to be one of the good guys. You aren't if you do this. You're just like him, destroying whenever it suits you."

He narrowed his gaze. "We're hardly the same," he said. "Kray's entire life is based on getting what he wants at any price. He lives in a world outside normal rules and boundaries."

"Won't you be doing the same thing?"

"No. I'm here to kill my enemy, no one else."

She spun back to face him. "And that makes it all right?"

"You're the one so concerned with semantics. A few minutes ago it was fine because I was part of a mission and had my government's permission to take him out. Now that I'm on my own, it's wrong? Explain the difference."

"Now it's personal."

"It's always been personal. He killed my wife and child. How can it not be personal?"

She shook her head. "You're twisting my words. I know what he did and how it hurt you. However, that doesn't give you the right—"

He took a step toward her and stared down. "Don't talk to me about rights. You weren't there. You didn't see the car explode, or smell the burning bodies. You don't know anything about this."

She couldn't meet his gaze. She stared at the ground. "I know, Jeff. It's hard, but you've got to see—"

"No." He grabbed her arm. "I don't have to see anything. I've sent men to their death before. I've killed before. What do you think happens in the field? It's not like the movies. We're not exchanging bits of microfilm in cigarette boxes. People do die and sometimes it gets ugly."

"But then it's for a reason."

"I have a damn good reason for wanting him dead."

"You have no purpose in doing this except for assuaging your guilt."

They glared at each other. She blinked first and looked away. He dropped her arm. "Are you saying the world won't be a better place without Kray in it? That you won't be better off? You should be pleased about this. If I succeed, then all your troubles are over."

"If you don't succeed, Kray will see you dead."

"I might be dead anyway. If Kray's men catch me, they'll kill me."

She flinched. The color drained from her face. "What happens if you get away?"

"Our government won't take kindly to a rogue agent acting on his own. I'll be arrested and brought to trial."

"You'll risk everything to destroy Kray?"

"Wouldn't you?"

The sun had risen over the jungle and now shone down on the pool area. Heat from the ground swirled up and surrounded them. Jeff could feel a trickle of perspiration beginning between his shoulder blades and running down his back.

Andie sank down in the middle of the chaise lounge. Her long hair spilled over her lap. She brushed the blond strands away impatiently. "As easily as that?" she whispered. "I can't reconcile what you want to do with the man I've come to know here."

"You never knew me. You made me into what you wanted me to be. I'm the white knight here to rescue you. You didn't want to know anything else."

"I can't connect your willingness to kill in cold blood with the man who risked his life to save me and Bobby."

"What about reconciling your former loving husband with a man who killed Jeanne and my son?"

She raised her head and stared at him. Sorrow filled her face. "You must hate me. I never understood how much before now. Everyday, watching Bobby and me. You've been so nice, but it's all a facade. You want us dead, too."

"Not anymore."

She went on as if he hadn't spoken. "Would it be enough, do you think? Our deaths, an eye for an eye? Maybe our families should die, too. I don't have any relatives, but if I did, should they die? Would that be enough? Where does it end? How much payment do you need?"

"It's not like that," he said loudly. "That's not what this is about. It's between me and Kray."

She stood up. He could see her body shaking. She balled her hands into fists. "You're wrong. It's about all of us. I can't believe you're going to do this. Even more than that, I can't believe you don't think it's wrong."

She turned and started toward the house. He thought about calling out to her, but he had nothing to say. She didn't understand. She was a civilian. She didn't know all that he knew, all that Kray had done. If anyone deserved to die, it was that man.

Who are you to decide? a voice in his head whispered. It had been there from the beginning, since he'd first come up with the plan. He wasn't sure if the voice was his conscience or perhaps even the faint echo of Jeanne's ghost. Sometimes he was willing to admit to himself she wouldn't have wanted him to do this. She would have counseled him to let the wheels of justice slowly grind Kray to dust.

But Jeff wasn't willing to wait. He wasn't willing to listen to the voice in his head. Kray had to be stopped and no one else was willing to take a stand.

He walked off the pool deck and onto the beach. The tide was out. Damp sand stretched toward the waves. Small bubbles and pockets indicated life beneath the surface. There was a small outcropping of rocks near the shore. He sat on the largest one and stared at the sea.

Andie was right about one thing. He had always been on the side of the good guys. Even though he knew he was right, it pained him to cross the line. He didn't think he would like living on the other side.

But did he have a choice? Once Kray was dead, he wouldn't be able to hurt anyone again. His reign of terror would end. Was that so bad? Did the end justify the means? Did it really matter if he, Jeff, crossed the line or not? It was unlikely he would live long enough to suffer from guilt. Kray's men would shoot him on sight. If they didn't get him, then the local law-enforcement officers would take him into custody and he would live out his days in some small prison cell.

He thought about the price he would pay, he weighed the consequences. He had no other choice. He'd sworn to see Kray pay, and he would risk everything to see that through. It didn't matter about crossing the line or what Andie thought of him. All that mattered was Kray's death. But before he could take care of that, he had to get her and Bobby off the island.

He walked to the house and entered the living room. He could hear Andie and Bobby fixing breakfast in the kitchen. Quietly he moved down the hall to his bedroom. After closing the door behind him, he went to the small closet. When he'd first taken up residence in the house, he'd pried up several floorboards to create a hiding space. Now he popped up the boards and pulled out a small black box.

He carried it over to the bed, then lifted up the cover. Inside was a sleek phone attached to a computer keyboard. He punched in several numbers. When the red lights on the console began to flash green, he picked up the receiver.

Modern electronics would scramble his signal before sending it skyward to bounce off a satellite. The call was coded and untraceable. Unfortunately, it also put him back in touch with the agency.

Jeff waited a few seconds, then heard a sleepy "'Lo?"

"Aren't you up yet?" he asked, grinning.

Cort Hollenbeck cleared his throat. "It's not even six in the morning. The kittens don't expect breakfast much before seven."

"Sorry, buddy. I had to be sure I got a hold of you."

"No problem." He heard the sound of rustling covers. "Hold on and let me change phones."

The receiver clicked as it was placed on the nightstand. It was picked up immediately. "How's my second favorite spy?" a female voice asked.

"I'm fine, Faith. How are you?"

She chuckled. "We're doing great. Everyone is either pregnant or giving birth. Sparky is beside himself acting as a surrogate father to all the cats."

Jeff could picture the stocky black leopard showing off for all the new arrivals. Cort worked for the agency, while Faith ran a breeding center for endangered snow leopards. "What about your baby?"

"Sara's perfect." He heard the smile in her voice. "She misses her favorite uncle."

"I miss her, too."

"Will we see you soon?" Faith asked.

There was a click on the line. "I've got it," Cort said. "You can hang up now, Faith."

"How did you know I was on the line?"

"Because I know you. Now say goodbye."

"Bye, Jeff." She hung up the phone.

For a moment Jeff fought the pain in his gut. He envied Cort and Faith their happiness. Not only because he missed his own family but because he and Jeanne had somehow lost their feelings for each other. They'd been unable to hang on to the love. In the end their marriage had been more about habit and duty than real affection. Andie didn't understand that. She thought it had been a perfect relationship. He didn't think he could explain that the flaws made it worse. The flaws were his fault. He'd been the one who'd cared more about his job than anything else. Jeanne had come to Lebanon to compete with his job. In the end, his job was the reason she and J.J. had died.

"Jeff? You still there?"

"Yeah, Cort. Sorry."

"So what's up?"

"I need a favor."

"Name it."

Jeff clutched the phone. That was the reason he'd called Cort. Because his friend wouldn't hesitate to help.

"There's this woman," he began.

Cort laughed. "A woman? About time. I knew this vacation would be good for you. You haven't taken any time off since—" Cort hesitated. "I'm glad you've met somebody."

"It's not what you think. I'm on St. Lucas." Jeff heard Andie's footsteps in the hallway. She tapped softly. He ignored her.

"Are you crazy?" Cort asked. "Do you have a death wish? If Kray finds out you're there, he'll hunt you down and kill you."

"He already knows, but that's not the point."

"The hell it isn't. What are you doing there?"

Jeff didn't answer.

Cort was one of his best agents. It didn't take him long to figure it out. "You're going to take him out." It wasn't a question.

"This woman—"

"I don't care about the woman. Jeff, have you lost it completely? You can't do this. It's wrong."

"I don't have a choice. Look, I don't want to talk about that. I don't want you involved. When I do it, there's going to be an investigation and the less you know the better."

"I could report you," Cort said quietly.

"But you won't." Jeff waited. When his friend didn't say anything, he continued. "I have a woman here. Andie Cochran."

"Why is that name familiar?"

"She's Kray's ex-wife."

Cort whistled. "What's she doing there?"

Jeff filled him in on the kidnapping and what had happened to the charter boat he'd arranged.

"So Kray's men have reported back to him by now," Cort said.

"Probably. I need you to come and get her and her son. I figure we've got forty-eight hours until Kray finds the house."

"I'll have to go through official channels."

"I want that. Andie is going to need the government's help to get out of here. I want you to bring the boat and personally escort her to the States."

"What about you? You coming out with us?"

"No. I've got business to finish."

"If you do this, you can kiss your career goodbye."

"There's not a day that goes by that I don't relive that explosion. I can't let it go forever, Cort. As long as he's alive, he's won. I know the risks I'm taking. I think they're worth it."

"You're wrong," Cort said. "Come out with us, buddy. Just get on the boat with the woman and the kid. No one has to be the wiser. You could—"

"No. I have to see it through. Will you be here?"

"You know what you're asking?"

Jeff knew. He was risking his career, his life, everything he'd ever worked for and believed in. He was also involving Cort. "I know. I'm sorry. I don't have another way of getting her off the island."

Cort was silent for a long time. "I owe you, boss. I'll charter something out of the Grand Cayman Islands and be there in thirty-six hours."

They agreed on a time and meeting place, then picked a radio frequency.

"I'll see you then," Jeff said. He heard the click as Cort hung up the phone; then he replaced the receiver and closed the box.

Only then did he look at Andie standing in the doorway.
He knew she'd been there for most of his phone conversation. He could have turned around and acknowledged her,
but figured she might as well know what was going on.

"As simple as that?" she asked. "You pick up your secret spy phone and make arrangements? No one cares what
you're going to do?"

"They care."

"But they won't stop you."

"I didn't call the agency, I called a friend."

She stared at him as if she'd never seen him before. "So
you're going through with this."

"Yes."

The late-afternoon sun filtered through the palm fronds,
shading Andie from the heat. She lay stretched out on the
chaise lounge. Sunglasses shielded her eyes. Her arms and
legs were dry, but her bathing suit was still damp from her
recent swim in the pool. She'd hoped the physical activity
and warm temperature would lull her to sleep. But she'd
been in the chair for almost forty minutes and she didn't feel
the least bit like resting.

She opened her eyes and stared at Jeff and Bobby playing Frisbee on the beach. Jeff wore baggy swimming trunks
and an open shirt. His muscled body moved easily and he
bent low to pick up the brightly colored yellow disc and
throw it back. Bobby raced forward and caught it. He
kicked up sand as he spun and threw the Frisbee.

Andie watched her son. He'd tanned. Zinc oxide protected his nose, while a baseball cap shaded his eyes. His
trunks hugged his skinny hips. Sometime in the last year or
so he'd changed from a plump toddler into a sturdy little
boy. He looked more like a miniature person now than a
large baby. He moved gracefully and with purpose. He was
active, growing, doing, changing right before her eyes.

The sound of his laughter carried to her and she smiled in
return. He was having a good time with Jeff. At least he

didn't understand the danger they were in. The explosion had frightened him, but he'd only heard the noise. She'd picked him up when Jeff had screamed at them to run so her son's face had been buried in her arms. He didn't know about the ship's captain dying, nor about the men who had been after Jeff. He was now curious but not afraid and she wanted to keep it that way.

She wished *she* didn't know the truth. It didn't make sense. As she watched Jeff play with her son, she tried to imagine him as a killer. She didn't want it to be true, and yet she remembered the rifle she'd seen him with when they'd first come to the house. She recalled the stark expression in his eyes when he talked about his wife and son. Kray killed them, now he would kill Kray. A life for a life.

She'd been so sure Jeff was the opposite of Kray. He worked for the government, she'd assumed. He was on St. Lucas to take her husband in, to see justice done. Her feelings had awakened, her heart had risked caring because this time, surely this time, she'd chosen wisely.

A shriek of laughter broke through her musings. She saw Bobby racing after the Frisbee. It had gone over his head and landed near the surf. Her son grabbed it and threw it back, as hard as he could. Jeff had to jump to catch it. His powerful legs thrust him high in the air. His shirt flapped open, revealing his chest. Her breathing increased. He reached up one hand and snagged the toy. Bobby crowed with delight. Jeff threw it back to him, this time aiming for the boy and making sure the Frisbee was level with the child.

He was patient with her son. He laughed and smiled. He was a good dad. He hugged easily and told stories about a magical bird named Echo. And he wanted to murder Bobby's father. She didn't dispute that Kray needed to die. But for Jeff to do it that way— She shook her head. It wasn't right. For any of them.

Bobby came running toward her. "I want a drink."

She pointed to the house. "There are small bottles of water on the bottom shelf of the refrigerator. Go ahead and take one."

"Okay." He tossed her a grin before running off. When he reached the porch, he turned toward the beach. "I'll be right back, Jeff."

"I'll be waiting."

The screen door slammed shut.

Andie glanced at Jeff. He was standing in the surf, staring out to sea. The waves surged around his ankles before retreating, then raced forward again. She wondered if he would speak to her. He didn't. He just stood there, looking out at who knows what.

Was he ashamed? Did he think she was still angry? Or was there nothing left to say? They'd each chosen sides and picked a position. What point of compromise could there be?

For a brief moment in time she'd thought he was the one. That she could safely care about him. He knew her worst and still seemed to like her. Yet she now knew that was a lie. He'd used her in his bed, then abandoned her. She should hate him. She should do a lot of things. Instead, she stood up and walked over to him.

The sun was hot against her body as she moved next to him. The saltwater felt more like a tepid bath. When he glanced at her she wished she'd thought to pull on her T-shirt. Then she reminded herself it didn't really matter. He'd seen all of her already.

"What will happen to you when you get back home?" she asked.

"Don't you mean 'if' I get home? Kray's men will be gunning for me on the island. It's unlikely I'll get away."

"I figured you had some sort of plan to escape them."

He didn't respond.

She stared at him. "You don't have a plan?"

"There didn't seem to be much point. I don't know when or where I'll get my chance with Kray. Thinking about escaping only makes it more complicated."

He expected to die. She didn't know why she hadn't figured that out before. He was going to sacrifice himself. Maybe that was how he justified the killing. It wasn't just one life he would be taking, it was two.

"You don't expect to make it back," she said slowly.

Jeff ignored her. "If Kray's men don't get me, the local police probably will. Then Kray's men will find me in jail and take their justice. But if I do make it back to the States, I don't think I'll be getting a promotion anytime soon." He folded his arms over his chest. "It won't come to that. Kray has the money to employ the best people. They won't let me get away."

"That certainly makes it nice and tidy," she said, her voice taut with anger. "You get your revenge, then someone else tidies up the mess. You won't even have to worry about the consequences because you won't be here."

"I don't think about that part of it."

Just like a man, she thought grimly. He was doing what he had to do, and damn the rest of the world. Damn what it meant to anyone, especially her.

She wanted to scream at him, to yell until he realized what he was doing was wrong. But it wouldn't do any good. She only knew one way to get his attention.

"What am I supposed to tell Bobby?" she asked. "How do I explain to him that you murdered his father?"

Jeff glanced down at her. His blue eyes were expressionless, his mouth a straight, forbidding line. "He'll understand in time."

"You really think so? Who's going to explain it to him? You're expecting to be dead and frankly, I don't think I'll be in the mood to give him both sides of the argument." She stared up at him. "He adores you, Jeff. He listens to everything you say, he tries to walk like you, talk like you.

You're everything he wants in a father. How can you do this to him?''

She saw the first flicker of pain behind his cool facade.

"I don't want to hurt him."

"Then don't. Let it go. Trust the system to handle Kray."

"The system isn't getting the job done," he said, the hurt fading. "I don't have a choice."

"We all have choices. You want to do this. You want to be the one."

"You should be pleased. If I succeed, your problems are over with Kray. Have you thought about that?"

She turned away from him. The sand was warm as she shifted her feet. The tide retreated, rushing only to her toes. "It's not worth it. I don't want your life to be the price of my freedom. Are you really willing to sacrifice so much for one man?"

"I'm not doing it for me, or even for you."

She spun back toward him. Her braid flew out and hit her shoulder before brushing against her back. She stiffened her spine. "Kray's death won't bring back Jeanne and your son. Nothing will. They're gone. You have to let them find their peace."

He bent at the waist, bringing his face close to hers. "You don't know what the hell you're talking about."

If he intended to frighten her, he was doing a good job of it. She wanted to back away from his cold eyes, from the warrior so willing to give his life in the name of the cause. She swallowed hard. "Would Jeanne want you to do this?"

He thought for a moment, then straightened. "No."

"Then why?"

"You don't understand."

"You're right. I don't. I don't always agree with what our government does in situations like this, but there are rules in place. We can't all do everything we want, all the time. Society doesn't work that way. If you kill Kray, it won't change anything. There will be another crime lord to take his place. Then another. Are you going to hunt them all?"

"They don't matter to me. This is personal."

"It can't be. The moment you do that, the moment you cross the line and turn your back on everything you've ever believed in and fought for, the second you ignore what you know is right and honorable and good, you become just like him. You'll be Kray. No better, no worse. Exactly equal."

He was silent. She waited, praying he would see the logic of her argument. There had to be a way to reach him. There had to be another way out of the situation.

He turned and started toward the house. At the pool deck he glanced back at her. She couldn't read his expression. Did he understand what she'd said?

"You can't change my mind," he said.

"Then you're just like him."

He looked past her, out to sea. "I know," he said at last. "I know."

Chapter 13

Bobby slept on his left side, with the sheet pulled up to his shoulders and the blanket bunched around his feet. His brown hair fell across his forehead and his eyelashes cast shadows on his rosy cheeks.

Jeff stared at the boy and wondered if the child dreamed. Would he think of the games they'd played that day? Of the Frisbee thrown in the sunshine? Of the taste of their dinner? Would he recall the silly jokes and the most recent installment of Echo's adventures in the land of pretend?

Or did Bobby dream of his father? He never mentioned Kray, yet he must have questions. Did he wonder about the man who had stolen him away from his life and all he'd known? Or did he simply trust his mother to make his world right again?

Jeff touched the boy's cheek. His warm, smooth skin reminded him of another child. Of J.J. and of how many times he, Jeff, had come home late and crept into his room to watch his son sleep. Jeanne had often chided him, telling him that the boy was even more interesting when he was awake and perhaps he should try to get home a little earlier. Soon, he'd promised to appease her. Soon.

But he'd waited too long. He'd chased the bad guys and won his citations and he'd thrown away the little time he was to be allowed. When he'd finally realized how much he was missing, it was too late and the boy was gone.

He closed his eyes against the pain, but it didn't help. There was nothing he could do to bring him back. Not even Kray's death would fill that emptiness. God, he missed his son.

The pain surrounded him, filling him until there was nothing left. Losing a child had to be the worst thing for a parent to experience. At least Jeanne had lived longer; she'd experienced more of what life had to offer. His eyes opened. She'd lived but not enough. Her parents no doubt missed her as much as he missed J.J.

He should have called them more often, he realized. In the past five years he'd cut himself off from his family and hers. He hadn't wanted to talk about the past with anyone. He hadn't wanted to relive those last horrible seconds when the car had blown up. He'd avoided holiday get-togethers. He hadn't even gone to the memorial service.

There had been no bodies to bury, nothing recognizable to be flown home. Both families had put off the memorial service, hoping he would finally be willing to begin the mourning. But he never had. Finally he'd told them to go ahead without him. He'd never gone to see the plaque, or brought flowers. He'd never tried to explain any of what he was feeling to Jeanne's parents or his own. He'd held it all inside, using the rage and pain to feed his hate. Those ugly dark emotions kept him alive. But was it a life? He lived only to kill another. To cross the line and become the enemy.

He stood up and left the bedroom. The hallway was dark. A single light burned in the living room. He paused there and looked around. Bobby's toys were scattered everywhere. A hardback novel had been left open on the coffee table. Andie had been reading earlier. He could hear the faint squeak of the swing on the porch.

If he got out of this alive, if he made it back to the States, he would go to his family and speak with Jeanne's parents. He would visit the plaque with them and talk about what had happened. He would share some happier memories, tell his parents he cared about them and Jeanne's family that she'd always loved them. It was really all they'd wanted to know. When he got home, he would unpack the pictures he kept in boxes and look at them. Maybe then he would be able to recall Jeanne's face.

He'd loved his wife. Their relationship hadn't been perfect, it wasn't what they both wanted it to be, but he had loved her. Almost as much as he'd loved J.J. It would be hard to let go of them, but maybe it was time.

He bent down and picked up a battered action figure. It was amazing what one five-year-old boy could do to a plastic toy in just a couple of days. Bobby was a good kid. Jeff saw a lot of Andie in the boy.

If he got out of this alive—

He didn't complete the thought. He didn't have the right. He'd been a jerk from the first moment he'd seen Andie. He'd punished her for having been married to Kray, and for a few other things that weren't her fault. An apology wouldn't make up for what happened in his bed.

He set the toy down. He couldn't let go of the thought. If he got out of this alive, he wanted a second chance. He wanted to find her. Maybe if they both put the past behind them, they could find some common ground. He respected her courage and her strength. He admired the way she admitted her mistakes and refused to take the blame for what wasn't her fault. She wasn't a fool. She was smart, mouthy and gorgeous as hell. For some reason that he would never understand, she cared about him.

If he got out of this alive... He shook his head. She would never forgive him, and even if she would, he could never be a part of her life. If Kray's men didn't kill him and the local authorities didn't arrest him, if his own government didn't lock him away, he still would have crossed the line. Once he went to the other side, there was no finding his way back.

He walked out of the living room and onto the porch. The squeak of the swing slowed, then began again. He turned toward the sound. Andie sat in one corner. The seat was wide enough for two, so he settled next to her.

"Is Bobby asleep?" she asked.

"Yeah, he's fine."

She pushed off against the wooden porch. The swing began to move slowly back and forth. He stretched his arm across the back. His thumb was inches from her shoulders, but he didn't touch her.

Beyond the overhang he could see the clean night sky and millions of stars. The moon was shaded by the palm trees. Cool, tropical air caressed his arms and legs.

"You're really going to do it?" she asked without warning.

He didn't want to talk about that, but she had the right to her questions. "Yes. After you're gone."

"You still haven't said how I'm supposed to explain it to Bobby. He really likes you. He looks up to and admires you. You're the closest thing he's ever had to a dad in his life."

His throat tightened. "I know. If there was another way out, I'd take it."

"Of course there's another way. Just don't kill Kray."

"I have to."

He glanced at her. She sat with her hands folded on her lap. Her long, loose hair hung around her shoulders, concealing her breasts from him. He could feel the warmth of her body and inhale her sweet scent. It was wrong to want her, but that didn't lessen the heat flaring in his groin. He shifted on the seat.

"What am I supposed to say to him?" she asked. "Gee, Jeff didn't mean to kill your father, it just sort of happened. You think he'll understand that?"

"I don't know. We're not going to agree on this tonight."

"I'm not going to stop trying to change your mind." She glanced at him. "I don't care how mad you get."

"I never expected anything less. You're a very determined woman."

She grimaced. "You'd better be careful, Jeff. That last comment almost sounds as if you like me. I might get a swelled head."

He brushed her hair aside and rested his hand on her bare shoulder. His fingers rubbed against the skinny strap of her tank top. "I do like you."

"Excuse me if I don't believe you. For the past week or so you've done a great imitation of someone who despises me."

"Okay, maybe at first I could have done without your company, but you've shown me you're not so bad."

"I'm overwhelmed by the compliment."

"I can't help that I'm a charming kind of guy."

Instead of smiling, she looked serious. She glanced up at him. "Are you being nice to me because I'm leaving tomorrow?"

"Partially." He decided it was time to be honest. He might never get another chance. He'd spent the last five years living with regrets. He didn't want any more in his life. "But I'm not that altruistic. I'm also doing it for me. Because I don't want you to be angry when you leave."

"I can't approve of what you're going to do. I think it's wrong."

"I didn't mean that. I meant me, specifically." He drew his arm back to his side, then leaned forward on the swing. He rested his elbows on his knees and let his hands dangle. "You have this image of me. Most of it's not true. I'm not the guy in the white hat. I'm just a man."

"I never thought you were perfect."

"You thought my marriage was. You think I'm mourning something that can't be replaced. It's more complicated than that."

She didn't say anything. He glanced at her. She was staring straight ahead.

He looked back at the porch flooring. "We met in college. I was three years older, a senior while Jeanne was a freshman. I already knew what I wanted out of my life. I was going to work for the government and save the world. We dated, then I graduated and went into training. I was gone for several months. When I came back, Jeanne was still waiting for me. We got married."

"I'm sure it was lovely for both of you."

He ignored the sarcasm. He knew it came from her pain. "Jeanne had one goal in life, and that was to be the perfect wife. At first we were in love and it was easy to be together. Then my work began to consume me. She tried harder, but I didn't notice the effort or her perfection. I was too busy getting promoted or being in the field. Too many months apart began to wear on the marriage. I thought maybe we should split up or something. Then I found out she was pregnant."

He drew in a deep breath. He remembered that day as if it had just happened. He'd been home about a week, after being gone for two months. Already he was itching to be somewhere else. The walls of their small house seemed confining. Jeanne's endless chatter about wallpaper and gardening had bored him. He'd wanted more, an adventure, but when she'd looked at him he'd seen the love in her eyes and he couldn't say the words. Then she'd told him about the baby.

"I never thought about having children. Jeanne hadn't told me she'd stopped using the Pill. I was surprised, and thrilled. But I didn't change my ways." He closed his eyes against the memories, but they were there anyway. "I wasn't with her when J.J. was born."

"J.J.?"

"Jeff Jr." He grimaced. "Pretty egotistical."

"I think it's sweet."

"Yeah, right. I loved my son and my wife, but they eren't enough. I wanted to be in the field. I wanted to be a the center of the action. Jeanne used to beg me to take a esk job. I'd reached the point where the next promotion ould bring me inside. I didn't want to go. I liked what I as doing. Our marriage was obviously failing. When I got ssigned to a post in Lebanon, Jeanne showed up as a last-itch effort to hold it all together. I wanted her to go home. he said if she went, she was filing for divorce. So I let her tay. Because I couldn't face the consequences of her leav-ag. I wasn't willing to lose my son."

He shook his head. "That's what haunts me. I was self-sh. I wanted it all. I wanted my family and my job. In the nd, I lost them both."

"Jeff, don't." She placed her hand on his back.

He ignored her. The words came faster now. "If I'd just ent them back, J.J. would be alive now. I think about that ll the time. It's my fault. I killed them as much as Kray did. ecause they were there and an easy target. Because I was n his heels and I refused to back off, he murdered them. I as right there when the car exploded. Less than twenty feet way. Pieces of metal and some wood from a nearby stand ained down on us. People were screaming. Fire was every-vhere."

She slid across the bench seat and leaned over him. Her ands clutched at his shoulders, her forehead pressed gainst his back. "I'm sorry," she whispered.

"I tried to get to them, but the heat drove me back. My nee was busted, some other things broken. I knew they lied instantly. But I kept imagining I heard them calling out or me. It was months before the dreams stopped coming very night."

She didn't say anything, she simply rocked against him, *ffering solace and comfort. He let her hold him because he ad no energy left to fight her, and because right now he needed to be held. So many others had tried to reach him. His parents, Jeanne's parents, friends. It hadn't worked. Perhaps because they'd used kindness. Andie had gotten inside with a combination of fury and determination. He'd been so busy hating her, he hadn't noticed she'd slipped past his defenses.

"The thing I regret most is the time I lost with J.J. I was never there for him. Work got in the way and I assumed I had enough time. Now that I know what I've lost, there's no way to get it back."

Her long hair spilled over his bare arm. He reached up and fingered the silky strands. "You're so damn beautiful."

She laughed, although it came out slightly strangled.

He glanced at her. Tears filled her eyes and spilled onto her cheeks. "Why are you crying?"

She sniffed. "It's so sad. I wish I could make it better for you. I wish there was a way to bring J.J. and Jeanne back so you could tell them you love them and miss them."

"You're the most incredible woman I've ever met."

She flushed and turned away. "Don't say that."

"It's true. After everything that's happened between us, you're still generous enough to want me to see my wife. How can you forgive me for what happened in my bed?"

"I don't want to talk about that."

She started to move back, but he grabbed her arm and held her in place. Gently he touched her chin until she was looking at him. "I'm sorry, Andie. I was out of line. Please forgive me."

"All right."

He smiled. "As easily as that?"

"I don't have time to hold a grudge. I'll be gone soon, and then I'll never see you again. Spending these last few hours being angry at each other seems like a waste of the time we have left."

Especially when they could be making love.

The thought came from nowhere, but once it lodged in his brain, he didn't want to let it go. His arousal was instant. Blood raced through him, heating by the second, bubbling with need and intensity. He remembered the feel of her next to him, under him. Her sweetness surrounded him. His gaze was drawn to her mouth.

She didn't notice. She stared at her hands resting on her lap. "I want to convince you not to go through with it. Because when you sell your soul to the devil, you can't get it back."

He leaned against the swing. "I don't have any more explanations for you. I have to do this. I know you don't understand. Hell, half the time I don't understand, either. But my decision is made. This is who I am. A couple of days ago you said I'd seen the worst part of you. Now you've seen the worst part of me. I'm a killer, just like Kray. I know that, but I'm still going to do it."

She flung herself at him. "I don't want you to die."

It was a cry from her soul. He wrapped his arms around her and held her close. "I'll do my best to survive."

"Don't make a joke of it."

"I'm not," he whispered, stroking her hair. "I swear I'll try to get out of here."

Her breath was hot against his shirt, her tears damp. "But if you—"

"Shh. No more words, Andie. Not tonight. I can't say what you want to hear and you can't convince me. You're right. There's not much time left. Tomorrow you'll be gone."

"Hold me," she said softly. "Hold me."

He pulled her onto his lap. She snuggled close. Her cheek rested on his shoulder. He could feel her warmth and the faint beating of her heat. Her hip pressed against his arousal. He thought she didn't notice. Finally she shifted slightly and looked up at him.

He read the questions in her eyes.

"I want you," he said simply.

He expected some kind of response. Maybe agreement o
a quick slap on the face. He hadn't expected her to duck he
head in shame. "Are you sure?"

"I'm a complete bastard." He slid his hands up her arm:
to cup her face. When she tried to turn away, he held he
still. Their eyes met. "I'm sorry. I know you said you for
gave me and all that, but I want you to know I mean it.
never wanted to hurt you. I was reacting to my own feeling:
about Kray. I don't think you're a whore. You're right.
wasn't thinking about you, I was using you, but it wasn't o
purpose. I didn't set out to be a jerk. It just sort of hap
pened."

"I didn't set out to marry an evil man."

"I know he deceived you. I know it wasn't your fault.
know you left as soon as you found out the truth."

Andie stared at him. She wanted to believe him. She'c
been waiting six years to have someone say those words tc
her. To hear them from Jeff was more than she'd ever hoped
for. She knew she was a fool when it came to him. Probably she should hate him for what he'd done. The problem
was she understood what he was thinking. If the situation:
had been reversed, she would have been just as angry at him
for being alive. She would have assumed the worst about
him.

His eyes were dark in the night, a deep midnight blue. He
was close enough that she could feel his warm breath on her
face.

"I'm sorry," he said, as he stroked her face. "If I could
take the words back, I would."

She felt his pain for her, and it was enough. Without
thinking about what she was doing, she leaned forward and
kissed him. Her brief touch was meant to comfort and offer atonement. Instead, at the first brush of his lips, her
body began to tingle. She became aware of their position,
of the fact that she was on his lap and he was already
aroused. Her hands rested on his chest, her bare thighs
touched his. They were both hungry for love.

"Come with me," he said.

She slipped off his lap and stood up. He rose and took her
and. Together they walked into the house and toward his
edroom. At the door she hesitated. She didn't want a re-
eat of what had happened before.

Jeff understood. She supposed that was one of the things
he liked best about him—he often read her mind.

"There's just the two of us," he said, stepping into the
edroom. "No one else. I promise."

She trusted his promises, just as she trusted him. She fol-
owed him inside, then closed the door. She couldn't imag-
ne leaving this place without being with him one more time.
he wanted to love him with her body, to silently speak the
vords she wasn't sure she had the courage to say aloud.

He bent over and clicked on the light beside the bed, then
tood in front of her. He was tall. She had to tilt her head
ack to look at his face. She liked the way the shadows and
ollows of his face made him dangerously handsome. She
iked the way her heart beat faster when he was close to her.

He reached out and touched her hair. "You're so beau-
iful, Andie. I know what you look like, but every time I see
ou, your beauty takes my breath away."

She knew her nose was a little small and her mouth un-
ven, with a fuller bottom lip. Her eyes were okay, but she
lidn't have great cheekbones. She'd spent a couple of years
as a model and was intimately familiar with her physical
aults. Yet Jeff didn't notice. She could point them out to
him and he would simply shake his head in amazement and
ell her she was crazy. What did any of that matter?

He was right, she acknowledged. It didn't matter. As long
as he thought she was attractive, she didn't care about the
est of the world.

He slipped his fingers through her hair. She reached for-
vard and began to unbutton his shirt. When she was done,
he pushed the material aside and pressed her lips to his bare
chest.

He tasted of man and the sea. She could smell the scent of tropical sunshine, of the sand and the wind. He was hot against her lips. She flickered her tongue against the golden hairs angling down his chest toward his belly. They tickled her mouth. He caught his breath, then twisted her hair around his hand and held her head in place.

She smiled against him. She had no plans to move away. She wanted to touch him, taste him, everywhere. She wanted to be close to him.

She wrapped her arms around his waist and moved her mouth to his collarbone. She licked the length, then slipped lower to his flat nipple. She nibbled at the slight crest, circling until she felt the shudder that raced through him.

The night was still, the air sultry. The heat between them grew and intensified. He released her hair and grabbed her shoulders. She looked up. He face was taut with anticipation and pleasure. He wanted her. His arousal pressed against her belly.

As he bent down toward her, she reached around and cupped his rear. The muscles there flexed against her hands. Her palms hugged the fullest part of the curve, her fingers squeezed. Then his mouth found hers.

Hunger swept over her as his lips searched hers, touching everywhere, seeking her sweetness. She opened for him. He teased her by not entering. Instead, his tongue traced her lips, over and over again. He licked the tiny corners, then worshiped the soft inner skin. She squirmed against him, wanting more, needing more.

Desire, fueled by the danger, by the fear that their world was about to explode, filled every part of her body. Her thighs trembled, her breasts ached, her chest was tight as if she couldn't catch her breath.

She angled her head, then in desperation thrust her tongue into his mouth. They touched, tip to tip. Excitement raced through her. Jeff laughed low in his throat, then retreated, as if expecting her to follow.

She did. She tasted his moistness, his heat. She reveled in the clenching of his muscles. She moved her hands up his back, under his shirt. Warm skin met hers. He was strong and broad. A man. Hard to her soft, but matching her tenderness with his own.

It wasn't just about the sex, she thought as he began to tug on the hem of her tank top. It was specifically about him, about the feelings she had for him. She needed him, she cared about him. She loved him.

Love. Her eyes opened. She raised her head as he pulled up the tank top. The material slid up her torso, then over her head and down her arms. He fingered the strap of her bra.

"I would have pictured you in satin, but the cotton looks just right," he said.

She smiled. "I'm not really a satin sort of person."

"You don't need it to look sexy. You just are. All the time."

"Oh, right. You haven't seen me when I have the flu."

He laughed. She reached up and shoved his shirt off his shoulders. It fell onto the floor behind him. Jeff kicked it aside and stepped back to the bed. He sat on the edge, then urged her to straddle him. Her knees and calves rested on the bedspread, his hands locked behind her back. She could feel his arousal pressing against her heated center. With a quick flick of her head, she shook her hair off her shoulders. It stretched down her spine, tickling her bare skin.

"You're not so bad looking yourself," she said.

He shrugged. She leaned forward and nipped the end of his chin. "A little shy, are we?"

He cleared his throat. "Guys aren't supposed to, well, you know."

"Guys aren't supposed to do a lot of things, but being handsome isn't one of them."

"Andie." His voice came out in a growl.

"What?" She moved lower, kissing his neck, licking the line where stubble gave way to smooth skin.

His hips arched against hers. She could feel the length of him, the hardness. He was ready.

"Undo your bra," he said.

She looked up, startled.

"The catch is in the front and if I let go—" he released her briefly and she started to slip back "—you'll fall."

She glanced down at the white cotton bra. The fastener sat low between her breasts. It gave with the slight flick of her finger. She did it every night without a second thought. But she'd never undressed for a man.

It was no big deal, she told herself. She squeezed the catch and it popped open. The cups slipped to the sides, but the edge of the lace caught on her nipples.

"Don't move," he ordered, staring at her chest. His organ surged against her. The muscles in his arms tightened.

She couldn't help herself. She wiggled slightly. The bra came loose and she shrugged it off.

"You leave me weak," he said, then fell back on the bed. He pulled her with him.

The action caught her off guard. She shrieked and braced herself with her arms. She straddled him. Her bare breasts were inches from his chest. Laughter and need darkened his eyes. He drew her up until her breasts were over his mouth; then he reached up and captured one hard nipple.

At the moment his lips closed over her, she felt the tingling start. It filled her chest, then moved to her feminine place, finally moving out to her arms and legs. Her hair spilled around them, over his neck and face. He didn't brush it away. Instead, he shifted her so he could reach her other breast.

His tongue traced her nipple; then he licked her pale skin. He moistened her and blew on the dampness. Again and again, going from breast to breast, he suckled her until her arms refused to support her. Only then did he let her roll on her back.

Before he could move over her, she reached for him, pulling him close. She wanted to press against him, feel all of him near her, around her, in her.

His weight rested on her for a moment, then he slid down, trailing kisses along her belly. He pulled off her shorts and her panties and tossed them behind him. He kissed her knees, her thighs and her hipbones. While he dipped his tongue into her belly button, his fingers found her waiting moistness. With one quick stroke, she was already near the moment of surrender.

But he kept her from her release. When she got too close, he stopped, letting her body cool down. She reached for him, wanting to taunt him the way he taunted her, but his shorts prevented her.

"Take these off," she ordered.

"Yes, ma'am. That's what I like—a woman who knows what she wants." He stood up and pushed them off with one quick thrust.

"Wait," she said before he could get back on the bed. "I want to—"

She flushed. She couldn't say it, but she wanted to look at him. He read her mind. Instead of joining her, he spread his feet slightly and placed his fists on his hips.

He was beautiful the way wild animals are beautiful. Hard muscles, power and need sleekly wrapped in golden skin. His blond chest hair caught the light. She reached toward him and placed her palms on the center of his belly. He didn't move. She got to her knees on the edge of the bed. Slowly she worked her hands up his chest to his shoulders, then down, lower and lower to the darker blond hair that surrounded his need.

She touched him then. She held him firmly and stroked back and forth. His breath hissed from between clenched teeth. She lowered her head and, holding him still, licked the smooth sensitive tip.

He flinched. She circled him, then drew him into her mouth. His audible groan made her smile. Before she could find a rhythm, he drew back.

"You'll make me embarrass myself," he muttered.

"Maybe you need a little embarrassing."

"Later."

He knelt in front of the bed. While his hands cupped and kneaded her breasts, he trailed kisses down her belly. She knew what was coming and braced herself for the sensual assault. His tongue slipped between her curls to lightly caress her most sensitive place. She cried out his name. He moved there until she knew she was close to her peak. Then he stopped and wrapped his arms around her.

And so it went. Tender embrace to tender touch, they each brought the other closer and closer to their moment of mutual release. With hands and mouth, he traced every inch of her body, whispering against her skin, promising paradise with his fingers. Then she explored him. The hard and soft places, the shape of his muscles, the different textures. She found what made him grow still, what made him pant, what made him not breathe at all. She wasn't sure how long they continued their tender exploration. She didn't know if they were trying to pretend if they had forever, or were just clinging to their last moments together. She didn't want to know.

He moved over her humming body. She was so close, her muscles quivered in frustration. There was one place he hadn't touched yet, one part of her hungry and ready for him. She parted her thighs and he moved closer. His hardness swept over her tiny sensitive spot. She fought against exploding right then. When she was under control, he moved inside of her.

She stretched around him. She could feel the slickness that welcomed him. He whispered her name. She opened her eyes.

He watched her. This time there was no accusation, no hatred. This time his expression tightened only with need. She drew her legs back, forcing him deeper inside of her.

She felt the first spiraling promise of her release. She tried to hold back. She wanted the moment to go on longer between them. She wanted it to last forever. But her body could not be denied. He pushed in again, then withdrew slowly, so slowly she almost cried out loud. It felt too good, too perfect. She couldn't survive.

He thrust into her, deeper, and touched some sacred place. She climaxed without warning, her muscles contracting, her hips arching, her eyelids drifting closed. She felt him withdraw once more, then bury himself in her and shudder.

It was as if the fire consumed them whole, leaving nothing behind but the essence of their mutual pleasure.

When she stopped quivering and he was still, he settled next to her and pulled her close. She liked the feel of his arms around her, his legs tangling with hers. He brushed her hair away from her face.

"I love you, Jeff," she said quietly.

For a long time he didn't answer. She thought he might get angry, or not want to hear about her feelings. There were still so many questions between them. He might think she was trying to take Jeanne's place. She wasn't. She didn't even want him to say anything back. He had too much to resolve for her to believe he returned her feelings. She didn't expect saying the words to change anything, but just wanted him to know.

He drew in a breath. "I needed to hear that."

She raised her head slightly and looked at him. "You're not mad?"

"Never." He kissed her briefly. "I don't care if it's the dangerous situation, or the fact that you think I'm some kind of hero. I don't even care that three months from now you won't remember my name."

"After all we've been through, I think I might remember your name."

"You know what I mean."

"You think it's not real?"

He settled down and rested his hand on her bare shoulder. "It's real tonight, Andie, and that's all that matters. I need you to stay with me."

"Good." She snuggled closer to him. "I wasn't planning on leaving."

His eyes closed and his breathing became more regular. As she stared into the dark night she thought that sad goodbyes might make for great country music, but they hurt like hell in real life. They had less than twelve hours together. Then she would be gone and Jeff would once again stalk his prey.

A sharp pain cut through her heart. He was lost to her. That was the worst of it. If he killed Kray, he was gone. It didn't matter if Kray's men caught him or not, if he lived or died. Once he pulled the trigger and crossed the line to the other side, the man she loved would be gone.

Chapter 14

It was the middle of the afternoon and Andie felt as vulnerable and exposed as a duck sitting in a very small pond. She fought against the need to twist around in her seat and check the road behind them. The last time she'd done it, Jeff had threatened to tie her in place.

She brushed her damp hair from her face. Sometime in the night a storm had rolled in. The clouds produced more mist than actual rain, but it was hot and muggy. In the middle of the day, there was no point in trying to hide in dark clothing so both she and Bobby were dressed in shorts and T-shirts. Once again she'd packed everything in her soft-sided bag. A pistol rested at the small of her back.

"Is it going to be a big boat, Mommy?" Bobby asked.

"I'm not sure. Big enough to get us to Florida."

"You'll like Cort," Jeff said, glancing at the boy over his shoulder. "His wife, Faith, runs a breeding center for snow leopards."

Bobby looked puzzled.

"They're big cats, like tigers or lions," Andie explained. "They have thick fur coats and live in a very cold part of the world. They're endangered. Do you remember what that means?"

Bobby nodded. "There's not enough left so we gotta protect 'em," he said proudly.

"That's what Faith does," Jeff said. "She has several breeding pairs. After the cubs are all grown up and know how to survive, some of them will be introduced back into the wild."

"Can you pet them?"

"Not the snow leopards. But she does have a black leopard named Sparky. You can pet him."

"Can we go see him, Mommy?"

Andie smiled. "Not on this trip. We're going to Florida, first, then we have to fly somewhere else."

Fortunately Bobby didn't ask where. He saw a colorful bird dart around a tree and that distracted him. Andie didn't know where they would go when they left Florida. Whichever plane left first to a large city would determine their destination.

She was scared. Her damp palms and rapidly beating heart didn't let her pretend any longer. She was afraid of Kray, of leaving the island, of staying on the island, of losing Jeff, of the future and the past. Except for Bobby, there wasn't anything in her life that didn't frighten her.

She glanced over at Jeff. He drove competently, constantly checking the mirrors and the road and staying at the speed limit. They'd spent the night together, making love, talking and sleeping some. In the morning they'd made breakfast with Bobby and played outside. Like a family on vacation. It was all pretend, but she hadn't wanted it to stop. Apparently neither had Jeff. He'd stayed until the last possible minute. Now they'd begun their journey and there was no turning back.

Jeff's profile was familiar to her. Dark sunglasses hid his thoughts, but she didn't mind. She'd touched every part of his body, had loved him to exhaustion, had held and been held, had told him she loved him. She had no regrets save one.

That she would lose him. She'd spent her whole life waiting for the right man to come along. She'd been too young when she'd met Kray. She hadn't had the experience to see him for what he was. The next six years had passed in a blur, with her looking over her shoulder wondering when he would come and destroy her fragile happiness. Instead of taking responsibility for her own life, she'd been waiting. Reacting instead of acting. For the first time she was ready to act and it was too late.

In a few hours Jeff would be dead. Or a killer on the run.

She couldn't even come up with a decent wish. If only they'd what? Met sooner? Met under different circumstances? She wasn't sure Jeff was over Jeanne enough to be in a relationship, but it didn't matter. Even if he got away with it, the second he pulled the trigger, he would be destroyed inside. He wouldn't be able to live with himself. She believed that with her entire being. He was too honorable to survive crossing the line.

A faint lazy breeze stirred the afternoon's heat. She wiped the perspiration from her forehead. Once again St. Lucas had changed her life.

"If something happens, get away from the dock as quickly as possible," Jeff said. She started to interrupt, but he silenced her with a quick shake of his head. "Listen to me. This is important."

He glanced over his shoulder at Bobby. Her son was staring at Jeff, his eyes wide. "Mommy, are we in trouble?"

"No, honey." She reached back and patted his hand. "We're fine. Jeff is telling me what to do in case there's a problem, but everything is going to be fine."

"Am I going to be with Daddy?" She could hear the fear in his voice.

She turned in her seat and stared at her son. "I promise you won't have to go back with him, ever."

Bobby stared at her for a long time. His mouth twisted in confusion. Finally he gave her a slight smile. "Will I have my toys on the boat?"

"Of course you will, honey. We'll play all the way to Florida."

She settled back in her seat and returned her attention to Jeff. "What else?"

"You'll be safe back at the house for no more than three days, so don't stay there longer than two. The cruise ships will come in the day after tomorrow. Go down by the port when it's crowded and use a pay phone to call this number." He reached in his shorts pocket and pulled out a small piece of paper. "Call collect. Tell them who you are and that you need help getting off the island. Tell them you're with me."

"Won't they ask any questions?"

"No. Use my name and everything will be fine."

She took the paper and studied the number.

"You have to memorize it," he said. "It doesn't matter if anyone else has the number, but you can't afford to lose it."

"Anything else?" she asked.

"No."

She stared at the phone number and repeated it silently several times. Then she closed her eyes and tested herself. When she could recite it perfectly without hesitation, she tucked it away in her shorts. With a little bit of luck, she wouldn't have to use the number. Jeff's plan had to work. If it didn't, he would likely end up dead.

They continued to drive along the coast. They passed several cars but no one seemed to notice them. She was grateful. She didn't think she would be able to fake her way through anything right now. If the police stopped her, she would probably just blurt out the truth.

They drove around a small village then came out onto a road that paralleled the shore. She could see the ocean stretching out to the horizon. It was gray, like the clouds, but smooth. At least their journey wouldn't be a bouncy one.

She could see the small marina up ahead. Several boats were tied up, with more scattered out at sea. Jeff pulled off the side of the road. He grabbed his binoculars and scanned the moored boats. A man stood on the front deck of one of the larger cabin cruisers tied at the end. He bent over something, then straightened. A flash of light caught her attention. She saw that he'd dropped some kind of reflective buoy over the side of the craft.

"That's him," Jeff said. "Let's go."

He parked the Jeep and got their suitcase out of the back. Bobby clutched his bag of toys. Jeff left them by the vehicle for a couple of minutes while he checked out the path.

Andie tried to catch her breath. She felt as if she'd been running for hours. It was nerves. Her stomach fluttered and her palms were damp. They were really getting out of here.

She supposed she should be happy. Once they were in Florida, they had a chance of escaping Kray. Yet she didn't want to go. It wasn't just because she was going to miss Jeff. Of course she was; he'd become a big part of her life. But the worst part of leaving was what he was going to do when she was gone. Whether Kray's men killed him instantly or he found his way back to the States, he was dead to her. The man she loved, the man she'd spent the night with, would be gone forever.

She wanted to sit down and cry, but there was no time for tears. Besides, she didn't want to scare Bobby.

As Jeff walked down the dock, she placed her hand on her son's shoulder. Bobby glanced up at her. His face was solemn. She gave him a half smile. "It's going to be okay."

He nodded. "Jeff told me I have to be brave for you, Mommy."

"You're very brave. I'm proud of you."

She squeezed his shoulder, then bent down and took his hand. When Jeff turned back toward her and waved for them to come toward him, she bent down and pulled Bobby against her, then started toward the boat.

The morning was steamy. As she hurried along the wooden dock she felt perspiration break out on her forehead and back. Jeff moved toward her and met her halfway. He took Bobby from her and led the way to the boat. The closer they got to the vessel, the larger it appeared. It had to be at least forty feet long.

Jeff stepped into the boat and set Bobby down, then turned and assisted her. The deck shifted beneath her feet. She had to hold on to him to keep her balance. Jeff wrapped his arm around her waist.

A man stepped onto the deck from below. Andie stared at him. He was tall and muscled like Jeff, with blond hair. But the stranger's hair was more golden and hung just past the collar of his polo shirt.

"You'll get your sea legs soon enough," the man said, then grinned. He was handsome, although not as good-looking as Jeff. His eyes were brown instead of blue and there was a scar on his face, from the corner of his mouth down across his chin. "I'm Cort." He held out his hand.

"Andie." She glanced at Jeff. When he nodded she shook the other man's hand. "This is my son, Bobby."

Cort squatted down in front of the boy. "Hey, kid, how's it going?"

Bobby straightened. "I'm brave."

"Good for you." He glanced at the bag the child held. "Are those your toys?"

Bobby nodded.

"Why don't I show you where to store them, then we'll leave. Okay?"

He was asking the question of Bobby, but looking at Jeff.

Bobby hesitated.

"It's all right, honey," Andie said. "Go explore the boat, then come back and tell me what it's like. We're going to be on board for a couple of days."

Cort stood up and took the bag, then led the way down to the main cabin. Andie could see through the open door and the large windows flanking either side. There were two small sofas in the salon, a television and even a narrow coffee table. Beyond that, she saw part of a kitchen.

"Cort's a good man," Jeff said. "You'll be safe with him. The boat is large enough to be comfortable."

She didn't want to hear about being comfortable. She stared into his familiar face, then leaned against him. Instantly his arms wrapped around her. "Don't go," she pleaded. She touched his shoulders, his back, his sides, then felt the pistol tucked in the waistband of his shorts. "Come with us."

"I can't."

"You won't." She pushed away from him and folded her arms over her chest. "There's a difference." His blue eyes met hers unflinchingly. "Why do you have to be the one to do this?" she asked.

"There's no one else."

"Entire governments are looking for Kray. They'll catch him. Don't you see? If you kill him, he wins. He'll make a mistake eventually. He has to. Everybody runs out of luck. Don't destroy your life over this. Don't destroy us. Or me."

He touched her face. She wanted to duck away, but she couldn't. His fingers stroked her cheek. "I know how hard this is for you."

"You don't know anything about what I'm feeling. I've spent the last six years living in hell. I finally find a little peace and comfort and you want to destroy it." The anger gave her strength and she did step back then. "I won't wait for you. If you get away, if your government forgives you, don't bother coming to find me. What you're going to do is wrong and once you do it, you won't be a man I can love anymore."

He didn't move, but she saw his muscles tense at her words. A flash of pain lit his eyes; then he blinked and all emotion was gone. "I understand."

She flew at him and started hitting his chest. "Don't understand, damn you. Get angry, change your mind, stay with me."

He grabbed her wrists and held them to her side. "I can't do that. If there's anything else, anything, I'll do it or say it. Just tell me what it is."

He wouldn't be swayed. She hadn't thought he would, but a small part of her had continued to hope. If only she could make him see what the price would be. Yet he knew the price. He was willing to pay it. He would do what he felt he had to do, then face the consequences. He would risk everything, even her.

She tried to think of some last words to convince him. Instead she blurted out, "Tell me you love me."

He stared at her.

She flushed. "I know you don't. You're still in love with Jeanne, and you can't forget who I was married to. I know it's not true, but please, say the words. Just once."

She needed to hear them. They would keep her strong. He stared at her for so long, she started to tug to free her wrists. Then he let her go. Before she could turn away, he hauled her up against him and kissed her.

His mouth was hot and hungry. His lips pressed hard against hers, his tongue invaded, demanding her surrender. They clung to each other as if they would never see each other again.

They never would.

At last he released her. She had to fight back the tears. "I love you," he said, then took her hand in his and kissed her palm.

Before she could answer, Cort came out from the salon. "Bobby is having some juice and a graham cracker," he said. "We're ready to go. You sure you don't want to come with us, boss?"

"Thanks, but I've got to take care of business."

Andie didn't care about being strong. She grabbed his arm. "Don't do this. Don't throw everything away."

He bent down and kissed her cheek. "Take care of yourelf, Andie. Don't hate me forever."

"I don't hate you at all. I love you."

He stepped away from her, then vaulted over the side of ne boat onto the deck. Her chest felt as if someone were ipping out her heart.

"I can't do this," she whispered.

"You have to be strong for your son," Cort said.

She looked up at him and saw compassion in his oddly ecked brown eyes. "I know. It's hard."

He moved to the steering wheel on the left side of the eck. He turned a key, then pushed a red button. Instantly, owerful engines started beneath the deck. She felt the imble and bent her knees to stay balanced.

Jeff loosened the ropes holding the boat to the dock and ssed the lines back to them. The boat began to drift out to a.

She stood at the side and stared at him. "Damn you, Jeff. don't even know your last name."

He grinned. "Markum. Jeff Markum." The engines nade it hard to hear. He stood there, then called out, "I asn't lying, Andie. I do love you."

Then Cort increased the power and they were moving way. Andie raced to the stern and screamed Jeff's name. ut the wind caught the sound and carried it back toward er. Jeff stayed on the end of the dock, growing smaller and naller. His figure blurred. She brushed away her tears. She tood there until she couldn't see him anymore.

"He'll be all right," Cort said. "He always seems to land n his feet."

She nodded but didn't answer. No point in explaining it ouldn't matter if he landed on his feet or not. Once he rossed the line, the Jeff she knew would be gone.

"There's a couple of things you should know about the oat," he said. "If you're up to it, I want you to practice andling her. Also, there's a special compartment below. If ray's men catch up with us, we can hide Bobby. They'll never find him. As soon as we're away from the pleasure boat traffic I'll show it to you. All right?"

"Fine."

She turned back to look at the island. She could see the pale beaches and lush foliage, but the dock had disappeared. Jeff was gone. Now she only had herself and her son. Somehow she would have to stay strong enough to keep them safe.

Jeff waited until the boat rounded a curve and was lost from view, then he hurried up the dock to his Jeep. Once inside, he started the engine, then paused. She was really gone. He didn't have to worry about her or the kid. He was free to get on with his own business.

He should have felt relieved. Instead, he found he already missed her presence and Bobby's chatter. The Jeep felt empty and large without them.

He reached in the glove box for his baseball cap. When he pulled it out, a small, plastic action figure fell on the floor. He picked it up and held it. Just a cheap toy, he told himself. Bobby wouldn't even miss it. Jeff tucked it into his shorts pocket and shifted into gear.

As he drove down the road toward Kray's villa, he wondered how long it would take to get over her. He had no way to reconcile his feelings for Andie with his mourning for Jeanne. Maybe Andie was right. Maybe what he was mourning wasn't his wife, it was simply an excuse to wallow in guilt. Maybe he used the pain to keep him going because it was easier than actually facing life and his responsibilities. He couldn't take back what he'd done, but he could try to do better in the future. Not that he was going to have much of a future when he was done with Kray.

He approached the villa the long way, going by the expensive hotel on the edge of Kray's property. He parked in the guest lot, grabbed his binoculars, then strolled through the grounds. There were plenty of vacationers around. On the west end, a walking path meandered through the thick growth. He took it, then cut through toward the ocean. He came out on the beach.

A wall of rocks and boulders hid Kray's villa from the hotel guests. Jeff wasn't ready to take action. He simply wanted to get a look at things and start making a plan.

He glanced around the beach. The small stretch of sand was empty. He could hear vacationers beyond the sandbar, but this little cove was deserted. He walked toward the rocks and started up.

The climb was easy. Well spaced boulders provided foot- and handholds. When he reached the top, he paused and looked around. No one was stationed at the top of the bluff. Slowly he pulled himself over and lay flat on the ground. He didn't want to get caught. Depending on who saw him, he might be able to bluff his way out of any trouble, but he didn't want to take the risk. Not until Andie was safely away.

The house was about a hundred feet away down a grassy slope. Jeff picked up his binoculars and scanned the property. There wasn't anyone around. No bodyguards, no staff, nothing. He carefully checked out all the windows but couldn't see any sign of life.

He rose to his knees, then to his feet. Quickly he hurried toward the shield of growth to the right of the grassy slope. Using it for cover, he made his way down to the house. He was on the opposite side from where Andie had entered through the French doors. Back here there were only windows. She'd probably come out this way with Bobby.

He circled around the house, toward the French doors. The silence was unnerving. He checked again for signs of anyone, but everything was still.

He crouched in the low brush. What was Kray up to? Before he could come up with an answer to the question, he heard Andie's voice telling him even if he made it out alive she didn't want to see him. He believed that she loved him. He also believed she meant what she said. If he killed Kray she wouldn't see him again.

He understood her feelings. He wasn't sure how he was going to live with himself. But he didn't have a choice. Kray had to be stopped and no one else was lining up to get the job done. Kray's death would solve all their problems.

But it wouldn't bring Jeanne and J.J. back to life.

He closed his eyes against the anguish. In that moment, with the hot, humid air stealing the breath from his lungs, with his fingers gripping the binoculars so tightly, his knuckles were white, with his heart pounding and his chest tight with pain, he knew the truth. His wife and child were gone forever.

All the mourning, the guilt and blame he could muster wouldn't bring them back. Kray's death wouldn't bring them back. He could scream at God about the unfairness, he could punish himself forever, but they were gone.

He wasn't sure how long he crouched there. Finally his legs started to cramp. He rose and walked toward the villa.

The French doors stood open. He hesitated before entering. Was it a trap? He listened to the silence, waiting for his instincts to warn him of the danger. He felt nothing. He reached behind him and pulled out his pistol. He lifted the binocular strap over his head and let them hang against his belly. Then he stepped into the villa.

The main room was empty. Jeff listened for the sound of conversations, or footsteps on the tiled floor. There was only silence from inside and the faint crash of the waves from the shore. He went from room to room, half expecting to find a bleeding corpse, but there were only made beds and tidy piles of clean laundry.

He returned to the great room. Half-filled glasses and dishes sat on a table by the bay window, as if the people there had been unexpectedly called away from their meal. He moved closer and saw several documents sitting out. He picked up the first one and scanned the sheet. It contained a schedule for laundering money at one of the local banks. Jeff set it down and picked up another piece of paper. Bribe information. There was enough here to lock Kray away for the rest of his life.

He grinned and started to grab the documents. Before he could pick them up, he reminded himself he was gathering evidence illegally. Not only couldn't it be used in court, but it went against everything he believed in. If he took the papers—

The battle of his conscience stopped abruptly. He could plan to kill Kray, but he would quibble about picking up a few papers left lying around? Was he crazy?

If you kill Kray, Kray wins this round. Andie's words. He picked up one of the papers again and stared at it. He could easily take the lot and get them into the right hands without anyone questioning where they came from. It could simply be an anonymous tip.

But it was wrong. Just like killing Kray was wrong. Here was the line—was he willing to cross it for good? Was he willing to go to the other side, to be just like Kray? Or would he rather fight the decent way, following the laws and keeping his honor in one piece?

He put the paper down and walked out the front of the villa. He had a radio in the Jeep. He would call Cort and have him bring the boat back to collect him. There was nothing he needed at the house. Together the two men could work on a plan to capture Kray legally. He turned to start back along the beach when he heard a noise. A large pleasure craft came around in front of the house. It was flying across the water.

Jeff started to turn away, but there was something familiar about the boat. He grabbed his binoculars and looked out at the vessel. He focused, then swore under his breath.

Kray and three of his men sat in the back of the boat. They were all heavily armed. He lowered the binoculars. Somehow they had found out about Cort's boat and they were after them.

* * *

Andie glanced through the big glass windows toward the salon. Bobby sat in the middle of the floor watching a cartoon video. He hadn't seen TV in so long, he was beaming with pleasure. She was glad he was happy. After all he'd been through, he deserved a treat.

Andie turned back toward the open ocean surrounding them. She sat in the same seat, at the rear of the boat. The warm tropical breeze tugged at her neat braid. She'd gone below to inspect the hiding place for Bobby and to grab a snack. Now she sipped on her soda and tried not to think.

Cort sat in a high captain's chair and handled the boat. In a couple of hours she would spell him; then she would rest while he took the first night watch. Together, they would make their way to Florida and safety.

It would be easier if she could cry again, she thought. But ever since they'd lost sight of St. Lucia, she hadn't been able to do anything but breathe through the pain. She knew in time it would dull to a manageable ache. In a few weeks, she would go hours at a time without thinking about him.

Before they landed in Florida, she was going to make Cort promise to keep her informed. She wanted to know if Jeff made it out alive. She wanted to know what happened. She wanted to know when to start her mourning.

A soft beeping caught her attention. She turned and saw Cort picking up a headset. He spoke briefly, then set it down and turned to her.

"That was Jeff," he said, his expression grim. "Kray's after us."

Jeff twisted the wires together, then hit the starter. The speedboat's engine leapt to life. He leaned over and untied the lines holding the boat to the temporary mooring facility outside the hotel, then pushed off the dock. The needle showing the fuel level registered full. He breathed a sigh of relief. At least he had enough diesel to find them.

He turned the small steering wheel toward the open ocean, then pushed the throttle a quarter of the way forward. The boat started moving through the water. When he was clear of the dock and small sailboats, he pushed the throttle all the way and the slim speedboat soared over the waves.

From behind him he could hear the faint calls of the disgruntled owner of the boat. No doubt the harbor patrol would be after him. Good thing. By the time the police arrived at the scene, the battle with Kray would be in full swing. He and Cort would be able to use the assistance. Thank God this small craft could outrun Kray's bigger, more expensive boat.

Jeff settled in the seat and checked the compass. Cort had given him their position. It wouldn't take him long to catch them. He only hoped he made it before Kray did.

That line of thinking made him worry about Andie, so he distracted himself by figuring out several different plans of attack. If Kray beat him to Cort's boat—which was likely, he had a big head start—then he, Jeff, would have to come in quietly and surprise his enemy. No matter what, he couldn't let Kray get hold of Andie and Bobby. They were depending on him.

He continued to watch the horizon. Occasionally he brought up his binoculars and scanned the sea, searching for the large boat. Nothing. His stolen craft glided swiftly over the waves. How ironic. He'd finally made the decision not to break the law by killing Kray and his first act after that had been to steal a boat.

He checked the compass again. He should be getting close now. He looked through the binoculars and saw two small dots on the horizon. Then over the loud rumble of the speedboat's engine, he heard the echo of gunfire. He swore under his breath. Cort and Andie were alone on their boat, but Kray had three men with him.

He angled toward the two spots on the horizon and prayed he wasn't too late. Gradually he was able to make out individual features of the boats, then the people standing on deck.

As he got closer, he powered back and started to circle around Kray's boat. The man still on board saw him and aimed a lethal-looking rifle in his direction. Jeff ducked. The bullet hit the side of the small speedy craft. He reached up and nudged the throttle forward. He aimed the boat toward Kray's yacht, then locked the steering mechanism in place. The man took aim again. As gunfire sprayed the approaching speedboat, Jeff slipped off the other side and silently began swimming toward Cort's vessel.

Andie shook with terror. Her ex-husband stared at her with the cold, deadly eyes of a killer. The gun in his hand pointed directly at her chest.

"You'll tell me what I want to know," Kray said.

"I told you, I don't have Bobby with me."

"Liar."

She saw him raise his free hand. Even as she told herself to duck, she was too slow. His palm slapped the side of her face. Pain exploded in her cheekbone. She staggered back a couple of steps before regaining her balance.

"You bastard," Cort growled. "What kind of man gets his thrills from hitting a woman?"

Kray didn't spare his prisoner a glance. "I didn't do it to amuse myself, but to get her attention. Andrea was always very stubborn."

She glanced at Cort. He struggled, but the two men holding him didn't loosen their grip on his arms. His face looked worse than hers would. Kray's men hadn't caught him easily. "I'm okay," she said.

Kray moved closer to her. She studied him. No gray marred his dark hair. Even after six years, he still looked like a handsome businessman, although now she could see the lines of cruelty around his mouth. His eyes darkened with temper.

"You *will* tell me. The question is how much do you want to suffer first?"

"I sent Bobby home four days ago."

"No!" Kray roared. "Two days ago my men saw you helping Jeff Markum escape. Where is the American and where is my son?"

"Your men only saw me. They didn't see Bobby. Ask them. There was no child with me. I'd already sent him home."

She darted a quick glance around, trying to find a way out. If only his men hadn't searched her when they'd first come on board and taken her pistol. She and Cort had fought, but they'd been outnumbered and outgunned. At · least they'd had enough warning to put Bobby into the hiding place. Kray's men would never find the child. She had to hang on to that thought.

"Kray, look," the man still on Kray's boat called.

A small, fast speedboat was circling toward them. "It's the American," Kray said. "Kill him."

Instantly gunfire erupted. Andie spun toward the sound. She had to cover her mouth to keep from screaming. It couldn't be Jeff, and yet, no one else knew to rescue them. As she watched, more gunfire hit the smaller craft. It turned toward them, apparently undamaged. She waited, wanting to see Jeff stand up to jump off the side.

"He's going to ram us," the man screamed, and started toward Cort's boat.

Everyone's attention focused on the small boat heading directly for Kray's vessel.

Andie saw Kray look away from her. She ducked down and started to go behind him. Cort broke free of the two men holding him. They tried to grab him again. He kicked one in the ribs and punched the other in the face. Kray spun toward her, his pistol pointed at her head. She rolled to get away. A bullet flew past her into the deck of the boat.

Then there was a horrible crash as the speedboat drilled into Kray's larger craft. His vessel bumped hard against theirs. Everyone was knocked down. Lines, cushions, glasses and equipment fell onto the deck. Andie kept rolling. She came to a stop against the narrow walkway that led to the front of the boat. As she started to stand, a man vaulted over the side in front of her. He was wet, but she recognized him. Jeff!

Before she could say anything, he covered her mouth with his hand and motioned for her to keep crawling toward the front of the boat. He slipped past her toward the fray. Andie started to do as he'd asked, then hesitated. She turned back to look at the deck.

The speedboat was half submerged. Kray's boat spun around. There was a huge hole in the side and it was already listing. The man who had been left there was clinging to the side of Cort's boat. Jeff reached him first. He grabbed the man's pistol, then pushed him into the ocean. Cort was still fighting the two men. Kray was on his knees searching for his gun.

"Don't even think about it," Jeff said, coming to a stop beside Kray.

The crime lord looked up. "Ah, Markum. I've been expecting you. As soon as my men told me you were on the island and with my wife, I knew what you'd come for."

"She's not your wife."

Kray smiled. Andie flinched. She hated that cold, ugly smile. It reminded her of death. "She once was. It's enough. A life for a life. A bride for a bride. Although I expect you're too much of a coward to kill my son as well as me."

"Damn it all to hell, will you stay down?" Cort said, frustrated. One of the men who had been holding him was unconscious, but the other staggered to his feet and came at him again. Cort ducked and the man went sailing over him. There was a brief splash. Cort straightened, then looked at Jeff.

"Now what?" he asked.

Andie moved closer. "Jeff?"

He turned toward her. She met his gaze, determined to deal with whatever she saw in his eyes. She loved him. She trusted him. He'd come back to her. Pray God he'd changed his mind.

The blue depths flared with anger, but it was controlled. He was furious at what had happened, but not deadly. She bit her lower lip, not sure she was willing to believe.

"It's okay," he said. "You were right. I can't cross the line and be like him. When the local authorities show up, we'll have him arrested for what he did to you and Cort. Then we can get a search warrant for the villa. There's enough evidence there to keep him locked up for a long time."

"Never!" Kray said. "I won't allow it."

He lunged forward on the deck, as if he'd found what he was looking for. Andie saw the dull black of a pistol under a coiled line.

"No!" she screamed.

Jeff turned toward Kray. He raised his arm, aiming directly at Kray's chest. She waited for him to fire. It was all right now; he would just be protecting himself. But he hesitated. Kray laughed, then pulled his hand up.

A single shot cut through the still afternoon. Andie turned toward the sound. Cort was crouched by the unconscious man, holding a gun in his hand. Kray slumped to the deck. She didn't have to look at the wound to know he was dead.

Jeff walked over to her and pulled her close. "It's over," he whispered.

No, she thought with relief as she clung to him. It had just begun.

Three days later Jeff stood next to Andie in the Fort Lauderdale airport. Cort had taken Bobby to get a hot dog at the snack stand. Around them, passengers waited for their planes to be called, airport employees chatted and the loudspeaker announced departures and arrivals. But at the far end of this unused terminal, they were alone.

"You'll be in L.A. by nightfall," Jeff said. "You must be excited about getting back to your life."

"I haven't had much chance to think about it," Andie said. She tucked her blond hair behind her ears. "We've been so busy answering questions."

"Yeah." He leaned against the podium and tried to think of something to say. What he wanted to tell her was that he loved her and couldn't imagine being without her. The thought of his empty life looming in front of him made him break out in a cold sweat. He wanted to ask her to marry him and come live with him in Washington. But he didn't.

He stared at the tall, slender woman standing in front of him. She'd bought some clothes at the hotel. He was used to seeing her in shorts and T-shirts, but now she was dressed in a white silk suit with a blue blouse that matched the color of her eyes. She looked like a model posing for a magazine cover. Or an elegant businesswoman about to make a million-dollar deal.

She had law school. Commitments. Friends in L.A. What did he have to offer her? His apartment was conveniently close to work, but had little else to recommend it. There was only one bedroom. They could buy a house, of course, if she wanted to, and Georgetown had a great law school, but it wasn't just the logistics that kept him from proposing. It was him.

He wasn't done mourning Jeanne and J.J. He knew that now. In the next few months he was going to have to lay the past to rest. She wouldn't want to be around for that.

"You must be glad these last couple of days are over," he said.

"Yes. Spending ten-hour sessions with government agents and answering questions about Kray wasn't fun. But it's done."

He touched her smooth face. She was wearing makeup. Something that made her eyes looked bigger and mysterious and her mouth a kissable shade of pink. "You were a

ig help. With his men being rounded up, you won't have to
vorry about anything."

She wrinkled her nose. "Except what to do with the
money. I wish they'd confiscated it all. How am I supposed
o explain to Bobby that his father left him a million dol-
ars?"

"The government only takes what they can prove came
rom illegal ventures. Kray had some legitimate businesses,
oo."

"I don't want any of it. But I suppose I should take it for
Bobby. At least I know he'll be able to go to the college of
his choice."

Jeff smiled. "He's a good kid. He'll be fine." He tugged
it the cuff of his shirt. He was wearing a suit, too. When he
got back to Washington, he was going directly to work.
He'd already spoken with his boss. As he hadn't actually
done anything illegal, he wasn't going to be disciplined. If
anything, his boss had sounded pleased with the outcome of
eff's unorthodox trip to St. Lucas.

"Just say it," Andie told him.

"What?"

"Whatever you brought me over here to say." She tilted
her chin up slightly. "We just spent two nights in the same
hotel and you didn't once come to my room. I assume
here's a reason. You regret what you said on the boat."

Only the faint edge to her voice gave away her pain. He
took her hand and brought it to his mouth. After kissing her
palm, he squeezed her fingers. "I didn't come to your room
because there were guards in the hallway and I didn't want
o start any talk."

"And?"

"And I don't regret what I said on the boat. I do love you,
Andie. I hated you at first, for who you were, but I can't
imagine anyone more right for me. I admire your courage,
your determination, your loyalty. You're everything I've
ever wanted."

"But?" She pulled her hand free and smoothed her skirt. "I know there's a problem. I can see it in your face."

He swallowed. This was harder than he'd thought. "Go home," he said at last. "Live your life. Be happy. Find someone else. Someone whole."

"You're giving me the brush-off?"

She was oddly calm, he thought. "No, I'm doing the right thing. You deserve so much more than I can give you. I've come a long way, but I'm still not over Jeanne and J.J. I'm going to have to deal with that. I live in Washington. You would grow to hate my job. Most wives do. You've got a life, friends, Bobby. You don't need me."

"I see." She folded her arms over her chest. "I suppose I'll get over you in time."

He nodded. She was taking this really well. Too well. He'd thought she might at least be sad.

"A year from now, you'll give me a call," she said. "If we're both not involved, we might meet and see how it goes. Is that part of the plan, too?"

"Well, I thought maybe—"

"Bull. You didn't think anything except for what was easiest for you." She leaned toward him and poked her finger in his chest. "If you think I'm going to walk away from you and wait for a year, then you're crazy. My whole damn life has been on hold. I've spent the last six years looking over my shoulder, praying for a miracle. Something to release me from Kray." She poked him again. "He's gone and I don't ever want to think about him again. I'm not waiting for you, Jeff Markum. Do you hear me? I'm not waiting a single day."

He couldn't breathe. She was going to walk out on him, just like that? All this time he'd been worried about his feelings, when hers were the questionable ones.

"You guys about ready?" Cort asked as he walked toward him. Bobby clung to his new friend's hand. He had a stuffed dolphin under one arm and mustard on his mouth.

"Yes," Andie said. "Do you have my tickets?"

Cort handed them to her.

Jeff stared at her. "I already gave you tickets."

"I know. They were wrong."

"Wrong?"

Cort glanced down at Bobby. "I think we came back too soon, buddy. Let's go get an ice cream, okay?"

Bobby beamed. "Strawberry? That's my favorite."

"Strawberry it is." Cort picked him up and set him on his shoulders. "Tell me which way to go."

"Over there," Bobby said, pointing toward the snack stands.

Andie opened the tickets and handed Jeff one. He scanned the destination. "Washington? What are you going to do there?"

"Apparently beat some sense into you." She grabbed the ticket back and stuffed it in the envelope. "You're supposed to be so bright, too." She looked at him. "I'm not leaving you, Jeff. I know you have feelings to work through about your late wife and son. I have things to work through, too. We'll do it together. I've come too far to lose you now. You're stuck with me. For always. I love you."

She wrapped her arms around him. He was stunned. Then he hugged her back, squeezing hard, knowing he would never let go. "Thank you," he murmured.

"For what?"

"For not letting me be noble."

She looked up at him and smiled. "Don't be silly. This wasn't about you, it was about me. I was being selfish. I couldn't stand the thought of losing you now."

"I love you, Andie." He cupped her face. "Will you marry me?"

She reached up on tiptoe and kissed him. "I thought you'd never ask."

Epilogue

Three years later

"We're going to be late," Andie said, as she bent over in the closet. Everything in there was a mess, as usual. She'd kept promising herself she was going to give their closet a good spring cleaning. This was the third springtime that had gotten away from her. "We're going to be late and I can't find my black pumps."

"Did you mean these?"

She turned slightly and saw Jeff dangling a black patent-leather shoe from each index finger. She blew a strand of hair off her face and straightened. "Those are the ones. Great. Is everything else ready?"

"We're just waiting on you."

She pushed back the sleeve of her black robe and glanced at her watch. "Oh, we're going to be late."

"We're not going to be late," Jeff said, handing her the shoes. "Everything is ready. Jamie is dressed, Mitchell's bag in the car and Bobby is keeping watch to make sure no one ets dirty."

Andie rolled her eyes. "He's the one who gets dirty the nost." She slipped on her shoes and tugged at her gown. "How do I look?"

Jeff grinned. "Like a lawyer."

Andie turned and glanced at herself in the full-length nirror. Her long hair hung down the back of her black raduation robe. "I feel old. Do you know how long it's aken me to get through law school?"

Jeff came up behind her and wrapped his arms around her vaist. "Yeah, I know. But you had a few distractions along he way." He nudged her hair aside and started nibbling on er neck. "And I can hear one of them in the living room."

"Mo-om, Mitchell's crying" came the confirming call.

"Bobby, check his diaper for me," she yelled back.

"That's gross."

"I'll check," Jeff said, giving her a quick squeeze before valking into the other room.

Two-year-old Jamie came toddling in. "Mama, we go in he car," she said.

"I know." Andie smiled at her daughter. Two children, new house, a husband and now a law degree. It had been busy three years. She resisted the urge to glance at her vatch again. They wouldn't be late for her graduation, she old herself. They couldn't be.

"He's dry," Jeff said. "But we'd better go."

Andie grabbed her purse from the dresser, then picked up amie. Her daughter had white-blond hair and big eyes the ame color as her father's. Six-month-old Mitchell looked nore like Andie. She thought all her children were beautiul.

Jeff stood by the front door. He had Mitchell's baby seat nooked over one arm. He was holding Bobby's hand and propping the door open with his heel. Her oldest stood tall nd proud in his new suit.

"Don't forget your hat, Mom," he said, pointing to the flat black graduate's cap on the hall-tree shelf.

She grabbed it as she went by. Within minutes, they were all strapped into the car and speeding down the highway toward the university. The spring air was warm, almost tropical. It reminded her a little of St. Lucas.

"What are you smiling at?" Jeff asked.

"Just thinking about how we met."

He reached for her hand and brought it to his mouth. He kissed her palm. The tingles had never gone away. Even now they raced up her arm and made her wish they were alone.

"There they go again," Bobby grumbled. "Gettin' all mushy."

Jeff read the desire in her eyes. "Tonight," he promised. "After the party celebrating your graduation."

"Tonight," she agreed.

Tonight, and tomorrow and for all the nights left to them. He loved her with a passion that made her catch her breath. They'd survived the mourning and the pain. They'd found their way out of the past, toward a future filled with promise.

"I love you," she said, smiling at him.

"I love you, too," he answered.

"Ah, you guys," Bobby complained. Little Jamie just giggled.

*   *   *   *   *

INTIMATE MOMENTS®
Silhouette®

COMING NEXT MONTH

HIS ACCIDENTAL ANGEL
SANDRA PAUL

No sooner had Bree Shepherd entered heaven
than she was sent back down, this time as an
angel, to reform cynical lawyer Devlin Hunt.
Difficult and charming, Devlin was a man to test
an angel's patience—and somehow still be
able to steal her heart.

**SPELLBOUND: BECAUSE LOVE
CAN CONQUER ANYTHING**

AVAILABLE THIS MONTH ONLY FROM

▼ *Silhouette* ROMANCE™

He's Too Hot To Handle...but she can take a little heat.

SILHOUETTE
Summer Sizzlers

This summer don't be left in the cold, join Silhouette for the hottest Summer Sizzlers collection. The perfect summer read, on the beach or while vacationing, Summer Sizzlers features sexy heroes who are "Too Hot To Handle." This collection of three new stories is written by bestselling authors Mary Lynn Baxter, Ann Major and Laura Parker.

Available this July wherever Silhouette books are sold.

He's an everyman, but only one woman's lover. And we dare you not to lose yourself—and your heart—to these featured

In May: NIGHT OF THE JAGUAR, by Merline Lovelace. Jake MacKenzie was a seasoned operative used to calling the shots. But when feisty Sarah Chandler and her three young charges became his newest mission, he knew he'd lost all control—along with his heart.

In June: ANOTHER MAN'S WIFE, by Dallas Schulze. Gage Walker had only intended to get his best friend's widow back on her feet. His idea of help had *never* included marriage—or fatherhood. Then he learned that Kelsey had a baby on the way—*his!*

In July: WHO'S THE BOSS? by Linda Turner. Riley Whitaker *never* lost a good fight. So when single mom Becca Prescott threw down the gauntlet in the race for sheriff, Riley accepted her challenge—and offered a seductive one of his own....

Heartbreakers: The heroes you crave, from the authors you love. You can find them each month, only in—

INTIMATE MOMENTS®
™ *Silhouette*®

ROMANTIC TRADITIONS

Romantic Traditions sizzles in July 1995 as Sharon Sala's THE MIRACLE MAN, IM #650, explores the suspenseful—and sensual—"Stranger on the Shore" plot line.

Washed ashore after a plane crash, U.S. Marshal Lane Monday found himself on the receiving end of a most indecent proposal. Antonette Hatfield had saved his life and was now requesting his presence in her *bed*. But what Lane didn't know was that Toni had babies on her mind....

Lauded as "immensely talented" by *Romantic Times* magazine, Sharon Sala is one author you won't want to miss. So return to the classic plot lines you love with THE MIRACLE MAN, and be sure to look for more Romantic Traditions in future months from some of the genre's best, only in—

INTIMATE MOMENTS®

Silhouette

SIMRT8

ANNOUNCING THE

PRIZE SURPRISE SWEEPSTAKES!

This month's prize:

L-A-R-G-E—SCREEN PANASONIC TV!

This month, as a special surprise, we're giving away a fabulous FREE TV!

Imagine how delighted you and your family will be to own this brand-new 31" Panasonic** television! It comes with all the latest high-tech features, like a SuperFlat picture tube for a clear, crisp picture...unified remote control...closed-caption decoder...clock and sleep timer, and much more!

The facing page contains two Entry Coupons (as does every book you received this shipment). Complete and return *all* the entry coupons; **the more times you enter, the better your chances of winning the TV!**

Then keep your fingers crossed, because you'll find out by July 15, 1995 if you're the winner!

Remember: The more times you enter, the better your chances of winning!*

PRIZE SURPRISE
SWEEPSTAKES

OFFICIAL ENTRY COUPON

This entry must be received by: JUNE 30, 1995
This month's winner will be notified by: JULY 15, 1995

YES, I want to win the Panasonic 31" TV! Please enter me in the drawing
and let me know if I've won!

Name_____

Address _____ Apt. _____

City   State/Prov.   Zip/Postal Code

Account #_____

Return entry with invoice in reply envelope.

© 1995 HARLEQUIN ENTERPRISES LTD.   **CTV KAL**

PRIZE SURPRISE
SWEEPSTAKES

OFFICIAL ENTRY COUPON

This entry must be received by: JUNE 30, 1995
This month's winner will be notified by: JULY 15, 1995

YES, I want to win the Panasonic 31" TV! Please enter me in the drawing
and let me know if I've won!

Name_____

Address _____ Apt. _____

City   State/Prov.   Zip/Postal Code

Account #_____

Return entry with invoice in reply envelope.

© 1995 HARLEQUIN ENTERPRISES LTD.   **CTV KAL**